FRIENDS WITH MORE BENEFITS

A Friends With... Benefits Novel
Book Three

LUKE YOUNG

Cover Art by Once Upon a Time Covers
V1

ALSO BY LUKE YOUNG

SHRINKAGE
CHOCOLATE COVERED BILLIONAIRE NAVY SEAL
CHANCES AREN'T

The Friends With... Benefits Series:
FRIENDS WITH PARTIAL BENEFITS
FRIENDS WITH FULL BENEFITS
FRIENDS WITH MORE BENEFITS (Excerpt Included)
FRIENDS WITH EXTRA BENEFITS
FRIENDS WITH WAY TOO MANY BENEFITS (releasing
12/17/2013)

To contact Luke or to be placed on a mailing list to receive updates
about new releases, send an email to lukebyoung@gmail.com

To find out more about the author and his work, see
http://www.lukeyoungbooks.com/

1

Brian Nash was lying naked on the bed, rubbing his hands together impatiently while he craned his neck, struggling to peer into the bathroom. He sighed. "Come on."

Poking her head through the door, Jillian Grayson smiled. "Just a second." She disappeared and called back, "Hey, did you send the prenup to your lawyer friend?"

"No, I signed it. I trust you and I just want my birthday present."

"I really wish you'd have someone look it over."

"Please get out here so I can look *you* over."

She appeared in the doorway wearing a white lace teddy, her full breasts busting out of the top, and her pink nipples showing through the sheer fabric. Standing there for his pleasure, she traced her fingertips over her breasts. "Do you like?"

"I do."

"How does it feel to be twenty-seven?"

He smiled. "Awesome, now."

Grinning, she slowly made her way over to him. "I've got a surprise for you—a couple actually."

"Really, what?"

"One at a time."

He eyed her up and down, and his penis began to grow as a result. "Is that new?"

She nodded. "This is the first surprise." She ran her hands down over the lace fabric and stopped between her legs. "It snaps way down here, if you need to open this up for some reason."

He swallowed hard. "That's, uh, good to know."

Her eyes traveled down his lean, muscular body to his erection as she climbed on the bed. After sliding her tongue over her lips, she gasped, "Wow, you're ready to go!"

He nodded, as she knelt between his legs and took hold of him with both hands. Suddenly, his cell phone rang on the nightstand. "My mother said she'd call tonight." He sighed. "She has the worst timing."

She gave him a sexy look. "It won't bother me if you get it."

"If I don't, she'll keep calling and calling."

"I insist." Her expression morphed into an evil grin.

He answered the phone. "Hey, Mom."

Jillian chose that moment to engulf him in her mouth.

He gasped softly. "Uh, what's that?"

She lifted her head and grinned at him, then began licking all around his thick head.

"Oh, I'm having a good birthday. Just staying home tonight... Jillian? Yeah, she's good."

Just then Jillian took him back deep into her mouth and sucked him hard. Brian said quickly in a cracking voice, "Actually, she's great—she's absolutely great... couldn't be better."

Getting into a rhythm over him, Jillian's eyes glazed over, and it became more and more difficult for him to concentrate. "What... Yeah. Oh, sorry, Mom. Can I call you back tomorrow? We're just in the middle of a movie, and I really want to see how it ends."

Jillian pulled up from him and stared into his eyes, as he said, "Okay, Mom... bye." Putting the phone down, he widened his eyes. "What's gotten into you?"

"Whenever I think of your mother, I feel like really taking care of you."

"I wish she would call more often then."

Moving up beside him on the bed, she unsnapped the bottom of her teddy, and the front end retracted up, exposing her completely shaved parts. "Wow!" He exhaled deeply. "You shaved."

"It is your birthday." She pulled the teddy up off her body and tossed it onto a nearby chair. Straddling his chest, she lifted up on her knees, eight inches from his chin. His eyes traveled down from her face to her breasts and settled between her legs.

"The second surprise is in the pool."

Tearing his eyes away from her playground, he gave her a curious look. "Really the pool? But where's Rob?"

"Out all night."

"You're sure?"

"I'm positive." Dipping down, she moved her body to within a half an inch of his lips.

His eyes returned to her beautiful parts and he sighed. "You, uh, don't want to stay here?"

"I think you'll like what I have for you down there."

He extended his tongue to lick her, but just before he made contact she pulled away and climbed off of him. He gave her a sad look. "Hey."

"I bought a huge raft. I want to lay in it and float around the pool for like an hour while we do sixty-nine. It's a big boat—it matches your big cock."

Leaning up on his elbows, he smiled at the compliment. "That sounds like fun."

"You go get in the boat and stay hard. I'll be right behind you."

He rushed out to the pool, jumped into the water, and climbed onto the giant three-man raft. He lay there waiting with a goofy smile, while touching himself and gazing up at the beautiful starlit Miami sky. He heard the door open and close, then a splash in the pool. Seconds later Jillian grabbed the raft and poked her head up over the side to look at him.

She grinned, and said in a bad English accent, "Has your boat sunk, dear sailor?" He glanced at her, confused, as she continued, "I'm a mermaid sent up from the bottom of the sea to save you."

"How exactly am I supposed to perform oral on a woman with a fishtail bottom?"

She rolled her eyes. "I get my legs and everything as soon as I get out of the water. Just go with it, will ya?"

"Okay." After pausing, he took a shot at his own accent. "Why, yes... fair mermaid..." He stepped out of character. "Um, why the English accent?"

"This thing just feels British to me." Shrugging, she gave him a tired look.

He cleared his throat. "Why yes, you are a sight for sore eyes, for my boat has sunk, and I'm thirsty. I need a drink from your sweet quim."

She smiled brightly. "*Quim*—nice touch."

"Thank you."

She climbed up onto the raft, with her head toward his groin. They struggled to get into the right position and went to town. What started off silly, soon became one of the hottest oral sex sessions they had ever had. It didn't last an hour, but instead a good thirty minutes. The warm night, the gentle waves, and the intense passionate oral sex left them panting and spent.

As they lay back, floating lazily together, he said, "That's a keeper. We should put that in the regular rotation."

She began stroking his penis; it soon responded and was at full size. She slipped her hands behind his balls and traced a finger over his perineum. "I've got one more surprise for you."

Closing his eyes, he melted with her touch and moaned. "Really? What is it?"

"I want to do that thing to you that Victoria is always raving about." He knew instantly what she meant, and his face lit up at the thought of it. "But let's take a bath first—a good bath."

After flopping out of the raft into the water, they swam to the edge of the pool and climbed out. Standing on the edge, he asked, "Where are the towels?"

"Oh, shit. I forgot!"

He shrugged, and they walked up to the back door. Turning the knob, he found it locked and sighed. "Again? No fucking way."

"It must have been locked when I pulled it closed."

He made a face. "Well, why'd you pull it closed?"

She glared at him. "Well, I was rushing out here to put your penis back in my mouth, and I wasn't thinking of much else."

"Sorry." He sighed and moved right and began checking windows to see if they were locked while she did the same to the windows on the left. They, of course, were all secured. They met back at the door, and she said, "I guess you'll just have to go to Victoria's to get the key."

"No way," he grumbled. "I'm not walking through the neighborhood completely naked for the third time."

Her eyes brightened. "What about those clothes you hid out here in that plastic bag months ago?"

"That's right." Wearing a big grin, he headed over to an outdoor bin. "And you thought I was nuts. Well look who's not crazy and has something to wear." Opening the bin, he pulled out a shredded plastic bag, and looked at it in shock. "What the hell?"

She walked over with her mouth wide open. "Some animal must have gotten in there and—"

"Shit." He opened up what was left of the bag and pulled out two pieces of shredded fabric, and a pair of flip-flops that were still in good shape. He turned his head slowly toward her. "Fuck me."

"This sucks," she added with a frown.

"Don't you have towels out here in that other bin?"

"I just took them in to be washed."

"You sure?"

She nodded apologetically.

"So we're locked out again? How's this even possible?"

She returned a shrug. After shaking his head, he headed back to the door, paused a moment before putting his shoulder to it, hard.

"Don't hurt yourself. I guess you'll just have to walk to Victoria's. I'd go with you, but I don't have any shoes. You know how sensitive the bottom of my feet are."

He exhaled deeply. "You can wear these. How about you go by yourself, and I'll wait here. I took the first two trips. It's your turn."

She gave him an angry stare. "Fine. Give me the shoes. I'm sure I'll be fine…a naked woman walking two blocks at night. I can hear Nancy Grace interviewing you now." Jillian did an amazing impression, as she said in a high accusatory voice, "Let me get this straight—you sent your *buck naked* fiancée… out in the middle of the night to get a *key*, and you were shocked to find she was kidnapped, gang raped, tortured, and brutally murdered."

He rolled his eyes. "Of course, I wouldn't send you." He paused to think. "How about I break a window? We can get it fixed."

She shook her head in disappointment and moved behind him. Standing on her tiptoes, she put her mouth to his shoulder. In a soft, sexy voice she said, "It's only two blocks." She kissed his shoulder blade and moved a little lower and kissed him again, as she held him by the hips.

Groaning, he melted with the gentle brush of her lips as he craned his neck, desperate to see what she was up to.

"I really want to make this special for you." Settling down on her knees, she placed tiny kisses all over his lower back. She grinned and put her tongue where his back met the cleft of his ass and slid it down half an inch.

Reaching back blindly to touch some part of her, her face, her hair, anything, he let out an audible sigh.

She moved back before he could lay a finger on her and whispered, "Hurry back."

He turned to discover her gazing up at him with eyebrows raised. "Okay. I'll be five minutes max." Then he took off toward the gate.

Jillian glanced around the backyard, looked at the stars for thirty seconds, then lifted a rock, took the key, and unlocked the door. Grabbing her cell phone, she hit a button and waited for an answer. "Yes... okay." She ended the call and rushed to the powder room.

Standing in front of the mirror, she groaned at her appearance, and quickly towel dried her hair and body. She put her hair up in a ponytail and opened the cabinet to pull out some clothes and shoes she had stashed there. As she pulled on her clothes, she figured Brian was about half way to Victoria's.

2

Brian moved stealthily from one tree to the next; he knew the drill. There was very little activity on the street, yet it was only about 9:00 p.m. After peering out from behind a tree, he took off for another nearby. Lights flashed behind him, and he heard a car door open. He slipped behind the tree with is heart pounding.

"It's okay. They didn't see me," he whispered to himself.

"Police! Step out from behind the tree with your hands up," A stern female voice called out.

"Fuck!" he said aloud.

"Now!"

He sighed, covered his junk with his hands, and slowly moved away from the tree. Two female police officers were holding guns pointed at him. "I said hands up!" one of them ordered.

"Look at me — I don't have any weapons."

One officer cocked her gun, and instantly his hands shot up in the air. Glancing down to his nakedness, both women widened their eyes.

"Let's see some I.D."

He grinned uncomfortably. "I, uh, left my wallet in my other pants."

The officers were not amused; they lowered their weapons, and one took out handcuffs and moved behind him. "Hands behind your back."

Closing his eyes, he followed the command. "Look, I was locked out of my house."

"Yeah. Okay, we've had complaints about a pervert running around naked in this neighborhood before." After tightening the cuffs around his wrists, the officer grasped him by the elbow. "This isn't your first time, is it?"

"Is it, perv boy?" asked the other officer.

He opened his eyes to find them glaring at him, waiting for a response.

"Well, no — but I can explain. It's, uh, really a funny story."

"Save it. You'll have a lot of friends to tell it to in the city jail."

The two officers sat in the front of the car with Brian sitting uncomfortably in the back—still completely nude with his hands cuffed behind his back.

One officer turned to him. "They'll like you down there in lockup— you're so fresh and young."

"Wait, we really don't need to do this, I—"

He watched nervously as one officer leaned over and whispered something in the other's ear. They turned to him, shined their flashlights down to his groin, and smiled.

"We might be willing to let you go," said one of the officers.

"Great! I would really appreciate it." He breathed a sigh of relief as he gave them a big, hopeful smile.

"You have a really nice penis."

"Uh, thank you." He shifted uncomfortably in his seat.

"Have you ever been with two women at the same time?"

After swallowing hard, he stammered, "Well, no. I mean, I've had offers—well just one actually."

"Officer Johnson's apartment is just a few blocks from here. What do you say we go there and take the cuffs off and—"

Johnson interrupted, "Or leave them on..." The officers both broke into a chuckle, and he returned a nervous giggle. With her eyebrows raised, Johnson finished her thought, "...and, uh, we have some real fun?"

"I'm flattered—really, I am, but I'm getting married in a few months. I'm in love—like insane, head-over-heels-crazy-about-her love. I just can't."

The officers exchanged a look of disappointment, then Johnson said, "Let's get back to the station then." Officer Johnson's cell phone rang, and she answered, listened for a moment, and hung up without saying a word.

He watched intently as the officers glanced at each other and nodded. He said, "It's not that I... I mean you both are gorgeous. I'd love to take you up on your offer, but I can't. I live one block from here. I was just on my way to our friend Victoria Wilde's house to get the spare key."

"You know Victoria?"

"Yes."

"Why didn't you say so?" He shrugged, and the officer added, "We'll take you there, but if she doesn't know you, you're going to lockup."

"Thank you so much." Slumping back, he exhaled deeply. "You wouldn't have anything I could wear in the car would you?"

The officers glanced at one another, and, fighting back a laugh, both said, "No."

The two officers stood behind Brian at Victoria's front door. Johnson said, "Looks like no one's home."

"Please be there, please be there," whispered Brian to himself.

Johnson knocked again, and a few seconds later the door opened. The house was completely dark as Victoria appeared in the doorway holding a lit candle. She looked at them in shock. "Brian, what the—"

"Do you know this man?" Johnson asked.

"I do… Brian what happened?"

"I kinda got locked out—again, and these police officers were kind enough to give me a ride."

"The power is out, but please come in."

Victoria led them inside, and they moved to the center of the living room.

"How long has your power been—"

Before he could finish that thought, the lights blasted on. As his eyes adjusted to the change, he squinted and looked around the room in shock at the more than forty people staring at him all wearing big smiles. He was, of course, completely naked except for the flip-flops.

The audience in unison called out, "NICE PENIS, BRIAN!" as Jillian yelled, "SURPRISE!"

Walking over to him, Jillian gave him a kiss on the cheek. "They were supposed to yell 'surprise.'"

Victoria said, "The change was my idea."

"Happy birthday," Jillian said, as she waited anxiously for his reaction.

He bent over, cracking up, then, after composing himself, gave her a serious look. "I'm going to get you back for this. It might take years, but I will one day, and it'll be good."

She chucked. "Sorry."

"You sabotaged my clothes stash, didn't you? You were the animal."

Jillian shrugged her shoulders and smiled.

Victoria announced casually, "Now, most of you know Brian, and quite a few of you have already seen him naked. Purely out of curiosity, could I have a show of hands for those who have." Victoria immediately raised her hand and Jillian did as well. Brian chuckled while shaking his head toward both of them. Brian's brother Jim raised his hand as did Jillian's son Rob. Brian turned his attention to Victoria's parents and said sarcastically, "Don't be shy. Put them up—come on, loud and proud." They slowly raised their hands.

Officer Williams had his hand raised; Brian recognized him and gave him a nod. "Officer."

Brian glanced around the room and noticed six of the neighbors who also had their hands held high.

He made eye contact with a woman and asked, "Really?"

"A few months ago I saw you sneaking over here in the middle of the night."

"Oh." Brian curled his lip, and his eyes went to each neighbor with a hand up.

"Me too."

"We did also."

Brian widened his eyes at the final couple, waiting. The man said matter-of-factly, "Uh, we live behind you, and there's a gap in the tree line, and we can see directly into your pool."

Jillian looked away, mortified.

Victoria rubbed her hands together. "Okay then, we should probably take the handcuffs off now."

"You think?" Brian said sarcastically. Johnson moved behind him and unlocked the cuffs. He rubbed his wrists a moment, looked down at his groin, then covered it with his hands. Johnson said to Jillian loud enough for all to hear, "Jillian you've got a good one here. We offered him a threesome to keep him out of jail, and he wouldn't take us up on it."

Brian said, "I, uh, I'm just crazy about her."

Jillian smiled brightly and she moved to him for a hug. He wrapped his arms around her, then, when they separated, he looked around the room forgetting to cover up. From the back of the room a man called out, "Got shrinkage?" Everyone in the room burst into laughter as Brian covered his groin.

When the laughter stopped, he smiled. "I was in the pool."

"Okay, Costanza, we believe you," someone called out.

"Jillian, isn't your pool heated?" another guest said, eliciting a groan from the group.

Brian frowned. "Now that's just mean." He looked at Jillian. "How the hell did you pull this off? This was some production, and the policewomen were a nice touch."

"Victoria's idea. We needed some way to delay you so I could get here."

"You *are* going to pay for this."

"Yeah, right." Jillian grinned. "I have some clothes in the back room for you."

He shook his head. "Knowing you guys it's probably a G-string and a tube top."

"It's not. Now go get dressed."

He gave Jillian a rebellious look. "I should probably say hello to everyone first. Can't just run away from my own party. That would be rude."

Putting on an insincere smile, he grabbed a pillow to cover his groin. He walked up to Victoria. "There are some people I don't think I know. Would you mind introducing me?"

Victoria grinned and, playing along, said, "Sure."

Jillian watched him while holding back a laugh as Victoria took his arm and walked him to an older couple. "This is my neighbor Craig and his wife, Emily." They glanced down uncomfortably at the pillow.

Brain said, "Good to see you."

The wife replied, "Nice to meet you."

Victoria spotted a man across the room. "Uh, there is someone you must meet." Jillian trailed along as Victoria guided Brian to the man wearing an expensive suit. "Brian Nash, this is Timothy Roberts."

"Hello."

Brian studied the man as if he recognized him but could not place him. Then it popped into his head, and he whispered to Victoria, "Is that Mayor Roberts?"

She nodded and Brian cleared his throat. "Mr. Mayor, love the work you're doing." He shook the mayor's hand and turned to Jillian. "I think... I think I'll get dressed now. The clothes are... ?"

Grinning, Jillian pointed toward Victoria's bedroom, and Brian took off. As he passed people, they glanced at his ass and whistled. The mayor looked down to his hand, grimaced, then asked Victoria, "The, uh, restroom?"

After giving him a weak smile, she indicated the way.

A few minutes later, Brian emerged fully dressed and headed to Jillian. Placing her hand on his chest, she gave him an apologetic look. "Are you okay?"

"Yeah, but I could use a beer or two."

Victoria yelled out, "Time for the gifts."

"No way — I don't want any gifts."

Brian reluctantly had a seat on the sofa; Jillian handed him a beer and sat next to him. After taking a big swig, he placed the beer on the table. Victoria handed him the first box. He removed the wrapping paper. "You guys didn't have to get me anything." He opened the box and smiled as he pulled out a swimsuit.

A man in front said, "You should try one." Everyone shared a chuckle.

Brian opened the second gift, and it was also a swimsuit. He opened six more boxes, and they were all swimsuits. His last box contained a tiny black Speedo bathing suit. He held it proudly over his head, which elicited a huge laugh from the crowd.

Brian smiled. "Finally, something I can use. Thank you all, and I promise I will never again skinny dip."

Jillian gave him a disappointed look.

The crowd giggled at her.

"What?" Jillian shrugged her shoulders, embarrassed. "It's kinda fun. You should try it."

"Maybe we'll just plant another tree," Brian quipped.

Later when they were alone in the kitchen, Brian took Jillian into his arms. He kissed her and whispered in her ear, "Were you serious about doing that thing to me tonight or was that just some ploy to get me over here?"

"I was serious. Plus, now I think I need to try extra hard to make this up to you."

"You're right about that."

3

About an hour later, Victoria heard voices in the massage room and moved to the door to listen from outside.

Jim was in there with his girlfriend Caroline. Caroline said, "I can't believe you put this together yourself."

"It wasn't that difficult."

Moving to Jim, Caroline wrapped her arms around him. "I wish you could give me a massage in here."

Victoria waited a moment, then walked into the room. She said, "So, he's showing you his creation."

Caroline smiled at her. "It's beautiful."

Jim gave Victoria an embarrassed smile. "I must have been channeling some HGTV creativity when I was down here because I can't even match my shirt to my pants normally."

Victoria said, "I was talking to Jillian earlier. If you guys wanted to stay here, you could, and let the birthday boy and his fiancée have some privacy."

"Oh, we couldn't put you out like that," said Caroline.

Victoria scoffed. "I insist. I just finished remodeling the guest room, and no one's slept in there yet. Plus you guys could try out the massage room either tonight or tomorrow. I have a lot of errands to run in the morning, so you'll have the whole place to yourselves." When Jim looked at her, unsure, Victoria added, "You do realize Brian and Jillian are both pretty drunk, and I don't know if you've ever been in the same house with them when they've been having sex while drunk, but, uh…" She shook her head with a sour face. "It can be a little frightening."

After Jim and Caroline shared a concerned look, Jim said, "They probably would like their privacy."

A few hours later with the party over, and the cleanup nearly complete, Jim walked to the car to pick up their luggage. When he returned, he found Victoria in the kitchen loading the dishwasher. The house was nearly put back together.

Victoria said, "Caroline said she was tired."

He gave her a hesitant look. "Do you need me to do anything else?"

"No, I only have a few more things to put away."

Grinning, she studied his body language. He was dying to get back to the guest room. "I'll bet you're *really* tired too."

"Well, I..." He cringed, busted. "This, uh, isn't too weird is it? I mean. It's weird, but not so weird that—"

She smiled. "You guys go have fun. At least someone should be getting laid in this house, if I'm not going..." She shook her head. "Sorry."

He looked at her, concerned. "Oh, I don't want to—"

"Oh, I'm just kidding."

"Seriously?" He bounced up and down anxiously on his heels.

"Go." She shooed him away with a wave of her hand.

"We'll definitely talk tomorrow." He took off toward the back of the house wearing a huge smile.

Victoria finished up in the kitchen, then went into the bedroom and closed the door. Once she was in bed, she lay awake thinking. She felt good about letting Jim and Caroline stay with her. She thought she'd be able to handle it. She had read that some women experience a period of incredible increased sexual desire during pregnancy. The article mentioned that it could last from a few short weeks to as much as seven months. Being a woman who was generally extremely horny to begin with, she feared the worst. Vowing to avoid sex throughout her pregnancy, she figured it would be pretty easy to pull off since she had absolutely no prospects. She wanted to avoid the complications of starting a new relationship as her pregnancy started to show. Luckily, she was barely showing at all at this point.

During the first few weeks, her sexual appetite seemed normal—for her anyway, but over the last few days she had found herself fantasizing about every attractive man she laid eyes on. Having the probable father of her child just a few feet from her in bed and most certainly having incredible sex with his gorgeous girlfriend wasn't helping the situation. A slight miscalculation, she thought.

She found her body temperature was off lately, always feeling either too hot or too cold. And at the moment she found herself horny, unable to sleep, and way too hot. After turning out the light, she kicked off her covers, pulled off her nightshirt, then moved her hand slowly down over her stomach until it came to rest between her legs. She touched herself, gently at first, as she floated away, exhausted, in a dream or fantasy or...

Victoria stood in the darkened hallway peering through the door at the young couple. Caroline was kneeling between Jim's spread legs as he leaned back against the headboard, simply watching her as she slowly worked her mouth over his straining erection. Victoria watched closely as the young woman tenderly licked Jim's engorged penis. His eyes were rolling back into his head, and his lids fluttered dreamily as Caroline worked over his throbbing manhood.

Glancing to the door, he noticed Victoria watching them from the shadows. He gently patted Caroline's arm, and when she met his gaze, he pointed toward the door. After wiping her lips, she turned toward the door. When she spotted Victoria, she smiled and motioned for her to join them.

Victoria moved through the door slowly as Caroline adjusted her position so she was lying off to the side of Jim. Glancing up to Victoria, she nodded with her lips parted and her fingers still wrapped around his shaft. Victoria slipped into bed on the other side of him, and both women stared closely at his prize. Then, their eyes met, and they moved slowly together for a gentle kiss with their chins hovering only an inch over his straining erection. Tilting to the side, Caroline guided their mouths down until his head was pressing against the sides of their lips. The women continued to make out with a random tongue slipping out occasionally to swipe at his rigid cock.

He watched them breathlessly. It was the hottest thing he'd ever seen. After moving apart an inch, both women slid down in unison to lick him. Without blinking, he witnessed as they slipped down his full length and back up in perfect rhythm, leaving a shimmering trail of saliva along the way.

Seconds later, Victoria woke in the completely dark room, torn from the vivid dream, and covered in sweat. She felt around the bed expecting to find Jim and Caroline's naked bodies next to her. When she didn't, she panicked, reached to the nightstand, and turned on the lamp. After glancing around the room for them, she shook her head and grinned, feeling silly. She turned off the lamp, curled up with her pillow, and struggled to get back to sleep.

4

As Victoria's dream fantasy was ending, the somewhat drunk Brian's real life one had yet to begin as he showered. He washed all the important parts with soap three times and with body wash twice; after drying off, he appeared at the bedroom door sporting a sizeable woody. The thoroughly tipsy Jillian was lying in bed wearing a matching white lace bra and thong panties.

"What took you so long?" she asked.

"I had things to wash."

Grinning, she got up on her knees, and he slipped into bed in front of her. "You just lie down on your stomach and relax birthday boy. Let me take care of you."

He exhaled deeply as he lay down flat, his exhausted body melting into the sheets. Spreading her legs, she pressed her pussy into his head as she leaned over and worked the muscles in his back. She moved lower to the cheeks of his ass; he spread his legs apart wide and groaned. Climbing over him, she sat on his shoulder blades as she leaned forward and placed tiny kisses along his thighs. He moaned and lifted his ass higher. She glanced between his legs to his erection and full, slightly hairy balls, then smiled.

"God, you're so cute. I could just eat you up."

"Go right ahead."

Dropping her head to the mattress, she moved her mouth to within a quarter inch of his manhood. Her warm breath washed over it, causing him to shudder. Extending her tongue to him, she purred loudly as she went to work. Pressing down on his back, she shifted her hips back and forth simply enjoying the sensation between her legs. She tilted her head to the side, kissed his inner thigh and took a deep languid breath.

Returning to her mission, she lifted up and ran her tongue slowly along his shaft until she reached his balls.

"Oh, fuck," he groaned.

She moved back and forth, slowly licking him as he gripped the sheets tightly with his hands. After taking one last trip down his length, she let her tongue completely circle around his sack over and over again. He spread his legs wider. She slid her tongue gently along his hair-covered perineum, and he stopped breathing all together. She licked him harder, getting lost in the moment until she felt a hair in her mouth. Grimacing, she lifted her head up and reached into her mouth as she struggled to retrieve the random hair.

Once free of the irritation, she glanced at the back of his balls and the tiny trail of hair that led to his little ass, and while she found it still pretty adorable to look at, she discovered licking it was another story. Victoria had warned her about this possible hair issue, but she decided to give it another try anyway.

Sliding back down, she planted tiny kisses all over his lower back. She moved to the cheeks of his firm ass and kissed them next. Spreading his legs wider, he lifted his ass higher in anticipation. She stared down at him breathlessly and placed her tongue at his cleft and ran it slowly to his seam.

"Oh, Goddddd," he moaned clenching the sheets tightly in his fists.

She swirled her tongue around his tight circle until she just couldn't do it any longer. The hair was just too much. She pulled back until her chin was resting on his lower back. After pausing a moment to think, she covered her finger with saliva and placed it gently on his hole.

"Oh, it feels so good when you… lick me there," he whispered.

She grinned. She didn't want to fool him, but if he thought she was still doing it, well then, that wouldn't be the worst thing in the world. She kept her mouth just a few inches from him as she slowly ran a finger masquerading as her tongue gently around his forbidden hole.

"Oh," he cried out again.

She reached down to his penis and took hold of it as she continued with her gentle tongue-like fingering.

"Oh, Jillian."

Less than three minutes later, Brian experienced the orgasm of his life. For a long time he lay there panting and struggling to recover, until he finally turned over and gave her a dizzied look.

She slipped down to her spot, curling up on his chest. "Happy birthday."

He sighed and drew in a deep breath. "That was… amazing."

"You liked it?"

He nodded and kissed the side of her head. "Do I need to wait a whole year before you do that again? Maybe we could do it on our wedding night."

She said, "Maybe," as she thought, *Do something about the jungle, and I'll think about it.*

The next morning Victoria slipped out of the house early and left her guests a note which read:

I actually have food in the refrigerator, so eat whatever you want. I won't be back until after one. Have fun.

After climbing into her car, Victoria sent a text to Jillian to see if she could come over. In her reply, Jillian asked her to come around back and meet her out by the pool since the birthday boy was still asleep. As she started the car, John and Mary approached, walking a dog. Spotting her, they smiled. Victoria rolled the window down. "Hey, you two."

Mary said, "Great party last night. Sorry we had to leave early, but all that male nudity made me want to get to bed early — if you know what I mean."

"I do. I really do." Victoria sighed. "Sorry we didn't get much of a chance to talk last night. I was crazy busy."

"So how did that summer class go?" John asked.

"It was really interesting. I actually learned a lot, and I'm looking forward to the fall semester."

"That's great."

"So, how's the team?"

"We're ranked number five in the country in the preseason polls. Things are looking good, and we're hoping for a major bowl bid this year."

Victoria glanced down to the dog. "I didn't know you had a dog. Did you just get it?"

"No. Mary kind of got custody of it during the divorce, but now were one big happy family again."

They all shared a chuckle. John turned his attention to the dog as Mary smiled at Victoria. He said, "Mary, you really can't tell she's pregnant. She looks as spry as ever."

Victoria's face dropped. She glanced down to her stomach and back up to John horrified. "Really how could you tell, I, uh—"

"She began acting strangely so we took her to the vet. He confirmed it."

Confused, Victoria shook her head until she followed his gaze to the dog. A smile spread on her face. "Oh, congratulations."

"Thanks. She's a purebred Golden, but we're not quite sure who the father is. We didn't breed her or anything, she just got out one day and, uh…"

Victoria thought, *There's a lot of that going around lately!*

John smiled at her. "Hey, do you want one of the little ones when they're born?"

"Oh, God no," she replied with a huge smile. They gave her a horrified dog-lover look, and she tried to repair the damage. "Oh sorry, I'm just not much of a… I've got my hands full at school and everything. No time."

"Well, if you know of anyone, just let us know," Mary said.

Victoria nodded. "I think Brian loves dogs. I'll ask Jillian. Maybe she'll want to get him one as a wedding present or something."

"Okay, great," John replied.

After sharing good-byes, they were on their way.

Minutes later, Victoria entered the Grayson backyard through the gate and found Jillian sitting at the table drinking tea. Across from her was another steaming mug.

Jillian smiled at her. "Thought you might want some tea."

Sitting down, Victoria warmed her hands around the hot cup. "Thanks."

"You want anything to eat?"

"No."

"The party was a hit," Jillian said.

Victoria nodded in agreement. "He was a really good sport."

"He was, almost too good... I wonder if he's really planning to get me back somehow?"

"He could never pull it off without a lot of help."

Jillian's eyes widened. "Hey, if he does come to you with some crazy plan, just go along with it and let me know — then we'll really get him good."

Victoria smiled. "Deal."

After each sipping from their teas, they shared an evil grin.

Jillian said, "Thanks for letting Jim and Caroline stay with you. Things got a little loud around here last night."

Sitting up straighter, Victoria's eyes brightened. "So did you?"

Jillian looked away a moment and pursed her lips. "Sorta. I started and everything was good. I mean he's adorable and everything, but..."

"But what?"

"He's just a little too hairy to, you know."

Victoria gave her a knowing nod, "I thought there might be a problem. I asked him to show me, and he refused. He can be such a baby sometimes."

"Show you what?"

"His ass," Victoria replied nonchalantly.

Jillian narrowed her eyes. "You asked him to show you his ass?"

"Uh-huh." Victoria shook her head then sipped from her tea.

Jillian said sarcastically, "And he refused. What a shock."

Victoria scowled. "You don't understand. He had just showed me his balls so it seemed like a natural progression to check out the rest."

"Oh." After nodding matter-of-factly, Jillian took a sip of tea. Pondering that a moment, her face contorted. "But wait."

Victoria gave her a tired look as she prepared for the inquisition.

Jillian asked, "He showed you his balls? When?"

"When you forced him to sleep over. The morning after you agreed to marry him."

"Oh, oh... okay, but why?"

Victoria exhaled deeply. "Okay, we were talking about sex, and I think he told me you'd put both of his balls in your mouth, under my suggestion, of course." She widened her eyes as if waiting for a response. When there was none, Victoria asked, "Right?"

"Um, yeah, that was your suggestion."

"So he told me how much he liked it, and I told him if he wanted more ball attention that he better make sure those boys were hair free."

"That makes sense," Jillian mumbled to herself semi-convinced, but still a little taken aback.

After taking a sip of tea, Victoria continued, "So then he reluctantly showed me. You know how shy he can be." They made eyes at each other in agreement.

"Well, when I inspected everything..." Victoria cringed. "Let's just say I found he needs some work. I told him he was too hairy and that he could use a shave. I then asked to see the back of the boys and everything else, and he flat out refused." She scoffed. "Can you believe it?"

"That bastard," Jillian said jokingly.

Victoria glared at her. "Go ahead, make fun of me for trying to help. I know we've talked about going the whole ten yards there... and forgive me for trying to head off a problem, but I was right. You headed down the path, and were a tad scared by the foliage I take it."

Jillian nodded with her lips curled. "Uh, yeah maybe a little."

"I knew it was going to happen." Victoria shook her head, disappointed. "What could have been a beautiful, unforgettable, mind-blowing moment, turned into a horror movie."

"Well, it wasn't that bad. I just pretended to keep going." Victoria gave her a confused look, and she elaborated, "I, uh, let my wet finger stand in for my tongue and he seemed to not know the difference."

"Good thinking. I'm proud of you," Victoria said with a smile.

"Thanks. I think I might be able to do it again if he takes care of the problem. He's so cute, and he seems to really, really like the attention back there."

"All men do," Victoria began smugly. "Most are too homophobic to admit it… not to mention too freaking lazy to keep that area—let's just say *visitable*."

"Visitable?"

"Yeah, visitable. It's a word, I think." Victoria said defensively.

They both broke into a chuckle. After Jillian composed herself, she shook her head, wearing an odd look.

Victoria asked, "What is it?"

"I can't believe he showed you his balls. You can get people to talk about and obviously do things that no one else can."

"I don't get what the big deal is. For example if I needed you to look at my ass because I couldn't see it or needed another opinion, you would do it right?"

Opening her mouth to speak, Jillian had nothing and instead gave her half a nod.

Victoria continued, "Like if I wanted your opinion on whether or not I should have my anus bleached, you would check it out and tell me, right?"

Jillian looked at her hesitantly. "You're not going to ask me to look at your ass this morning are you?"

"No, but we should totally go in together to have that done."

"What?"

Victoria rolled her eyes. "Have our anuses bleached."

Jillian frowned. "I'll give it some thought and let you know."

"You really should. If we end up on the nude beaches of St. Barts, you're going to wish it was bleached."

"Good point."

Victoria took another sip of tea and gave her friend a serious look. "Speaking of St. Barts… Do you think you could move the wedding up a bit. I sorta have a conflict."

"Really, what's that?"

"I'm going to be really, really not nude-beach worthy come late December." Off Jillian's completely lost look Victoria continued, "I'm, uh… I've been meaning to tell you. I'm, well, I'm… pregnant."

After laughing, Jillian took a sip of tea. "No, really why can't, uh—"

Looking at her with a completely straight face, Victoria nodded.

With her eyes widened, Jillian choked on her tea coughing and covering her mouth. After placing her mug on the table, she recovered and looked at Victoria in shock. "You're pregnant?"

"Yeah I am," she replied a little sadly.

"I…" Jillian moved to the edge of her seat. "So when did this happen?"

After performing some quick math in her head, Victoria padded a few weeks on to clear Jim. "About nine weeks ago."

"Wow, I can't believe…"

"I know. I don't know how it happened. I thought I couldn't."

"Is it Jim's?"

"No way. I, uh, said *nine* weeks. I was already pregnant when we met. I just didn't know it."

"So whose is it?"

Victoria took a deep breath. "It's John's."

"Coach John?" Victoria nodded, and Jillian asked, "Coach John who's now back with his wife. That Coach John?"

"I know I'm a bit of a slut." Victoria widened her eyes. "But he was the only coach I was fucking."

"Yeah, right. Sorry. Are you okay? Does he know?"

"No, absolutely not. He doesn't know. And you can't tell him."

"Oh, I won't."

"I'm going to tell him as soon as I figure this whole thing out. Please don't tell Brian. I'm not ready to tell anyone yet. Can you make something up about moving the wedding date? Tell him you just can't wait to marry him or…"

Placing a hand over Victoria's, Jillian gave her a comforting smile. "Sure, I'll figure something out. So are you keeping it?"

"Definitely. I never considered… and I thought about adoption, but I spent more than five years of my life obsessing over getting pregnant. Now, when it's the furthest thing from my mind, it happens. If God wants me to have this baby, well then I'm going to have it."

"Wow." Jillian stared off toward the pool thinking for a few moments. After shaking her head and taking a deep breath, she studied Victoria. "You seem happy. Are you happy?"

"You know, I am. I really am."

"Well then I'm happy for you."

"So about the wedding. If you don't change it, I'll be seven months pregnant and look ridiculous standing next to you at the wedding, and no one will want to see me naked on the beach so..."

"Oh, I'm sure we can do something."

"I looked at a calendar and most colleges get a few days off around Columbus Day. It's right in the middle of the semester so the workload might not be too bad for Jim and for me."

"When is that?"

"October tenth."

"Wow, that only gives me about eight weeks to plan everything." Jillian gave her a confident nod. "But, uh, I think I can pull that off."

"I hate to ask you to change everything, but—"

"Don't you worry about it one bit. We can work it out. It only takes one afternoon to get married. We can fly down there on Friday, and people can fly back on Sunday if they really need to get back. It'll be fine. I can't wait to hold a baby again and buy the little clothes and..." Suddenly overcome with emotion, a tear fell from Jillian's eye. "You've got to let me babysit all the time."

"Okay." Victoria gave her a skeptical look.

"I'm serious. I'll watch the baby while you're at class or whatever."

"Really?"

"Yes. I'm super excited about this."

With her voice cracking, Victoria began to lose it. "I, uh, I love you."

Standing, Jillian opened her arms wide. Victoria moved into her embrace, and they both sobbed uncontrollably.

Brian walked outside and gave them an odd look. "What the hell is going on?"

Victoria and Jillian turned to him while wiping their tears. Jillian said, "Oh nothing. We were just talking about some sad movie."

"Oh." Nodding, he shook his head baffled.

Victoria pulled herself together. "So how was your birthday? I heard it was a little harried."

Jillian glared at her and Brian looked completely lost. "What?"

"I mean, I heard you were stressed out by those two hot police officers."

"Oh, yeah. I, uh, was." The three stood in silence for a few awkward moments until Jillian said, "I'll be in in a minute, we just have some girl talk to—"

"Ok, sure. No problem, I'll just, uh, you know." With his words trailing off, he turned and walked back into the house.

When he'd left, Jillian said, "Don't tell him what I said about his you know."

"I was kidding around. I would never say anything," Victoria lied. She was already making plans to help him fix his little problem down there in time for their wedding night.

<u>**5**</u>

Waking before Caroline, Jim slipped out of bed. After putting on shorts and a T-shirt, he went to the massage room. He prepared the table, turned on the stone warmer, then went to the kitchen to put on the teakettle. He brought a cup into the guest room and placed his hand gently on Caroline's shoulder. Her eyes opened, and she smiled at him. "Hey, what time is it?"

"About ten thirty."

She yawned, stretching lazily while wearing a sexy grin. "Last night was incredible. You were just…"

"I know. I do my best work in this house." He grimaced. "Wow, that was inappropriate and a little creepy."

She nodded in agreement. "Maybe a little."

"Yeah."

After sharing a frown, he raised his eyebrows. "Did you forget what we're doing today?"

She looked at him confused.

"The massage. I've got the stones heating up."

"Oh, yeah I can't wait."

He handed her the mug of tea. "Drink this and then meet me next door when you're ready. Victoria's out and won't be back until this afternoon. I have a couple things to get ready."

A few minutes later, Caroline stood in the door to the massage room, completely naked. She found Jim checking the temperature of the stones. Smiling at her, he motioned toward the table. With a spring in her step, she hurried over and climbed on top of it. He exhaled deeply as he watched her beautiful breasts, which hung deliciously down from her chest as she relaxed on the table with her head in the rest.

After admiring her for another few seconds, he placed the first warm stone on her back. She groaned, and her body melted into the warm, padded table just a little more.

"That feels amazing," she whispered.

He placed five more stones in an S-shaped pattern on her back and after pouring some massage oil into his palms, he worked it all over his hands. As soon as he placed his hands on her, she sighed deeply. He proceeded to rub every inch of her back around the stones, then moved up to her shoulders and neck.

Five minutes into the session, she let out a long sigh. "You are so good at this."

"Thanks."

"Please never, ever stop."

After ten more minutes of working her upper back, he removed the cooled stones and moved to the other end of the table. He dribbled a thin line of warm oil from her firm ass cheek all the way down her leg and back up the other leg until he reached its perfect twin.

"Oh, my God," she groaned softly.

She spread her legs a bit, and he glanced at her gorgeous parts as he began to work the oil into her legs. Exhaling deeply, his eyes followed his hands up and down her faultless lower body.

Her moaning continued, and he bent over close to her ass for a better look. Licking his lips, he grinned. He wanted to taste her, but he couldn't break the rule. His rule was kind of stupid, but it was still a rule. Feeling his breath on her ass, she lifted her hips off the table toward him.

He shook his head. "God, you have a beautiful body."

"It's yours—do whatever you want to it."

Sliding his hands up her legs to her ass, he firmly massaged each cheek. Occasionally, he slipped a finger onto her tiny hole. With each swipe, her eyes rolled back in her head, and she gasped. She lifted her hips higher off the table, and he stared at her breathlessly, with his excitement growing in his shorts. "Do you, uh, want to get out of here and maybe take a shower?"

She whispered, "Or you could just slip it in right here."

"I really shouldn't."

"Why not?"

"This massage room is for relaxation only. There's a feng shui thing going on in here and—"

"Feng shui?"

"It's just a stupid rule that…"

Lifting her head out of the rest, she gave him a sexy look. "You don't need to explain. I wouldn't mind washing this oil off anyway. That way you could kiss every inch of my body."

"That was my plan." He smiled. "Let me just make sure I don't burn the house down then I'll meet you in the bathroom."

Moving away, he dried his hands on a towel and watched her shake her little ass as she took off out of the room. After he turned off the table and the stone warmer, he went to the bathroom where he found her in the shower washing her hair. He watched as the soapy water dripped off her body. Stripping off his clothes, he stepped into the shower with her. She lathered the soap in her hands and gently washed him, all of him, as he groaned with delight.

After rinsing him off, she turned to face the spray of the water. His erection pressed into the cleft of her firm ass. She reached back and ran her hands along his hips as she pushed back gently. Groaning, he pressed his lips to her shoulder. He trailed kisses down her back until he was on his knees staring at her twin pale cheeks. She spread her legs in anticipation. Breathing heavily, he watched the water cascade down her perfect backside. When he couldn't wait any longer, he moved his lips to her.

"Oh, God," she moaned.

He kissed her places she had never been kissed before. Jim continued pleasing her for a long time, with his neck straining and his tongue tiring. It went on and on, with spray from the shower slipping down his throat, but he didn't care.

After she experienced a huge climax, she looked back to him, panting and desperately wanting to please him as she struggled to catch her breath. "Wow, I... don't tell me she taught you that too?"

"No, I kind of came up with that on my own."

"Good." She smiled, then placed her hands on his chest. She ran them slowly down to his penis, slipped to her knees, then began to return the favor.

When she was done with him, he was left slumped against the shower wall with his heart pounding out of his chest. He wanted to tell her he loved her, but it was too soon. He felt like a moron. They had been dating for just a few weeks, but he wanted to spend every minute with her. She was perfect.

6

Victoria returned a few hours later, and she and Jim sat out by the pool as Caroline packed their things. He smiled at her. "Thanks for letting us stay here. She really enjoyed the massage."

Victoria grinned. "Were you able to stick with your no sex in that room rule?"

"We did, but it wasn't easy."

Her smile faded as the awkwardness of that exchange washed over them both. After sitting in silence for another few moments, he asked, "How are you doing? Are you seeing anyone?"

"Not really, but I did meet this hot guy on my flight back from Philadelphia. He owns a restaurant and is a little closer to my age."

"That's great." He glanced quickly to her firm legs. He sighed and thought, *Shit, I'm still in love with her. I love both of them. There must be something wrong with me.* He shook off those thoughts and said, "Just make sure he's a good guy before…"

"Oh, I will."

Caroline walked outside and approached them. They both smiled at her, and Caroline said, "Your house is beautiful. I appreciate you letting us stay with you. That massage room he put together is spectacular."

"You both can stay with me anytime."

Caroline gave her a slightly evil smile. "He has great hands. I almost couldn't make it through the whole thing without…" she bragged with her eyebrows raised.

With a twinge of jealously, Victoria glared at Caroline. "I know he does have great hands. When we, uh—"

"Okay then." Getting to his feet, he interrupted. "We'd better get on the road if we're going to make it to North Carolina before midnight."

After the two women exchanged fake smiles, they all headed into the house.

Two days later, Jillian was working on finalizing the arrangements for the expedited October tenth wedding. Brian had verified he could be away from the office, and they checked with

Jim to be sure he could make that date as well. She told Brian that she was having second thoughts about pulling everyone away from their homes around Christmas plus the timing worked better in October with some book promotion events that her publisher was planning.

By the end of that day, she had booked the wedding and reception at the luxurious Hotel Eden Rock and reserved a block of hotel rooms for the anticipated guests. She arranged for a charter flight from Miami to St. Barts and back. She also discovered a large, gorgeous beach mansion available for rent that would serve as a quiet spot for the wedding party to stay separately from the other guests. She thought it would be the perfect place to hold a rehearsal dinner. The wedding coordinator from the hotel helped her immensely in the whole process—everything from choosing a minister to finalizing the menu. In fact, everything was easy, but it was, of course, outrageously expensive.

After placing a rush order in for thirty invitations, she worked with Brian to finalize the guest list. She mailed the invitations out two days later, then told Brian it was time he made the call he'd been dreading for months. Although he spoke to his mother about every other week, he failed to mention the important fact that he and Jillian were about to be married. With the invitation on its way, he slept on it one more night, then made the call.

When his mother answered the phone, he just blurted his news out. She didn't say a word. He went on to explain that the wedding was going to be in St. Barts and that their airplane and hotel reservations would all be prearranged. He didn't apologize for not telling her sooner nor did she ask why he didn't. The call ended with Beverly simply saying they would be there. There were no congratulations, but there were also no tears, arguments, or questions. Brian breathed a sigh of relief.

In Kill Devil Hills, North Carolina, Jim and Caroline were a few days into their hectic beach vacation with Caroline's wild sister. With the house overflowing with guests, the two of them had absolutely no privacy. They were relegated to sleeping in the living area of the small rundown shack, but they were together and blissfully happy. They found they couldn't even go into the lone bathroom together without someone knocking on the door every few minutes.

That night they were craving each other as they walked along the beach hand in hand. Giving him a suggestive look, she led him toward the dunes. Once there, they slipped down to the sand and knelt as they kissed and explored each other's bodies with roving hands. Moments later, she cried out, "Ouch." Then she slapped at her calf. "Sorry."

She moved to kiss him again but pulled away, this time slapping her arm. "I'm getting all bitten up, let's get out of here."

They rushed back to the house and found six people there drinking, laughing, and having a great time. They joined in and, after downing a beer, they returned to eyeing each other hungrily. After one more drink, and with the booze accentuating their desires, they could barely contain themselves as the waited for everyone to retire to their rooms. Just after 3:00 a.m., they finally found themselves alone. They were both fully clothed as Caroline slipped on top of him. He ran his hands all over her ass as she placed her hand over his groin. He gasped. Just then, a random guy walked through the living room to the kitchen. Seeing what they were obviously up to, he looked at them, fighting back a smile. "Sorry."

They sighed and gave the intruder a tired look. When they were alone again, they went back to it. Moments later, just as she placed her hand on his zipper, her sister came through the front door with two other people. Jim and Caroline separated as her sister giggled drunkenly, "Wow, sorry about that. You mind if they crash in here on the floor with you?"

"Sure," Jim replied as they sat together on the sofa frowning. Widening his eyes, he leaned close to her and whispered, "Do you want to go for a ride?"

"Yes."

Two minutes later he was driving the car as she was busy with her head in his lap. He gripped the steering wheel tightly. "I can't do this." Pulling into a public parking area near the beach, he turned off the car. She sat up, and he moved on top of her. They kissed. Placing his hands under her miniskirt, he found she wasn't wearing panties. They both groaned as he plunged a finger between her legs. Unbuttoning his pants, she rushed to pull them down to his hips as he lifted her skirt up.

He adjusted her seat back, and they struggled to get into the right position as he slipped between her legs in the cramped car. "Shit, I don't have a condom. They're back at the place."

Pushing her head back against the headrest, she sighed. After closing her eyes, she gave him a hopeful look. "Just put it in for a minute and pull it out before…"

"Are you sure?"

"I'm just about to get my period, so we're go—" Before she could get the words out, he pushed inside of her. They shared a groan as their lips locked together with tongues exploring each other's mouths while he pumped into her with passion.

"Oh," she cried out. "I hate condoms. Your cock feels… I should really go on the pill."

"You really should." He pumped harder into her.

Staring deep into his eyes, she was close to orgasm. "Don't you dare stop. That's it… yes."

As the car windows fogged with the intense heat they were generating, he teetered on the brink desperately trying to avoid coming inside of her. He tried to focus on something, anything else as she held him tightly. With her mouth opened wide, she stiffened her legs pushing up higher in the seat. Suddenly she screamed out with a loud climax, pulling his hips closer to her.

With his face contorted, he fought back his orgasm. She moved once more and it was upon him. Pulling away from her quickly, he exploded all over her thighs and skirt. Their eyes met as she reached up to massage him with both hands. He groaned as she pulled the last drops of semen from him.

When he could take it no more, he moved to his seat panting like he'd just run a marathon. She slumped against the passenger door, desperate to recover.

Turning toward him, their eyes slowly met and she sighed. "Wow."

Gazing back at her, dizzied, he nodded slowly. "Yeah."

7

A week later, at around 7:00 a.m., after an evening of magical sleep-depriving, late-night sex, Jillian was wandering around the grocery store in a zombie-like fashion. As she headed down an aisle, struggling to remember what the hell she needed from this section, Coach John appeared in front of her pushing a cart with a few items in it.

"Jillian, how are you?"

She smiled. "I'm, uh, fine. How's everything with you?"

"Couldn't be better."

"Hey, tell Mary, it was a pleasure getting to know her at Brian's party."

"I will, and we all got to *know* Brian really, really well that night." He made a face, and they shared a laugh. "Oh speaking of… Victoria told me she was going to tell you the good news."

She looked at him a little confused until he added, "The pregnancy."

After widening her eyes, she smiled. "Oh, yeah sure. I, uh…"

"Mary and I couldn't be happier. I can't wait to hear the pitter patter of little paws running around."

"Paws? That's so cute." Her smile faded as she gave him a serious look. "And Mary's okay with all this?"

"She's overjoyed. She's always wanted another. Mary just hopes we don't end up with some all-black ones. No one wants to adopt those."

She looked at him, a little offended, hoping maybe she didn't hear him correctly. She shook her head in confusion. "Wait, so now she's not keeping it?"

"We'll probably keep just one."

"She's having twins?"

"At least!" He scoffed.

After trying to shake the cobwebs from her mind, she steadied herself against the cart.

He reached his hand out in support. "Are you okay?"

"I'm, uh… so I just can't picture Victoria taking care of twins. I offered to babysit, but wow, I'm not sure I can handle that. Mary is a strong woman. If my husband came home and told me he was having another baby—especially with a woman as attractive as Victoria... I'd kill 'em. Not to mention it's twi—" She shut the fuck up when she saw his expression.

He placed his head in his hands. "Victoria's pregnant?"

She looked away, horrified. "What's that?"

After glancing around the aisle to be sure they were alone, he whispered, "She's pregnant with my baby!"

"I'm sorry." She tried to repair the damage with a casual smile. "Um, what were *you* talking about?"

"Our Golden Retriever is having puppies, and Victoria said she would ask you two if you wanted one."

"Oh we would love one or two even. When, will, uh..."

He looked away sadly. "I can't believe she wasn't going to tell me." Abandoning the cart, he turned and walked away in a daze. She stood there, dumbfounded, and watched him go. When he turned the corner, she pulled out her cell phone, dialed Victoria's number, and it went directly to voice mail.

Five minutes later, John was knocking gently on Victoria's door while hiding a bouquet of flowers behind his back. He glanced behind him to be sure none of the neighbors were watching. After a few seconds, he knocked again and Victoria opened the door sleepily and looked at him surprised.

"May I come in?"

"Sure."

He rushed to the living room, plopped down on the sofa and fidgeted nervously in his seat. Sitting next to him, she curled up on the sofa, drowsy eyed. He handed her the flowers. "These are for you."

"Thanks." Her eyes went from the flowers to his face while she wore a look of confusion.

He cleared his throat. "I, uh, I'm not sure what to say."

"John why are you here? Is everything okay with Mary?"

"Yeah. I just want to tell you that I'll be there for you with whatever you need. I'll be as involved as you want me to be."

With the realization washing over her face, she sat up straighter.

He opened his palms to her and gave her a genuine smiled. "I can help out financially. Just let me know what you want from me."

Looking at him, flabbergasted, she asked, "Have you spoken with Jillian?"

"Oh, yeah, sorry. I could tell she didn't mean to tell me. It just slipped out."

"I'll bet."

"I'm serious. I'll find a way to break it to Mary, but I really think—"

"John...John."

He looked to be in a trance.

She widened her eyes. "John?"

Still nothing from him. She lightly slapped him across the face, finally bringing him back to earth. "John are you with me?"

"Yes, yes."

"It's not your baby."

"What?" He shook his head mystified.

She repeated slowly. "It's not your baby."

"Then why'd she—"

"I told Jillian it was yours."

"But why?"

"Because I didn't want to tell her the truth."

"Which is what?"

"That it's either her fiancé's brother, Jim, or Rob, her son."

His jaw dropped. "You *slept* with Rob?"

A second later Jillian burst through the door, and Victoria and John stared at her shocked.

Victoria covered John's mouth with her hand; she waited for Jillian to say something. Jillian finally said, "I'm so sorry. I, uh..."

Standing up, Victoria grasped John's shirt with one hand and coaxed him to his feet with her other hand, still covering his mouth. Jillian looked at them, obviously confused. "Look, I didn't mean to—"

Victoria pointed at her. "You sit right there and don't move. Don't say anything—don't speak. You can breathe but nothing else."

Rushing to the sofa, Jillian sat down, and curled her lip as Victoria dragged John out the front door. Jillian decided not to breathe since she wasn't exactly sure if Victoria said, don't even breathe or if she could only breathe. As she pondered that question, Victoria slammed the door.

Removing her hand from his mouth, Victoria led him halfway down the driveway. "Look, I promise you it's not yours. We used a condom every time, plus we had sex a few weeks before I got pregnant."

"Oh…okay." He took a deep breath.

"Look, I'm not sure why I told you back there that I had sex with Rob because—"

"Oh, good, so you didn't have sex with him, because Mary and I found him to be a little creepy. He's like—"

She gave him a tired look. "I was drunk, okay? I did have sex with him but only once." She sighed. "I meant I shouldn't have told you because if Jillian finds out, she's going to kill me. You cannot tell anyone."

"Okay, no problem. Are you sure you're going to be okay?"

"Yeah, I just need to get back in there and pretend like I'm so mad that she told you. I'm really going to let her have it. Why the hell did she tell you? How did it come up?"

"I was telling her about the puppies, and I guess she must have thought I was talking about your pregnancy." He shrugged his shoulders. "I mentioned you, and now that I think about it, I guess she could have reasonably assumed that I was talking about you."

Victoria broke into a chuckle. "I'm still going to really give it to her. This will be fun. You go back to that hot wife of yours."

John opened his car door as he said, "We'll be praying that it's Jim and not…"

Victoria glared at him. "Do not tell anyone. Not even the wife."

He nodded, smiled, then whispered, "Got it. I'll be praying."

"Thanks." After shaking her head with a grin, she went to the front door, paused a moment to prepare her words, then headed inside.

Victoria burst through the door and glared down at Jillian. She noticed her slightly blue face as she sat there, apparently holding her breath. Victoria cringed. "What the hell is wrong with you?"

Jillian exhaled deeply. "I wasn't sure if you said—"

"Never mind. What the hell were you thinking?"

"I, uh, I'm so sorry. I thought—"

"Just shut up." Turning away, she bit her lip to keep from cracking up, then put on an angry face as she returned her attention to Jillian. She sat down across from her on the other sofa and simply shook her head. After ten seconds of that, she said, "Do you know he was thinking about going home first to tell his wife that we slept together? Luckily, he stopped here first. She doesn't even know that we dated. She thinks I'm some kind of physical therapist. Now she might have been okay with that, but he was also going to tell her that I was having his baby. That... she might have had a slight problem with."

"I never meant to—"

"Why did you tell him?"

"I thought he knew. He was asking me if you shared the good news about the pregnancy. How the heck was I supposed to know he was talking about his stupid dog?"

"So, you think I'm a dog!"

"What, no, I, uh..."

"Look, you are lucky that I nipped this in the bud. You could have been responsible for a divorce."

"I'm so sorry."

Rising from the sofa, she walked over to Jillian and folded her arms. "I don't want you to mention me or my pregnancy or... in fact, don't even mention the word *baby* to anyone... or puppy for that matter. Actually, you are not to discuss the offspring of any mammal with anyone."

"Okay...okay."

"Just to be clear, if someone tells you his fish just laid like a million eggs, you don't ask what kind of fish it is or reply in any way. Just turn and run away. Got it?"

Jillian nodded like a frightened child. "I understand. Again, I'm so sorry."

"You haven't told Brian have you?"

"No, I swear."

After studying her distraught expression, Victoria nodded. "Okay, I believe you. Now, I want you to go. I need to be alone."

"Sure, I'll…" Jillian got up and rushed to the door. She looked back. "Is there anything I can do? Should I talk to John and apol—"

Victoria's angry glare answered her question.

"Right, I won't even…"

"Good!"

Jillian walked out and closed the door. Sauntering back to bed, Victoria slipped under the covers and burst into laughter. She felt guilty, but it was the most fun she'd had in months. Okay, so her life was pretty boring now—mainly because she wasn't having any sex.

8

The next Monday, Victoria began her fall semester at the U. She was incredibly horny and walking on a campus full of attractive men was not helping her situation at all. Luckily her classes featured mostly women and had only a few, not terribly attractive, guys. The workload was heavy, but she found it pretty easy to focus with no man in her life.

Brian kept himself busy at work and also spent a lot of time trying to come up with the perfect gift to give to Jillian as a wedding present. His job at the bank was thoroughly boring, and he found himself craving some form of creative outlet. When he was younger he had excelled in art. He could draw competently and also had some experience with watercolors. He had never been great at drawing the human body, but all the times he spent studying Jillian's perfect body made him long to improve. He signed up for a night class at the community college without telling Jillian and told her he was working late on the nights he had class.

It was an intermediate class in drawing the human form, and his goal was to complete a drawing of Jillian and to give it to her on their wedding night. The class met twice a week and on the first night the students drew a female nude with charcoal from a large video screen of an image of a live model.

At the second class, he sat at his station, along with the twelve other students, and waited. A young man in a robe entered the room, approached the chair, slipped the robe off, and sat on the stool completely nude. He was a shower — that was the first thing Brian noticed. The three male students, including Brian, rolled their eyes as the nine female students widened theirs in anticipation. Brian reluctantly drew the man, focusing on all the parts except his junk until near the end of the class, when he made a halfhearted, smaller-than-scale drawing of the man's parts.

On the third night of class, the same nude male model sat on the same stool, but this time the video camera was on and focused directly on his penis. The large television screen displayed it in extreme close-up detail. It appeared to be about two feet long. The assignment was to draw it in exquisite detail. After rubbing his head, Brian sighed and went to work.

When he returned home late that night, Jillian still didn't suspect that anything was out of the ordinary. After having sex, he and Jillian were both in bed, naked. She had just dozed off, and as he attempted to fall asleep, he found it difficult to get the image of the giant member out of his mind. When he woke the next morning he lifted the covers off of her, and, gazing underneath, he found her resting in a beautiful pose. After watching her for a few moments, an idea hit him. Running outside wearing only boxers, he rushed to the car, then grabbed his drawing pad and supplies.

Back in the bedroom, he found Jillian still in the same position laying on her side sleeping soundly with her hand lying gently under her face with her gorgeous breasts in a perfect position. After carefully sliding the covers off her a little more, he exposed the rounded curve of her hips then sat down to sketch. He worked quickly and made some progress sketching her hips, stomach, and breasts, but as he started to work on her face, Jillian began to stir.

Panicking, he quickly ran out of the room with his pad and charcoal. When he returned to the room, he found her still sleeping soundly. It was a close call. He made his way to the bathroom to shower. After getting dressed, he sat in his car in the driveway, grimacing at his drawing. He wasn't happy with it at all; it was a rushed, nervously prepared sketch, he definitely needed a better plan.

Victoria attended classes that morning and took an exam. When she returned home, she worked on a paper for a few hours, then proceeded to do something far more important. She searched the Internet for a plausible way to request a blood sample from Rob and Jim. She located a nationwide firm that she could contact to obtain the samples for her. That was the easy part. Then she pondered her story—that was the hard part.

First, she considered telling them that she had been diagnosed with some new strain of chlamydia that wasn't all that dangerous but needed to be treated. And rather than have them go to the bother of seeing a doctor, she would send a lab tech to get a sample. This she felt was an option, although an embarrassing one leading to more questions, and best used as a last resort.

She considered some other implausible scenarios and as she scrolled one last page from her Internet search she spotted it—an ancestry search required a DNA sample. Sure, it could be garnered from a cheek swap, but her subjects probably wouldn't know that. She would tell them both that she was planning on giving the wedding couple a gift of a full ancestry search and a blood sample from a close relative was the only way she could pull this off and keep it a surprise. Maybe it was an odd gift, but she knew she could sell it. She could sell anything. The company she found online produced this elaborate, framed ancestry family tree tracing back the roots of individuals hundreds of years. She would use these details only if needed.

A quick phone call to Rob and Jim left them confused and a little reluctant but onboard. Victoria made the arrangements with the lab and a few days later both Rob and Jim were visited by a nurse—Jim at his dorm and Rob at his office. Victoria's sample could not be drawn for another few weeks, but at least she had the potential fathers' part out of the way.

At Brian's fourth class, it was female nude night; the three male students were looking forward to the refreshing sausage-free change. All Brian saw of the tall woman in the robe as she made her way toward the stool was her back. When she dropped her robe and exposed her beautiful ass, he felt a sort of déjà vu vibe. As the woman turned, he recognized that it was Victoria. He was not at all surprised. She spotted him instantly and rushed over for a hug as the other male students looked on jealously.

When they pulled apart, she smiled. "Got to go. I'll talk to you after class."

For some reason, he broke out in a sweat during the entire remainder of the hour-long class as he sketched her body in full detail. He was really beginning to improve, and when he was done, he admired his sketch proudly. When the class had ended, Victoria unabashedly walked over to him, sans robe, and stood along with him appreciating his work. As the other members of the class packed their things, they gawked at them both. Giving her a nervous look, he whispered, "Aren't you going to put on your robe?"

She scoffed. "I've been sitting up their naked for almost an entire hour, and now I'm supposed to suddenly become shy?"

He shrugged his shoulders.

She held her chin as she studied his drawing. "It's really good. I had no idea you were an artist." Frowning a bit, she pointed to her crotch on the page. "You made my labia too big."

"What?" He took a closer look at the drawing.

"My labia, it's not right."

"Really?" He glanced down between her legs. She spread them apart and shifted her hips forward so he could get a better look. A student walking by nearly burst into laughter at the sight of them.

Brian shifted his eyes from the drawing to her actual labia back and forth twice before nodding in agreement. "I guess you're right. It's the first time I've ever drawn that part."

"Wait until next class when you get to do the close-up. Then you can draw it really big. That's my favorite class."

"I'm not surprised." After chuckling, he looked at her with concern. "You can't tell Jillian you saw me here."

"Why not?"

"She thinks I'm at work."

She smirked at him. "Are you secretly doing this so you can check out naked chicks?"

"What? No." He made a face. "I want to do something special for her as a wedding gift. I'm going to sketch her and have it framed. Something tasteful but sexy."

She smiled brightly. "That's a great idea. She's going to love it — I'm sure of it."

"I'm also going to get her these expensive diamond earrings in case the drawing sucks, or she thinks it's creepy."

"Good back-up plan."

Glancing around the room, he found them all alone. "I guess we should…"

"Oh, yeah." She headed over to retrieve her robe and as she walked away he gazed at her ass wearing a smile.

In the parking lot a few minutes later, Brian stood with her in front of her car. "I can't figure out how to draw her though. I need to do it so she has no idea. I tried drawing her while she was asleep, but she moved, and I had to run out of the room to hide. I need a picture or something, but I need her to pose, and I don't think I can pull it off."

"Maybe..." Pondering his dilemma, she paused. "I think I can help you. She and I are going on that girl's weekend thing next week. I can get you a picture."

He gave her a hopeful smile. "How?"

"I'll figure out a way."

Suddenly concerned, his smile faded. "You can't drug her or anything. I need something sexy and tasteful. I mean I don't need an extreme close-up of her, you know or some spread leg pose like in *Hustler* or anything."

"Just leave it to me." She gave him a wink. "I know exactly what you need."

"No, I'm serious. No beaver shots or—"

Sighing, she shook her head. "Trust me."

At the next class, Brian completed an impressive two-foot by one-foot drawing of Victoria's gorgeous vagina. Her labia, both major and minor, were nearly perfectly proportioned on his sketch. As she stood behind him studying it, she smiled approvingly. She, of course, asked if she could have it, and he agreed.

2

Jillian and Victoria drove down to Key West to spend some *girl time* together before the wedding, which was only three weeks away. On Friday, they checked into their room late, had a quick dinner, then went to bed. Jillian quickly fell asleep, but Victoria lay awake, plotting their activities for the next day, and how she would pull off the photo shoot.

In the morning, they enjoyed a late breakfast and spent a few hours ogling hot guys at the pool. Victoria did most of the ogling. Next it was off to the spa where they each got a massage and assorted spa treatments. Victoria insisted that Jillian have her hair done and a full makeup session and when she was finished, Jillian looked breathtaking. They both dressed in beautiful, sexy dresses and went to an expensive restaurant for dinner. Jillian was going to avoid alcohol that night out of respect for the pregnancy, but Victoria again insisted. In fact, it was a key part of the plan. After Jillian's second cosmo, she headed off to the bathroom. Once she was out of sight, Victoria quickly summoned the waiter for a refill for her friend. When Jillian returned, she frowned. "I didn't want another drink." Flopping down onto her chair woozily, she shook her head. "I'm already… wow…"

Victoria said casually. "Oh, the waiter came by, and I figured… Go ahead, live a little."

"But they are good." Jillian smiled and took a big sip.

"I know, I miss them. So, have you decided what wedding gift to get for Brian?"

Jillian smiled brightly. "I've thought a lot about it, and I think I've come up with the perfect gift or gifts."

Victoria gave her a hopeful look even though no matter what was said next, she would shit all over it.

"You know that tennis vacation I took him on before graduation?"

"Yeah." Victoria muttered indifferently.

"We didn't get to really play on the grass court very long because we spent too much time in bed." Smiling, Jillian raised her eyebrows suggestively.

Victoria didn't smile at the sex reference, simply returning a stoic look instead. Jillian lost her own smile as she added, a little less enthusiastically, "Well I'm going to book us a trip out there again."

With her jaw slacked, Victoria painted on a huge frown. "Seriously?"

"Well…" Jillian gave her a weak smile. "Oh, and I'm getting him a couple of these new really expensive tennis racquets that he wants."

"So basically it's a tennis-themed gift extravaganza?" Victoria asked sarcastically.

"What? Not good." Jillian took a huge sip of her drink.

After looking away, Victoria sighed, and shook her head. "It sounds kind of lame."

"Seriously, I thought it—"

"That's the most impersonal wedding gift I've ever heard of."

"Really? He loved it when we played on a grass court and I thought—"

"Please stop talking," Victoria added with a tired look.

"Okay, but…" Jillian exhaled deeply. "So do you have a better suggestion?"

"I do, actually." Victoria's expression brightened. "I read about this woman who did like a professional sexy photo shoot, had this incredible centerfold spread put together, and gave it to her husband on their wedding night. The husband was blown away."

After downing the rest of her cosmo, Jillian grimaced. "I don't know."

Victoria repeated with over-the-top enthusiasm, "Blown away."

"Like naked pictures?"

Victoria nodded. "But tastefully done."

"Where would I get something like that done?"

"I could do it for you."

"You, you're a photographer now?"

She looked at her insulted. "Yes, I can take pictures."

"And you can put this layout together so it looks good? Or would you be sending the pictures out… oh, they'll probably end up all over the Internet."

"I can do all of it."

"How?"

"I've been taking a class," Victoria lied with the most sincere yet offended face she could generate.

Jillian gave her an unconvinced look.

"Okay. You know." Victoria sighed. "You try to help someone avoid a huge mistake on their wedding night and..."

Jillian gave her a devastated look. "What do you—"

"Your gift is the equivalent of Brian giving you like a, I don't know, a vacuum cleaner on something. You wouldn't want a vacuum cleaner would you?" Glaring at her, Victoria waited for a response.

"Well, no."

"You see."

"You sure you could take the pictures?"

"Yes."

"And create the layout, and no one else would see them?"

"No one would see them." Victoria exhaled deeply. "I promise you they won't be leaked to the Internet."

"Okay, I guess. When could we do it?"

"I have my camera. We could do it tonight."

"Tonight?"

"Sure. You look gorgeous. Your hair... your makeup— everything. You look spectacular. Your tits look big, too... maybe you're ovulating."

Jillian glanced at her chest and smiled. "Really, I, uh thought they seemed bigger too, but..." Returning to Victoria, she asked, "Tasteful?"

"Definitely." Victoria nodded with a big smile. "Maybe you should have one more drink." Instead of waiting for a reply, she waved over the waiter.

An hour later they returned to their hotel room, and Jillian was pretty loaded. She went into the bathroom as Victoria got out a large red satin sheet and tossed it over the bed and headboard. After turning on every light in the room, she pulled out her big expensive new digital camera and sat on the bed waiting.

Jillian emerged from the bathroom wearing only a robe. After spotting Victoria with her giant camera, she scanned the staged room and returned a concerned look to the amateur photographer. "Um, I'm not—"

"Oh, you look beautiful." Victoria smiled brightly. "Why don't we start with some in the robe, then go from there?"

Jillian said hesitantly, "Okay." She slid on to the satin sheet and posed awkwardly as Victoria began shooting pictures like crazy.

"Amazing." Victoria pointed the camera down. "Whenever you're ready. Just have fun with it. Show a little here and there, then lose the robe completely." Adjusting her robe, Jillian revealed some cleavage.

Victoria returned to taking pictures. "Brian is going to absolutely *love* these."

Smiling, more at ease now, Jillian pulled the robe off her shoulders and exposed her full breasts for the first R-rated picture.

Pulling her eye from the camera, Victoria shook her head. "Gorgeous. You are a natural."

Within minutes the robe was completely lost as Jillian got more and more comfortable and immersed in the experience. The booze helped a lot! Jumping around the room like a professional photographer, Victoria took shots from every angle and in every pose. They stopped short of any spread leg extreme close-ups, but the pictures Victoria took were steaming hot. She knew Brian would love them.

When they were done, Jillian went into the bathroom as Victoria reviewed the amazing pictures. When Jillian came out wearing pajamas, Victoria quickly put the camera into her bag.

"So…" Jillian sat down on the bed.

"So, what?"

"Let's see them."

"What?"

"The pictures can I see them?"

"Um, no. You can only see them on a computer screen."

Jillian narrowed her eyes. "I thought your camera had one of those preview screens."

"It's broken."

"I sure hope they came out. Could you imagine if we went through all this and every picture was blurry or something."

Victoria nodded as she thought, that was exactly the plan. "Let me take care of everything. I'll load the pictures on my computer and let you know when you can see them."

"Oh, okay." Jillian climbed under the covers. "You really think he'll like them?"

"I know he will."

"Good night."

"Good night, Jillian."

Jillian was asleep seconds after her head hit the pillow.

The next morning, Victoria and Jillian enjoyed a leisurely brunch and climbed in the car. During the drive home, they vowed to do another girl's weekend soon. After Victoria dropped Jillian off, she drove to her house, and called Brian as soon as she walked in the door. When he arrived, she met him at the door wearing a huge grin. "I got some great shots. Wait 'til you see them."

At the computer screen the first image that appeared was an extreme close-up shot of a woman's vagina and ass—a gorgeous, breathtaking shot.

"What the hell is that?"

"What do you think it is?"

"I know what it is." He sighed. "But I said no beaver shots of her."

"It's not her," Victoria said smugly.

"Yeah, you're right, that doesn't..." He moved closer to the screen with his eyes narrowed. "But it does look familiar."

She smiled. "It's me. I was just testing out my new camera."

He nodded casually.

"Do you think I should have my anus bleached?"

"What?"

"Do you think I should have it bleached? Is it too dark?"

"Your ass hole?" he asked incredulously. He glanced to her face, she nodded with widened eyes waiting for a response."

"What do you think?"

He slowly returned his gaze to the screen. "Um, I think it looks fine."

"Fine?"

"I mean it looks cute. I don't think it's too dark or anything. It's pinkish. I like it."

"Pink—ish!"

"Did I say ish?" He gave her a hesitant look.

"You did."

"I meant it's pink, and it's adorable."

"Really?"

She returned to looking at the screen. "You can have the picture if you want."

"Why would I want a picture of your ass?"

"I figured you did such a good job sketching my pussy that you might want to sketch my ass too."

"Gee thanks, but if we're done with your ass can I see the pictures of my fiancée?"

She rolled her eyes. "You really are no fun." As Victoria flipped from picture to picture, Brian was blown away. There were more than one hundred shots, all sexy, with varying degrees of explicitness. None of them appeared tasteless.

He smiled and kissed her on the cheek. "You're amazing. This is just what I need."

"Great."

"How the hell did you get her to do this?"

"I asked what she was going to get you for a wedding present and after she told me, I told her it was the dumbest present ever."

"Yeah, then…"

"Then I told her I read about this woman who did a sexy photo shoot layout for her husband as a gift."

"She believed that?"

She grinned. "After a lot of alcohol and compliments."

He nodded matter-of-factly.

Returning her eyes to the screen, she said, "She wouldn't be the first woman to fall for the old casting couch, but she's probably the most intelligent though."

He chuckled. "Is there anything you can't get someone to do?"

"No." She gave him a smug look. "Not that I know of."

After popping the card out of the computer, she handed it to him. He kissed her again on the cheek. "And your pussy and ass are gorgeous. I wouldn't change a thing. Thanks again." He walked away, leaving her beaming.

About an hour later, Victoria picked up the phone and dialed. Jillian answered. "Victoria. So can I come see the pictures?"

"Uh, I'm... I don't know what happened. I'm a complete moron. All the pictures are blurry. You can't even tell what they are. It was the lighting or the camera settings or something."

"Oh, no. Should we try again?"

"I don't think I'm going to be able to pull it off."

"Really?" Jillian sighed. "So what should I get him now?"

"Oh, that whole tennis thing sounds amazing."

"What?"

"The tennis vacation and racquets and all will be perfect. He loves all that crap."

"But you said it was the worst gift ever. You made me feel—"

"I did not," Victoria interrupted.

"You certainly did."

"I don't know what you're talking about. You were drinking last night weren't you?"

"Yes, but—"

"You were drunk, right?"

"I wouldn't say I was drunk."

"Seriously?"

"Okay, maybe I was, but—"

"Look I think the tennis idea is great. You really should let this go. I might not have been completely on board with it last night, but it's starting to grow on me."

Jillian stared straight ahead completely lost.

10

After six weeks of working long hours at his first ever real job, Rob was doing bench presses in the workout room of the Blue Stone Apartments on a Sunday afternoon. He'd been able to get some of his workouts in, but mostly at odd hours when the gym was virtually empty. On this day, the room was crowded. There were two other men in the room along with ten young women. Some of the women were on treadmills, others were stretching, and a few were using the weight machines, but all were gorgeous and dressed in revealing, sexy outfits. Rob had forgotten about the pre-workout masturbation suggestion from Gary, and this was the first day it really would have come in handy.

He and Gary stared at a woman with a perfect body as she climbed onto a reverse leg curl machine and proceeded to put on a show. Rob moved his glance slowly back to Gary. "Wow."

"I know, right. At least out here they wear clothes."

"Rob scoffed. "What do you mean?"

"The steam room," Gary said like he should already know about it. Off Rob's confused look, Gary shook his head, flabbergasted. "Follow me."

Two minutes later, Rob and Gary were sitting in the steam room with towels wrapped around their waists. They were alone.

"I didn't know this was here. So, what, uh, they come in here in their tiny towels?"

Shaking his head, Gary gave him a tired look.

"I'm not sure I can handle that. I didn't jerk off like you sug—"

Just then a completely naked gorgeous young woman entered the room carrying her towel. Rob shut up as his jaw dropped. After nonchalantly opening up his towel, Gary smiled at her.

"Hey, guys," she said.

Rob glanced down to Gary's display, and Gary whispered, "Don't be shy, they don't like it."

Rob quickly opened his towel; his penis had built up a little size to it already due to the free show. Moments later, Carl Rodgers entered the room, unabashedly carrying his towel with his nub of a penis displayed for all of them to see. Rob nearly grinned but held back.

Carl let his gaze linger on the naked beauty a long time before he turned his attention to the Rob and Gary. "Hey, boys."

"Mr. Rodgers," Rob said.

Gary said, "Hey, Carl."

Smiling, Carl sat down really close to Rob. "Call me Carl, Rob. We're naked for God's sake."

"Sorry, Carl."

Rob could feel Carl's eyes on his groin. Rob broke out into a big sweat deciding whether to cover up or move or just act casual. Unable to make up his mind, he sat frozen.

Carl said, "This steam room is a wonderful way to relax."

Rob nodded quickly and tried to focus on not getting an involuntary erection. He glanced at the young woman; she smiled at him and leaned back and closed her eyes. Rob's eyes traveled from her perfect breasts to her gorgeous vagina. His mouth was wide open. After watching Rob gawk, Gary elbowed him in the ribs. Rob glared at him, and Gary made a face that screamed, "Knock it off."

Sighing, Rob struggled to put on a casual expression.

Two more hot naked women entered. Carl's eyes were all over them for a few seconds, then his gaze traveled back to Rob's groin. Rob felt it go there. The women exchanged greetings with the lucky guys and took their places in the hot steamy room. Ignoring Carl, Rob just casually enjoyed the view.

They all sat in the room without saying a word for a few minutes until Carl put his hand on Rob's knee. "Rob, I think I know a girl who would really like a guy like you." He glanced once more into his lap. "Yeah, I really think you're her type. Would you like to meet her?"

After pausing to look where Carl was looking, Rob moved his knee. "Uh, sure."

Removing his hand from Rob, Carl looked him in the eye. "Great. I'll call you next time she's here."

"Cool," Rob muttered uncomfortably.

Carl stood. "Well, I'll see you guys at the office."

After their boss left the room, Rob raised his eyebrows to Gary. Gary returned a confused shrug and neither one mentioned a word about it. A few minutes later, two more gorgeous naked women strolled into the room, and Rob glanced around utterly mesmerized. He folded his towel up to partially cover his groin as he vowed to workout during normal peak hours from now on, but only after a quick jerk-off session, of course.

After returning to his apartment, Rob showered. He slumped on his sofa, depressed, and thought about the fact that he hadn't had a single date since he'd moved to Orlando. He'd been too busy, but here he was, surrounded by amazingly hot and seemingly single women, and he wasn't dating any of them. He had talked to a few, but none returned enough interest for him to ask out. He realized he hadn't had sex since Kara and her roommate gave him that spectacular blow job almost two months ago. He hadn't spoken to Kara much since that amazing night, but he had seen her occasionally by the pool.

Rob dressed in nice pair of shorts and a polo shirt, slapped on some cologne, then headed to Kara's apartment. When she answered the door, she didn't appear all that happy to see him. He walked in, and Kara led him to the sofa.

"I was wondering if you wanted to go out some night?" Taking a seat, he spread his arms out along the back of the sofa, seemingly hoping for a repeat performance.

She sat as far away from him as humanly possible with her legs curled up in front of her. "I kinda have a boyfriend."

"Oh, is that a new development or… ?"

She ignored the question. "How's work going?"

"Pretty good. The hours are long, but, uh—"

"Have you gotten one of those big bonus checks yet?"

"No, not yet."

"When you do, let me know, and we'll celebrate."

She stood and stared at him. When he didn't get the message, she sighed. "My boyfriend is coming over soon, and I've got to get ready."

"Oh, sorry." Rising to his feet, he headed for the door.

Once he reached his apartment, Rob slumped on the sofa, depressed. After falling asleep, he was blasted awake by his cell phone ringing. He checked the display, and it was Laura. They hadn't spoken since the cruise. While waiting through two more rings, he slapped his cheeks a few times to avoid sounding like a loser who was napping in the middle of the day, then answered, "Yo."

"Rob?"

"Oh, hey, Laura."

"What are you doing?"

"Just lounging by the pool."

"I was driving back from Tampa, and I saw a sign for Orlando and I just kinda turned off. I think I'm right by your apartment building. Your mom gave me the address. Mind if I stop by?"

"Um, I, uh…" He rose to his feet in a panic. "No, that would be great. Just follow the path through the palm trees to the pool."

"Great, I'll see you in a few minutes."

He ended the call and rushed toward the bedroom, stripping off his clothes along the way.

Four minutes later, Rob was catching his breath as he relaxed on a lounge chair near the pool. His breathing was almost back to normal as Laura walked through the gate. She gazed in awe at the bevy of tiny-bikinied super model types as they frolicked around the pool. Spotting him, she smiled as she walked over.

He rose up to greet her, and they hugged. Laura said, "I'm so glad you were home. I would have felt like a complete moron."

"I can't believe you're here."

"Me neither."

Both were ignoring the obvious issue of Rob catching her blowing some other guy on the cruise ship, which led to him punching the recipient of the blow job, a huge public blowout between the young, volatile couple capped off by a return to their cabin for a slight property-damaging argument. There were eighteen complaints from passengers, a lawsuit threat from the guy who received the punch, and enough damage to the cabin to get them thrown off the ship on the island of St. Thomas. From there, they took separate flights home and hadn't spoken since.

"So, how've you been," he asked.

"Good… good." She glanced around the pool area while shaking her head. "This place is so nice." She scanned the crowd, raising her eyebrows probably because of the fact that there must have been twenty women compared to the three guys.

"It's okay." He shrugged. "So you were in Tampa?"

"Yeah, I was hanging out with some college friends."

Several women walked past them and said hello to Rob, he knew them all by name. Laura watched, awestruck, as one with a particularly spectacular ass walked by with nothing more than a string separating her cheeks. When Rob didn't even look at the girl's ass, Laura looked at him a little surprised "I shouldn't have stopped by like this, you're probably busy."

"No, no. Can you stay for a while?"

"I can."

"We could just hang out here. There's a bar, and we have this great carryout place like a block away."

"Awesome."

Twenty minutes later, Laura had gone up to his apartment and changed into her bikini while he went to pick up their dinner. They sat by the pool, eating, talking, and drinking until the poolside bar closed at 11:30 p.m. Neither of them mentioned the cruise, blow jobs given to random guys, Natalie, nor anything potentially negative. They simply enjoyed each other's company and had a good time catching up.

When they found themselves alone in the pool area, they went into the water, but she found it too cold and climbed out. As she was shivering, wrapped in a towel, he said, "They have this amazing steam room here. We could go in and get warmed up."

"Sounds good."

He led her inside the empty workout room and directed her to the door for the women's locker room. He told her she would see the door to the steam room from there and told her he would meet her inside in a minute.

He entered the steam room just seconds before she did. They both stood just inside their respective doors and wearing their respective towels. Inside the room were two naked young gorgeous women and a naked guy that Rob recognized from work but whose name he couldn't remember. He nodded to the crowd as she gawked around the room wearing a shocked expression. After pulling off his towel, he gave a sympathetic smile. She glanced down to his penis, and her lips parted. She shrugged and opened up her towel. Glancing over to the naked guy, Rob discovered him staring at Laura, and promptly gave him an evil look.

Rob and Laura made their way to an open bench, placed their towels down on it, and sat. Sighing, she leaned back with her eyes closed. He drank in her hot little body, and glanced down dreamily to the sight of her womanly parts. He really missed her. Turning his attention to his penis, he wasn't impressed with its cold pool water shrunken size. After scanning the room to be sure no one was looking, he gave it a few well-placed tugs. Ten seconds later, it had responded nicely and was putting on a respectable showing. Then he leaned back, sighed loudly with his eyes closed, then opened his eyes slightly so he could be sure Laura was looking at him. When he found that she was, he closed his eyes again and fought back the urge to smile.

Spreading his legs wider, he leaned back a little more, and flexed the muscles in his groin every five seconds or so to keep just enough blood in the target area to maintain its size without causing it to stand straight up. Laura stared at it desperately. Her eyes went to the crowd and thankfully no one was watching. After glancing to Rob's face to be sure his eyes were still closed, she gave his half-hard penis her attention. With her lips parted and her hands squeezing her knees in anticipation, she watched it closely. She noticed it moving every few seconds, and felt her excitement rising as well. Grinning, she knew what he was up to. She watched as one of the women stood and walked out of the room. The other woman spread out her towel and lounged back on the bench facing away from the creepy guy. Laura watched the whole production, fighting back a giggle as she caught the naked guy staring at the attractive girl longingly.

Following the other woman's lead, Laura spread her towel out along the bench and lounged back with her knees bent and pointed toward Rob. She relaxed back with her eyes closed, and Rob sat up and casually glanced around the room. Eight feet from him was a gorgeous tall woman with perky breasts and a tiny ass, and three feet from him was his completely naked ex-girlfriend with her gorgeous parts pointed right at his face. It didn't get much better than that, oh except that creepy guy was there as well. Ignoring the guy and the tall girl, Rob focused on Laura's body as she lazily moved her knees apart a few inches and back together over and over. Her foot gently brushed his thigh, and he found he didn't need to keep flexing his groin muscles any longer because his body was sending more blood than he wanted to his groin. Suddenly concerned, he covered it partially with the towel as he continued drinking in Laura's body.

The tall woman stood and left the room just as Laura's toes dug their way under his thigh. Exhaling deeply, he watched as she spread her legs wider. He leaned back and put his hands behind his head. Then, he made eye contact with the creepy guy who was now smiling. Rob glared at him, and the guy looked away, focused now on Laura's breasts. Rob's mouth dropped open as he continued to glare at the guy, and when the third wheel finally glanced back to him, Rob motioned with his head to the door and made a face that screamed, Hey, dude, get the fuck out of here.

Offended, the creepy guy stormed out of the room. Laura glanced around, saw that they were finally alone, and smiled. Rob grinned as Laura spread her knees far apart. He gazed into her crotch, and his penis grew even larger. Her toe gently caressed his thigh, and he took a deep breath. Moving one leg from the bench to the floor, she placed the other on the higher bench behind them.

He stood and spread out his towel directly in front of her. He lay down flat on the bench with his head just a few inches from her thighs.

She watched him breathlessly as his mouth moved toward her. When his tongue touched her, she nearly pulled away. Instead, she closed her eyes, as he pressed deeper into her. Twenty minutes later, after trading huge orgasms, they slumped back, recovering and just staring at each other.

He smiled breathlessly. "I've missed you."

"I've missed you too."

"I'm sorry about the cruise."

"Let's not talk about it. Let's just forget about it."

"Okay." Slumping his head back against the bench, he ran his fingers through her hair. After ten seconds of holding her, caressing her in that overbearing swamp-like room, he announced, "I've got to get out of here. It's hot as hell."

She pulled up from him. "I know."

"Pool?" he asked.

After sharing a quick nod, they each headed out of the room through opposite doors.

Two minutes later, Laura walked out to the pool and found Rob already in the water and no one else around. After jumping in, she swam to him. He gave her a serious look. "What exactly are we doing? Are we back or…"

"This was fun, but you're here, and I'm in Miami. Why don't we just not define it? Let's just have some fun when we see each other."

"Okay."

He took her in his arms, she wrapped her legs around him, and he moved around the pool carrying her. Feeling his growing excitement, she wrapped her legs around him tighter.

"You heard my mother's getting married, right?"

"Yeah, to your best friend." She chuckled.

"I know. It's weird, but somehow they are good together. She's happy, and he's actually a great guy."

"I know." She frowned. "He wouldn't sleep with me."

"He was in love with her even then. So the wedding is October ninth in St. Barts. My mother has a plane chartered, and we leave that Friday and come back Monday. Do you want to go with me?"

"I do." She gave him a sexy smile.

He returned the smile, and they kissed. The kiss intensified with the heat rising between them as he moved near the edge of the pool. Reaching down to her bikini bottoms, he moved them aside as he slid a finger between her legs. She gasped and looked around the empty pool area. "Rob!"

"What?"

"We're in a public place."

"I just licked you in a public steam room. No one's around." He raised his eyebrows suggestively.

She shrugged in agreement. After pushing his swim trunks down a little, he pulled out his erection. He guided it to her entrance, and she slid down over him, using her legs to pull him deep inside.

"Oh, fuck," he moaned. They kissed, their tongues exploring each other's mouths as she began moving her hips back and forth.

"God, you feel so good," she said.

They fucked like crazy in the pool. She felt nearly weightless as he moved her up and down on him. When neither could climax after five minutes of trying really, really hard, they went upstairs and finished the job.

11

The next day, Albert Blair sat in his office pensively reviewing, for the tenth time, the background report on the superflexible and also apparently anal-sex loving, Natalie Brookhart. He was torn, but only a little. Five copies of Jillian's new novel, *The Leg Thing*, sat on his desk. After pausing for a moment to reconsider, he pulled out an overnight envelope. Inside, he placed a copy of the book along with three articles on famous literary-related lawsuits and attached a Post-it note that simply said, "Enjoy this, Rebecca." He sealed and addressed the envelope, but did not include his return address information; he sent his assistant to drop it off. As he thought about the possibilities, most specifically his ten percent cut, his slight frown turned into a smile.

Over a thousand miles away, Jillian walked down to the bookstore at the mall, searching for her new novel. She wore sunglasses so she wouldn't be recognized and found a few copies of her book on a shelf with other new releases; there was no special display or promotion. She asked the clerk how it was selling, and he just shrugged and made a face, then got back to work stocking a shelf. She walked back home disappointed.

At just about the same time, on the campus of NYU, Natalie Brookhart walked into the campus bookstore and a display of books caught her attention. Her eye was instantly drawn to the silhouette of a ballerina in the exact pose that she made famous at Georgia State University. She couldn't remember how many times she was asked to get into the position, either at parties or in the quad outside of her dorm, but she was quite well known for it. Hardly anyone knew the technical name for the pose; everyone who asked always referred to it as the leg thing.

As she glanced from the image of the ballerina to the title of the book, which read *The Leg Thing*, her eye went quickly to the author's name, Jaclyn West. With her eyes bugging out, she nearly had an aneurysm. Rushing into the store, she looked around in a panic, and could not locate the book. She spotted a female employee. "Where is that Jaclyn West novel you have in the window?"

The woman replied, "Oh, it's wonderful. Such a great love story—funny too." Then she pointed toward the display. Natalie rushed over and picked up a copy, flipping the book open to read the jacket description:

Anastasia White is a disillusioned, recently divorced, world-famous fashion designer. Brice Nelson is a tennis-obsessed, college senior who's unlucky in love, and the roommate and best friend of Anastasia's son, Ryder. He's infatuated with a superflexible, ex-ballet dancer co-ed named Rebecca, who's toying with his affections. When Ryder brings Brice home for spring break, and Brice meets the surprisingly young and also tennis-passionate Anastasia, their shared interest quickly develops into an intense mutual attraction...

"Holy shit!" Natalie said as she stopped reading the jacket and began flipping through the book. She skimmed pages until she spotted the name Rebecca. She read a paragraph about Brice watching Rebecca get into the leg thing position that was written in exquisite detail. Shaking her head, she flipped through more of the book until she just happened on the term *technical virgin*. Her mouth shot open as she read all the explicit details of Rebecca explaining it to Brice. It made the Rebecca character sound like an off-the-wall lunatic. Scowling, she slammed the book closed, turned to the back cover, and studied the picture of the smiling Jillian Grayson. She glanced back to the display of forty copies of the slanderous novel, and her blood began to boil.

She headed to the door with the book in hand. The clerk standing nearby watched in shock as she walked past her and was a foot from the door. The clerk said with concern, "Is there anything else I can help you find?"

Stopping in her tracks, Natalie shook her head and sighed. "Oh sorry. I'll just take this."

The clerk held out her hand, Natalie handed over the book, then followed her to the counter. "Can't wait to dive right into it, can you?"

"Uh, no."

After scanning the book, the clerk held it up. "I just love the cover. That's a real ballet move you know?"

"Uh-huh."

"The Rebecca character is a real monster. I don't want to give anything away, but she's completely out of her mind." The clerk whispered, "Into this really deviant sex stuff. I, uh, couldn't put it down though." Switching gears, she smiled. "Are you one of our reward members?"

Natalie returned a tired look. "No."

"That'll be thirty fifty-eight."

Her jaw dropped. "Thirty dollars?"

"Yes. It would be about twenty-five, but you don't have a rewards card. I can sign you up if—"

"Are you selling a lot of this book?" Natalie asked with keen interest.

"We are. I think it could be her biggest seller ever. Her fans have been waiting almost two years for a new book."

Wearing an evil grin, Natalie handed over the cash.

Once she retuned to her dorm, Natalie dove into the novel. When she finished at 3:16 a.m. boy was she pissed. Rebecca was obviously based on her—she was Rebecca. Brice and Ryder and Anastasia were Brian, Rob, and Jillian. It was worse than she thought in the bookstore. She was painted as an anal sex whore, man-manipulating lunatic. She flipped to the copyright page and read:

This book is a work of fiction. Names, characters, businesses, places, events and incidents are the product of the author's imagination or are used fictitiously. Any resemblance to actual persons, living or dead is entirely coincidental.

"Coincidental my ass," she said out loud as she tossed the book on the bed then lay back in her bed, overcome with anger and struggling to fall asleep.

At 10:38 a.m. the next morning she was awakened by a knock at her door. After she signed for an overnight package, she tore it open to find another copy of *The Leg Thing*. Discovering the Post-it note with the name Rebecca on it, she frowned. She searched the envelope for a return address and could find none. Then she picked up the printed articles, enclosed with the book, and studied them curiously. Curling up on her bed, she read every word. One of the cases caught her attention. A case where a young man was awarded an undisclosed settlement rumored to be in the six-figure range with a complaint similar to hers. And that author was nowhere near as big as Jillian Grayson. An attorney from New York named Josh Roth handled the case and was quoted in the article.

She located the Web site for the law firm, clicked on Josh's picture, and found him to be young and attractive. She smiled when she located a recent article featuring Josh as one of New York's most eligible bachelors. What twelve hours ago seemed like a complete nightmare was looking more like a dream come true. She was already planning how to spend the settlement money.

<u>12</u>

Natalie stood at the reception desk of one of the most prestigious law firms in New York City. She wore a pair of supertight jeans and an equally tight top that showed off all her assets. Under her top, she wore a lace miracle bra, which made her look a full cup larger than her God-given Bs. She looked hot.

The young female receptionist glared at her. "As I told you twice before… without an appointment you will not be able to see Mr. Roth. He's in meetings all day."

Growling in disgust, Natalie picked up her copy of *The Leg Thing* from the counter and glanced around the busy lobby. She paused to think, then headed out to the bank of elevators. Leaning against a wall, she watched as attorneys and clients walked in and out of the offices. Nearly all the men who walked by gawked at her as they passed, but Josh Roth was the only attorney for her, and she would wait as long as it took.

Almost ninety minutes later, she saw him heading out of the offices toward her. Springing to life, she rushed to the center of the hall just as Josh hit the button for the elevator. She moved next to him and dropped the book on the floor. When she didn't make any attempt to pick it up, he glanced to her, smiled in surprise at her beauty, and happily reached down to retrieve the book.

As he handed the book over, she looked at him curiously. "Aren't you Josh Roth?"

"I am."

"I read about the Langley - Watson case. I was impressed."

"Thank you."

When the elevator doors opened she said, "Can I talk to you for a moment?"

After glancing at his watch, he caught her hopeful expression. "Sure." He sighed, and they moved away from the elevator traffic. "What can I do for you?"

"It's a private matter." Natalie touched his arm and leaned in close. "I promise it won't take more than five minutes."

He stole a quick look at her impressive cleavage. "Five minutes."

As she followed him back through the lobby of the firm, she shot a snotty look at the receptionist who was now watching her in astonishment.

Inside Josh's office, Natalie sat in an expensive leather chair that was placed in front of his desk. "Now what can I do for you Miss ?" he asked and looked at her expectantly.

"Natalie Brookhart." She placed the book on his desk, and he picked it up then glanced at the cover. She said, "That's me."

"What, you posed for this picture?"

"I might as well have. That picture on the cover represents my character in the story. The book is all about me."

"I don't understand."

Excitedly, she rattled off quickly, "I can do that ballet pose on the cover. I was dating Jaclyn West's boyfriend at the time she was writing this. Her real name is Jillian Grayson."

"Slow down. Relax. Now what?"

After taking a calming breath, she started again, "I was dating the author's boyfriend, her real name is Jillian Grayson."

"Okay."

"Inside this book are intimate details about my personal life and outright lies. You know how in a novel it says some crap about 'none of this is based on real people or events'?"

"Yes."

"Well it's mostly based on me and real events. I'm the author's *imagination*."

Picking up the book, he studied the cover, impressed. "You can really do this?"

She nodded, wearing a proud smile.

"Wow, you're flexible."

"A lifetime of ballet lessons. I'm very flexible."

"Did they use your real name in the book?"

"No, but it is based on me."

"Look Miss Brookhart, it—"

"Natalie."

"Natalie, it would be very difficult and expensive to prove that the character in this book is based on you."

"I can prove it in ten seconds."

"How?"

"By doing the leg thing—would you like to see it?"

After exhaling deeply, he folded his arms. "Sure I would *love* to see it."

Rising from her chair, she checked the logistics of the room. After giving the wide space an approving nod, she moved to the door. "Can I lock this? It would be embarrassing if someone walked in."

"All right."

She locked the door and moved to stand three feet from him beside his desk. "I also need to take off some of this—do you mind?"

Suddenly more interested, he widened his eyes waving his hand to give her the go ahead.

Grinning, she slipped off her shoes and jeans. She wore a tiny black lace thong, and he swallowed hard when he saw it. She stretched slowly from one side to the other. His heart beat faster as he watched her. She stood tall, paused, grimaced uncomfortably, then widened her eyes to him as she removed her top. "That's better." Her matching black lace bra appeared along with a clear view of her nipples through the sheet fabric.

"Sorry. I'm used to doing this either in a leotard or, well, nothing."

"It's not a problem."

He stared at her, mesmerized, as she slowly rose up on the toes of her right foot; she lifted her left leg until her foot pointed directly at the ceiling. The fabric of her black thong was disappearing, and his eyes were desperately trying to find it. He adjusted his suit pants a bit as his glance traveled slowly from her floor-touching toes all the way up to her ceiling-pointing foot.

"I can hold it this way for ten minutes at least."

"Wow."

"I used to be able to hold it a lot longer when I was sixteen."

"Sure… Uh, how old are you now?" His eyes seemingly screamed please be at least eighteen, please be at least eighteen.

"Twenty-one."

He smiled, relieved. With his mouth dropping open, his gaze traveled back down, stopping briefly at her tits then he tilted his head to drink in her ass, but only for a moment before his eyes locked onto the featured item—her beautiful almost fully on display womanly parts.

Without a hint of struggle in her voice, she said, "You see that is me."

He held up the cover, glanced at it, then back to her. "It, uh, sure looks like you."

After giving him a satisfied smile, she slowly lowered her leg and he, of course, followed it all the way down. She bent over away from him to pick up her top and flashed him a breathtaking view of her heart shaped, thong-covered ass. Panting slightly, he stared at her body then quickly slid his chair in closer to his desk to hide something possibly brewing in his lap.

He fumbled with items on his desk, stealing glances at her while she slipped on her top, jeans, and shoes, then returned to her chair. When she was seated in front of him again, he shook his head and gave her a sympathetic smile. "But even if we prove that this is about you, what—"

"Look, I'm made out to be some lunatic, man-chasing, anal-sex whore who uses men… and toys with their affections. None of it is true. I want her to pay."

"Proving damages will be very difficult."

"All I ask is that you read the sections that I have marked. Read all the stuff about Rebecca. It's all stolen from my life."

"Okay, I will read it and get back to you."

He stood, but she didn't make a move to leave. He gave her a look.

She folded her arms. "I can wait. It should only take you about twenty minutes."

"You want me to read it now?" He scoffed. "I was about to grab some lunch."

"I'll bring you anything you want. You stay here and read, and I'll be right back."

He sat back in his chair, defeated. Standing, she leaned over his desk with her breasts hanging down deliciously in front of him. He stared directly into the valley while she said, "I promise you, once you've read it, you'll see that I have a case. Just give it a quick read."

Tearing his eyes away from her cleavage, he looked to her face. "Okay, I'll take a club sandwich from O'Malley's on the corner."

"You've got it." She slipped out the door.

He read the marked pages and was a little shocked by all of it. He read how they made fun of Rebecca for being a technical virgin and how Anastasia and Brice made passionate love together. He was more than a little turned on by the combination of Natalie's live strip show followed by the erotic prose. It was a surprisingly fascinating show and tell.

When Natalie returned with his sandwich, she stopped at reception and wore a bright smile. The receptionist called Mr. Roth and showed her to his office while wearing a disapproving sneer.

Once she was back in the chair, he gave her an apologetic look. "It's a novel, so even if a fictional character is loosely based on a real-life individual, as long as the public cannot identify the real-life individual from the context in which the fictional character is portrayed, there is little risk of liability to the author."

"But what if the public can identify the individual?"

"Well, then you might have a slight chance of winning a case, but only if the individual is defamed in the work."

"Oh, I'm defamed all right."

"So this technical virgin thing and the other bizarre behavior from this Rebecca character… none of that is true?"

"Not a word," she said adamantly folding her arms and sitting back in her chair.

"You may very well have a case worth pursuing." He sighed. "But it's a long shot, and we would require at least a twenty thousand dollar retainer to begin the process. From there, depending on the path we choose, it could be much more expensive."

"Couldn't you take this on a contingency?"

He nearly burst into laughter. "We don't do that here. We're not a personal injury firm."

With a sexy evil glimmer in her eye, she stood, sauntered around the desk and spun his chair toward her. Falling down between his legs, she placed both elbows on his knees with her hands near his belt buckle. "I want you to sue her for every penny she's made off this book and every other book she's ever written."

He swallowed hard as he looked up to the ceiling. "You, uh, have to be realistic about this kind of thing."

She ran her fingers just over the waistband of his pants near his belly button. He looked down to her with his erection straining to be set free. She noticed his condition and grinned. "Don't you lawyers take those pro bono cases sometimes?"

"We do, but generally it's a completely different, uh—" He stopped talking when she held the top of his zipper with one hand and slowly unzipped it with the other.

"That book is full of lies, and I've been so traumatized from it lately that I've been acting out sexually." She gave him sexy smile. "She must pay for putting me through this."

"I, uh…"

"And I don't manipulate men. I love men and have too much respect for the gender. I would never… ever… do that."

"I do believe you."

He stopped breathing, as she reached into his fly and fished out his swollen penis from his underwear. Pulling it through the flap, she looked at it, impressed. "So will you take my case, counselor?"

"I would need to talk to my partners about it, but I'd say there's a real good chance that—"

She moved her mouth to the base of his penis, extended her tongue, then licked all the way to the head. Stiffing his entire body, he pushed his head against the back of the chair and gasped. Then he returned his eyes to her, amazed as her tongue traced three-quarters around the throbbing ridge and back again slowly.

"Fuck," he moaned.

She rose up a bit, leaned directly over him, then moved her head down over him, swallowing him in one motion. Pressing her lips down all the way to his pubic bone, she made him disappear. He gasped. Next, she worked her expert mouth up and down on his length. He struggled with every thing he had to keep from yelling out loud.

Pulling her mouth off of him, she wiped her lips. "A good chance or…"

"I'll, uh, definitely accept your case."

"Pro bono?" She began jerking him off. When he closed his eyes and didn't answer, she stopped.

His eyes shot open, and he met her gaze as she stared at him waiting. He nodded quickly and stammered, "Yes, pro bono. Yes."

Grinning, she plunged her mouth fully over him. He gripped the armrest of his chair nearly hard enough to peel off the expensive leather. His eyes locked on her beautiful lips as they performed their magic. When it was over, he glanced at her, dizzied from the experience.

"You file the paperwork, then we'll have another celebration." She smiled. "A bigger one."

He nodded slowly as she wiped her lips, stood, adjusted her clothes, then headed for the door. After putting her hand on the knob, she turned back. "I wrote my name, address, and phone number in the book." Then she was gone.

13

With three exams that week and a paper due on Friday, no one saw or heard from Victoria the entire time. She had an A in every class and intended to keep it that way.

Brian's figure drawing class had come to an end. He spent thirteen hours a day at the office that week—ten hours of each day were devoted to company business, but early in the morning, during lunch, and after hours, he would get out his laptop, open up the sexy nude picture of Jillian and sketch her in charcoal with his door securely locked. God, she looked good, and his drawing skills were getting better and better. After completing four sketches, he wasn't happy with any of them. However, the one he was working on currently was nearly finished, and it was perfect.

At Wealth Stone Investments, Carl Rodgers summoned Rob to his office. When he entered, Carl shook his hand, smiled, and handed over an envelope. Opening it up, Rob discovered a check for twenty thousand dollars. "Wow. What's this?"

"I've been tracking your sales. You are really killing it out there. It's just a little extra bonus." Carl patted him on the shoulder. "Keep it up."

"I don't know what to say."

"Don't say anything—just keep selling."

"If there's anything else you need, just let me know." Carl gave him a wink. "Do you have your eye on any of the girls over at the complex?"

Rob scoffed. "I have my eye on all of them."

Carl chuckled. "Well sure, but I have a little influence with them, so if there's one in particular that you like, I could put in a good word for you."

"I think Kara is just drop dead gorgeous."

"Oh yeah." While looking past him out the window as if caught up in some creepy daydream, Carl said slowly, "Kara, she's a real firecracker, that one. Um…"

Rob narrowed his eyes concernedly until Carl returned his attention to him. "I'll see if she's still *dating* that guy of hers. And if there's anything else you need, let me know."

"Maybe there is. My best friend is getting married soon, and I was thinking of having the bachelor party for him out by the pool on October first. Would that be okay? Is there some way to reserve it or—"

"How many guys?" Carl interrupted, breaking into a huge smile.

"Just six or seven."

"Do you want some strippers?"

"Sure, yeah. We'd love some."

"Are the guys, um, offended easily?" Carl asked with a hesitant smile.

"No, absolutely not."

"Good. Let me arrange everything for you. We have some special facilities over there, which you probably aren't aware of. Plus the girls know some other girls if you know what I mean."

"Awesome." Rob didn't, but he put on a smile anyway. "Are you sure it isn't too much trouble?"

"No, I insist we have it there—but only if I get to come." Widening his eyes, Carl waited for a response.

"Definitely."

"Just leave everything to me. Let me make a few calls, then I'll get back to you with the details."

"I appreciate it." Heading out the door, Rob took another peek at his big check.

As soon as he returned to his desk, Rob called Jim to give him the good news. Jim was lost when it came to planning the bachelor party. Problem solved, big time.

That night, Rob fell asleep while contemplating a possible new-car purchase. At just after 1:00 a.m. there was a knock on his door. His eyes opened briefly, and he drifted back to sleep until a louder bang brought him fully awake. Sighing, he headed to the door wearing only boxer shorts. He opened the door to discover Kara standing there wearing a short pink raincoat.

"Hey, what, uh…" was all he could muster before she opened her coat and showed him that she wore nothing underneath. Without saying a word, she slipped through the door around him. Closing the door, he turned just in time to see her drop the coat and head naked into the bedroom.

When he reached the bedroom, he found her standing near the bed wearing a sexy look. "Do you have a condom?"

Nodding, he pointed to his night table. She opened the drawer, searched for a moment, then pulled one out. Returning her gaze to him, she looked at him waiting.

"So did you break up with your boyfriend or…"

She shook her head slowly — first no then yes. Moving to him, she grabbed hold of his boxers with one hand, and guided him to the bed. She pushed him back, and he fell onto the mattress. He watched breathlessly as she tossed the condom down grabbed his boxer shorts and pulled them off. His manhood was already responding.

Kneeling on the floor, she took him into both hands, and expertly worked him until he was fully hard. She opened the condom package then slipped it over his length. Climbing over him, she guided his erection to her entrance, then quickly pushed down and he slipped inside.

"Oh, God," he groaned.

She rode him wildly, bucking up and down while wearing an almost bored expression. Rob was anything but bored as he reached up and cupped both of her sizeable breasts.

Reaching back, she massaged his balls as she quickened her pace up and down over him. He groaned, and after twenty more seconds he cried out loudly with a contorted face. It was over. She slipped down to kiss him on the cheek then slowly lifted off of him. He stared at her gratefully while also feeling a little used.

"Congratulations on your bonus." She gave him a smile.

"Uh, thanks."

"You want to stay or…"

"No. Can't." Turning, she headed toward the door. "I've got to go to work early, but thanks."

"Okay, should I—"

"Bye." She slipped out the door, and his eyes were glued to her ass as she disappeared into the hall.

The next day at work, Rob headed to Gary's office. After closing the door, he sat across from him and gave him a concerned look.

"What is it?" Gary asked.

"Oh nothing."

"Congratulations on the bonus."

"Yeah, Yeah..." Rob nodded dismissively. "Do you date any of the girls at the apartment building?"

"Date?" Gary nearly broke into a laugh. "No, I don't *date* them."

"Have you had sex with any of them?"

"Sure, everyone has."

"What?" Rob looked at him confused. "You see Kara and I—"

"Wait." Gary broke into a big smile. "You do realize they're all prostitutes don't you?"

"Huh?"

"Well some are strippers or wanna be porn stars, but—"

"Prostitutes?"

Gary scoffed. "You didn't really think all those superhotties were average normal girls who just happened to live in the same building did you?"

"What? No." Wearing a fake smile, Rob shook his head.

"Look, they're only a little reward here and there. Don't get so caught up in all that. Just be sure you wear a condom."

"Of course."

Gary's eyes widened. "Dude, don't tell me you went down on one of them."

"Oh, no... I, uh..."

"Good. Speaking of eating." Gary smiled. "Hey, what are you doing for lunch?"

Suddenly, Rob wasn't hungry.

The next day, with the wedding just under two weeks away, Jillian, Victoria, and the other two bridesmaids, Lisa and Brenda, decided to have lunch together before heading off to the dress shop to pickup their gowns. Jillian's wedding dress was a silk satin strapless tea-length dress—very chic and modern. While the bridesmaids' dresses were a light peach color and tasteful for bridesmaids dresses, with a ruffled area around the waist, which the heavyset Brenda appreciated, but was originally intended to provide the pregnancy-shielding coverage that Victoria needed.

Although the wait had seemed like an eternity to Victoria, the next morning was the first day that she could give blood for the paternity test. She was the first one in line at the lab.

14

That Saturday, the boys were heading north to Orlando for their party while Victoria was putting the final touches on her bachelorette party. There were a few surprises in store for the dozen women who were invited — and one really big surprise.

At the suite she had rented at the Mandarin Oriental Hotel in Miami, Victoria placed items in the twelve pink-striped party favor boxes. After a meal at the hotel restaurant, where more than their fair share of alcohol was consumed, the group headed up to the suite for more drinks and the real party. Everyone knew what Victoria was like, and they were anxious to see what kind of party she would put together. They all were expecting something crazy.

In attendance were Jillian, of course, the two bridesmaids, Lisa and Brenda, and seven of Jillian's other friends. Laura was also there, added to the list just a few days earlier after Rob had informed his mother that she was his date for the wedding. Victoria served champagne and was completely sober, but drinking a sparkling apple cider to complete the cover-up of her still hidden pregnancy. The other women guzzled the champagne as the party began to roll. The seating was arranged in a circular fashion, which created a large open area in the center. In front of each woman sat a pink-striped box. When Victoria gave them the go ahead, the women lifted the lids and peered inside.

Eleven of the women immediately snatched the large, realistic dildo from its fancy box that was emblazoned with a picture of the model — the famous porn star Antonio Steele. Victoria had introduced Jillian and Brian to Antonio's film work just a few months earlier during the initial phases of their backdoor lesson. Lisa was the lone abstainer and sat frowning and just gazing horrified into the box. Nine of the women opened the box, pulled out the replica of Antonio's monster penis, and studied it wearing varying expressions. Some were awed, some curious, some skeptical, and one was just outright horny.

Jillian gave it a quizzical look. "This looks familiar."

A woman called out, "Don't tell us Brian is that big." After all the women shared a laugh, Jillian turned to Victoria. "No, I mean where do I know this from? Victoria, help me out."

"Antonio," she replied slowly. "You know, Anton—"

"The anal-king Antonio?" Jillian narrowed her eyes.

"That's him."

Jillian's mouth dropped open. "I knew I'd seen this before."

Half of the women couldn't wrap their hands around the girth and still have their fingers touch. One woman said, "This can't be real. No one is this big around."

"Oh, it's real all right," Victoria began. "But more on that soon."

A few of the women kept inspecting the replica as others dipped into their boxes to explore the other goodies. Each box contained lube, condoms that had a battery-powered clitoral stimulation ring, padded handcuffs, edible panties, and a coupon for a Brazilian bikini wax. Each box also contained a smaller realistic-looking dildo that was completely average sized. All the women, except Lisa, pulled the smaller one out and held it up next to Antonio's. The little guy didn't stand a chance as he was completely dwarfed by the anal king's prize. Lisa sat uncomfortably watching as all the other women roared with laughter.

Victoria said loudly, "Now that one is the size of your average guy."

A woman called out, "So that one *is* Brian." More laughter from the crowd as Jillian shook her head, "no," with a suggestive smile.

In Orlando, Carl led Rob, Gary, Jim, Brian, and six other guys to a secret party room in the basement of the apartment building. The room was large and lavish. There was a fully stocked bar, a superlarge television screen on the wall, a full kitchen, and in the center of the room was a huge circular sofa that faced a black leather curved chaise lounge. Directly in front of the chaise was a single chair. As the men piled into the room, three catering employees were putting the final touches on a huge spread of food that sat on the counter, which divided the kitchen area from the large party room. The spread included huge steamed shrimp, pit beef and ham, pulled pork, chicken wings, and everything that went with it.

Carl tuned the television to some sporting event as some guys headed to the bar while others headed over to devour the food.

Back in Miami, Laura discovered latex gloves at the bottom of her box and held them up. "What are these for?" All the women pulled their gloves out as well.

An older woman called out, "There is no way I'm giving my husband a prostate exam."

After the laughter died down, Victoria said, "No, those are for the next surprise." Turning to Laura, she gave her a wink and pointed to the CD player.

"Oh, okay." Laura hit the power switch, and an upbeat song blared out of the speakers. Lisa sat frozen in her chair. She glanced at Victoria who stared across the room at a closed door wearing a huge grin. Following her gaze to the door, Lisa turned suddenly pale, then stood and headed out of the suite, leaving her box of goodies behind. All eyes were on her as she fled; Jillian turned to Victoria, and they shared a shrug. As the music continued, each woman turned her attention back to the closed door.

Just then, the door to the bedroom flew open, and out walked Antonio Steele, dressed in tight jeans and a T-shirt. Howling, the women watched him dance to the center of the group. The bulge in his jeans was very impressive, and many of the women's eyes were locked onto it. The rowdy women continued sipping their champagne as he ripped off his T-shirt, bent over, and made eye contact with the ones he could see upside down through his spread legs. Returning upright, he turned to face them, unbuttoning his pants and opening them up just enough so the first two inches of his manhood was showing.

The crowd reacted with whistles and obscene comments. Smiling, he danced over to the bride to be. He straddled her legs and danced with his partially uncovered penis only eight inches from her face. After stealing a few glances at it, Jillian looked away shyly. She shook her head with mock anger at Victoria then returned her attention to the main attraction, but this time looked him in the eye with an embarrassed smile.

He danced back to the middle of the room and quickly slipped off the jeans, exposing his huge flaccid penis to the crowd. The room exploded in screams and applause. Shaking his hips back and forth, his penis slapped each thigh in turn and grew with each blow. He reached down to it and stroked it a few times; as he returned to his gyrations, it expanded in size until it stood horizontally from his body and pointed right at Jillian. He spun around to give all the ladies a view as the music slowly faded away.

He stood there with a huge smile, matched only by his huge erection as he placed his hands on his hips and nodded to the crowd. Some of the women held up their replicas, and he approached so they could do a side-by-side comparison. Other than the color, it was a perfect match and no one was disappointed. The women laughed and squawked in loud conversation until Victoria stood to quiet the crowd.

Victoria began, "Antonio has agreed to do an interactive show-and-tell for all those ladies who are interested. This is what the gloves are for, but they are optional. One side note—he has been fully tested." Walking up to the star, she raised her eyebrows as she pointed down to the swollen monster. "Sorry, Antonio, some of us have seen where that has been."

Smiling, he said in a thick Italian accent, "Don't worry about it. Sometimes I'm scared to touch him myself."

The room broke into laughter. Victoria slipped on the latex gloves and returned to her seat. She said, "Now ladies, behave yourselves. You may touch him with your hands only within reason… this may be your only opportunity to handle equipment of this size so… don't blow it—no pun intended." The women all chuckled, and Victoria added, "I'm serious—keep your face away. I'll go first to break the ice."

As he made his way to her, his penis still stood straight out and was enormous. She reached out and cupped his massive balls with one hand and wrapped her other hand around him. Narrowing her eyes, she hefted it a bit she announced to the group, "Wow, I mean you can just feel the weight of it, and it's so heavy."

After Victoria played with it a bit more, she shook her head in disbelief. "Okay, who's next?"

Six hands instantly went up as others rushed to put on their gloves. In all, ten of the eleven remaining women took part in the exercise. Jillian simply watched the show with a confused grin. All who participated were for the most part well behaved, although during Laura's turn, the other woman began to get impatient when she wouldn't let go. Victoria was forced to intervene and gently pry his massive manhood from her white-knuckled, gloved hands.

When all were done, Antonio danced his way to Jillian. "Does the lovely bride wish to touch?"

Women began calling out, "You'd better do it."

"You'll never get to touch another."

"Don't miss this chance! It might be the last erection you ever see." This comment brought a roar from the drunken rowdy women.

Victoria said, "Don't feel obligated, but I did spend a little over one thousand dollars an inch to bring him here."

While all the ladies tried to do the math in their heads Antonio smiled. "Is worth every penny."

"It really is." Victoria nodded to Jillian as she gave her a hopeful look.

Back in Orlando, all the guys were completely stuffed from the fabulous food and their blood alcohol levels had all just blown through the legal limit when Carl announced, "It's time." Rob blindfolded the reluctant, but good sport, Brian and led him to the chair in front of the chaise. After being handed a beer, Brian sat quietly sipping it. All the other guys grabbed a fresh beer and planted themselves on the comfortable sofa. Seconds later, the hottest naked young woman on the planet walked slowly to the chaise and laid back with her legs spread. Brian could feel her walk past, and he certainly heard the murmurings of the guys in attendance. The young woman with long blonde hair stared straight ahead at Brian as she slowly ran her finger between her legs. All eyes, except Brian's, of course, were glued to her fingers as she touched herself.

Another young woman with fiery red hair, who just happened to be the second hottest woman on the planet, walked slowly toward the chaise. All uncovered eyes followed her. After stopping directly behind the chaise, the redhead smiled, then bent over and kissed the blonde.

Everyone except Brian gasped. All he could do was sip his beer as he listened curiously to the goings on. Reaching up, the blonde cupped the redhead's spectacular breasts as she rested her stomach on top of the higher end of the chaise, and leaned over so she could suck on the blonde's nipples. Next, the redhead climbed farther down the chair until her mouth was in line between the blonde's thighs, and her own target area was pressed into the face of her new friend. After a few minutes of reciprocal action, the blonde slid down to the flat part of the chaise, and the redhead followed after her.

Rob said, "Holy shit." Then, there were similar comments from the rest of the men.

Carl said, "Brian, you can take the blindfold off now."

Brian hesitantly reached to the blindfold. "I'm praying that it's not some woman doing it with a farm animal." He removed the blindfold, and his eyes adjusted to the light. As he took in the breathtaking sight of the striking redhead lying on top of the gorgeous blonde as they slowly performed oral sex on each other just two feet from him, all he said was, "Wow." Tilting his head for a better angle, he sighed. His gaze traveled down the redhead's perfect breasts as they dangled delightfully over the blonde's tiny waist, to the blonde's tongue as it disappeared just behind the tiny patch of perfectly coiffed red pubic hair.

Gary scoffed. "This is the best bachelor party ever."

Brian swallowed hard as he watched the passion unfold from his front-row seat.

Jim said, "I wonder what the girls are up to?" All men glared at him for a moment before returning to the action. He slumped down in his seat.

At the male review, all eyes were on Jillian as Antonio moved his stiff manhood to within six inches of her face. Focusing on the bulbous head, her eyes bugged out a bit. She asked him, "Do you feel faint or anything. Do you need to sit down?"

Shaking his head with a grin, he waved his prize in front of her. "Last chance."

Jillian rolled her eyes, shrugged, then began to slip on the gloves. The women cheered her on quietly. Once the gloves were secure, she frowned slightly as she hesitantly moved her hands toward Antonio's monster. Grinning broadly, he stared down at her. With her eyes widened, she took a good look at it while her gloved hands slowly closed in. All eyes watched as her fingers were less than an inch from him. Suddenly stopping, she grimaced, then pulled her hands back shaking her head. She tore her eyes from his manhood and looked up at his face. "Impressive, but I just can't. There's only one for me now, and it's a couple hundred miles away."

All the women, even Victoria, gave her a sympathetic and jealous smile as Jillian shyly looked away from the show. The smiles faded when Antonio turned and headed to the center of the room. With all attention, except Jillian's, returning to his groin, he flashed his eyebrows with a smile to the group, sauntered into the bedroom, and closed the door.

Jillian fanned her hand in front of her flushed face "All of a sudden I feel inspired to write a chapter."

Victoria said, "Yeah—a long thick chapter."

The women broke into laughter.

Back at the bachelor party, the girls were now sitting up on the chaise and making out. After a few moments, the redhead pulled her lips away and reached under the chaise. She pulled up a head harness complete with a large black dildo attached over the mouth area.

Jim instantly recognized it. "My parents have one of those." All men turned their shocked expressions to Jim for a moment. Even the girls delivered him a confused look. He shrugged. "They really do."

With the attention returning to the young women, the redhead carried the harness to Brian. She handed it to him, and he looked at it with curiosity.

"Put this on," she commanded.

Brian's face turned pale, and he looked more than a little horrified. "Oh, I shouldn't—my sinuses are really clogged… it's this humid air."

"Oh do it, Brian." Carl frowned. "If you don't, you'll regret it for the rest of your life."

Brian looked with dismay at the group of men who were obviously eager for him to strap on the harness. Only Rob, who appeared to be torn, and Jim, who appeared to be possibly relieving his horrific experience with Jillian in the closet, weren't trying to egg him on.

After taking in Brian's expression, the harness, and the naked woman, Rob grew immediately concerned. Maybe it was because he really didn't want to have the image of his mother's future husband wearing that harness and doing what he assumed would follow, or maybe he just wanted to do it himself. Either way, he would take the bullet for his friend.

"I've got this." Rob stood, and Brian looked at him gratefully.

"All right." Carl smiled proudly at his young protégé. "We have a man here."

After finishing off his beer, Rob handed it to Carl, then walked to the redhead. He placed his hand on Brian's shoulder, leaned in, and whispered, "You owe me one. Although, this might be fun."

The redhead handed him the harness, and he struggled to put it on his head. She spun him around and secured the straps. He looked ridiculous with his nose sticking out just above the long, thick, black dildo, but he was drunk and up for just about anything.

The redhead led Rob to the chaise and guided him down so that his head was closest to the crowd of horny guys. The blonde crawled over his face, held the black dildo as she placed it at her entrance and proceeded to slide down. She pumped slowly up and down for a few minutes as the crowd watched, completely captivated. Crying out in ecstasy, the rider neared climax. With everyone watching unblinkingly, the blonde brought herself to a huge orgasm. After, the redhead took her place and did the same, taking just over five minutes to orgasm, all the men looked on, dry-mouthed and gasping for breath.

When the girls were finished using Rob, they helped him remove the harness. With his eyes glazing over, he rushed to the bar and grabbed a drink. After the girls left, the guys all took a beer outside and watched as twelve other gorgeous women hung out around the pool and bar area wearing their sexy bikinis.

As one particularly hot young woman in a tiny white thong walked past them they all stared at her ass. One of Brian's friends said, "They say Disneyland is the happiest place on earth, but, uh, I think this really is."

"You can never move from here." Turning to Rob, Brian swayed back and forth a little. "Promise me."

"Yeah…" Rob muttered, still a little shell-shocked.

Another guy asked incredulously, "So you guys actually leave here to go to work each day — how?"

"Um, yeah it's not easy," Rob replied with a weak smile not wanting to destroy the fantasy as it had been destroyed for him only recently.

15

Brian returned to Miami on Sunday, and both he and Jillian described their respective parties simply as fine. No other details were given.

At work the next day, Brian was in his office when a call came in from the division vice president, Tom Myers.

"This is Brian."

"Brian, Tom Myers here. Can we go over the figures on the quarterly report?"

"Just give me a second to pull it up. You mind if I put you on speaker?"

"No."

After hitting the speaker button, Brian cradled the handset. As he struggled to find the directory on his computer, his boss, Richard Brown rushed into his office. He closed the door. "Hey look—"

Brian interrupted him. "I'm in the middle of something with Tom, can I—"

"Myers?" Richard asked with a frown.

"Yes."

"Fuck Tom. I need to talk to you now."

Brian's eyes widened, and he glanced at his phone to see the green light was indicating that he was still connected.

"But Tom is on—"

"Tom's on his way out of here. I'll be sitting in that office soon," Richard shot back.

Brian slowly moved a document so it was covering the green light on the phone. He leaned back in his chair, struggling to hide a slightly evil grin.

Tom Myers's jaw was wide open as he sat listening to the speakerphone in his office. He hit the mute button and rushed over and closed his door. Returning to his desk, he wore a big smile. Obviously, he wasn't a big fan of that prick Richard and was also looking forward to what might spill out of his fat mouth next.

Back in Brian's office, Brian asked, "So what do you need?"

Richard sat back in a chair. "Look, Brian, I like you. I think you have a future here."

"Okay."

"There was a problem with those loans you reviewed for me a couple months back. You didn't find any discrepancies, and after the regulators reviewed them—"

"I did find a bunch of issues. I detailed them all in the report I submitted to you."

"I didn't get any report."

Brian sighed. "I printed it out. It was on the stack when I placed it in your office, and I sent you a second copy by e-mail."

"Whatever." Richard waved his hand at him dismissively. "There was no report when the files went to the regulators, and now we're officially under investigation by the government for not reporting the—"

"I sent you the damn report," Brian interrupted.

Richard stood and glared at him. "Look, you little shit. It's your word against mine. You back me up on this, and there will be good things ahead for you. Especially when I'm sitting in Tom's big office. You fuck me on this, and I'll bury you here."

With his heart pumping wildly, and his anger boiling over, Brian glared at Richard. "I quit."

After looking shocked, Richard smiled. "Actually, that's probably best. I didn't think it was working out anyway."

Tom's voice blasted out of the speakerphone. "Richard, I need to see you in my office. Now!"

After glancing around the room, confused, Richard caught sight of the phone. Brian grinned as he slid the page away that had covered the green light.

"Richard?"

Richard took a deep breath and as his face turned pale white. "Tom, we were just—"

"Save it, Brown. Come to my office now."

The phone went dead, and Richard stood there, speechless. Brian said tentatively, "I guess you'll be sitting in Tom's office a little sooner that you originally thought."

Glaring at him, Richard ripped open the door, then took off. Brian stood and paced around the room with a sick feeling in his stomach, his hands clammy and his blood pressure sky high. He did hate that asshole, but he also hated being stuck in this office. He couldn't stand the job. Taking a deep breath, he felt a wave of relief pass over him. He had just quit. He had actually done it. Sighing, he slumped back in his chair and gazed out the window.

Ten minutes later Brian was packing his things in a small box when Tom Myers walked through the door.

"What are you doing?" Tom asked.

"I already quit. Richard is a complete—"

"Fucking asshole. I know. He's gone. Security ushered him out a few minutes ago."

"Okay, but I..."

"What?"

"I'm not sure if this place is for me, you know?"

Tom took a seat and looked at him sincerely as he said, "You didn't really quit. I mean, you told some guy who was about to be fired that you quit, so we won't hold you to that."

Brian moved to his chair. "I just don't think I want to do this anymore."

Tom scoffed. "You've been doing it what—four months?"

"Yeah."

"We like what we've seen from you so far. If you had a little more experience, I could see putting you into the *just recently vacated* director's position, but I can't justify it yet."

"I understand."

"Look, I'll need to fill that job now. I could bring in someone from another division, temporarily, then when you've been here a year or so, and if your stellar work continues, I'll definitely promote you. I give you my word."

"That's a great offer." Brian paused thinking. "I appreciate it, but I think I'm going to leave. I'm getting married on Saturday, and I just don't see myself doing this ten years from now. I've got to find something else to do—maybe something creative. I can't just stare at these documents and numbers all day without wanting to kill myself." Discovering Tom suddenly wearing a sad expression,

Brian gave him an apologetic look. "Sorry, I meant no offence. I mean, it's great—"

"Oh, no, it's okay." Sighing, Tom gave him a look like he was almost on the verge of tears. "Please take me with you."

Brian chuckled and Tom pulled himself together a bit. "Just kidding." As Tom's face morphed back into sadness, Brian knew he wasn't kidding and was even more confident now of his own decision.

Thirty minutes later, Brian arrived at home. He knew Jillian wanted him to quit, but for some reason he was a little scared of what she might think. She probably really wanted him to find something else to do before he left this job. After looking unsuccessfully upstairs, he searched the rest of the house. He finally discovered her in the workout room, stretching with her leg on the ballet bar. Wearing nothing but a tiny leotard, she looked amazing.

"What are you doing home?"

He moved to sit on the weight bench. "You know how you wanted me to quit my job?"

She pulled her foot off the bar. "Yeah." Her face wore a bright, hopeful expression.

Nodding, he flashed an insecure smile. She smiled widely as she rushed to him and knelt down to look him in the eye. "What happened?"

"Richard was blaming me for some problem that was his fault. I had the VP on the phone, and Richard didn't realize. It's a long story, but I quit. They fired Richard and wanted me to stay, but I just—"

After interrupting him with a long kiss, she pulled back and gave him a sincere look. "You know I love you and will support you in whatever you want to do."

He frowned. "I didn't really give it a chance. But I feel like if I don't leave now, ten years might go by, and I'd still be there and still be just miserable."

"Take some time and figure out what you want to do. You don't need to rush into anything."

"Okay, but I'm not going to have you pay my bills."

"What bills do you have?"

"The car and my school loans. Also I had my eye on this little gift I wanted to get for you and now—"

"I don't need any gifts from you—other than you, that is."

He smiled at her, unconvinced. "I've got to figure out how to keep myself busy. I won't be some lazy slob sponging off you like your ex-husband."

Moving away from him, she said suggestively, "You're nothing like George."

She pulled the straps of the leotard off her shoulders and slipped them down to uncover her breasts. His heart pumped faster as he stared at her, mesmerized. She smiled. "I think I can figure out how to keep you busy."

After slipping the leotard off completely, she moved until she was just under the strap that hung from the ceiling. She slowly lifted her leg until it was in *the leg thing* position and widened her eyes to him.

"Seriously?" he asked blown away.

"Why don't you come over and slip it in."

"But I thought you couldn't hold this position for very long."

"I've been practicing."

Rushing to his feet, he struggled with the buttons on his shirt. After stripping it off, he unbuckled and pulled down his pants. Wearing nothing except black dress socks, he looked a bit odd as he stood before her breathing heavily, but more than ready to go.

Her eyes locked in on his excitement. "Something tells me I won't need to hold this position very long."

Jillian was right. Less than three minutes later, it was over. Somehow they pulled it off with her in that position, and the pain was a not nearly as bad as she had anticipated. As she rubbed her hand over her cramping thigh muscle, she said, "Hey, if you're not going to be working, I insist that you give me more orgasms."

They shared a smile. Moving to him, she kissed him deeply.

He pulled his lips away from her. "Would you like me to start now?"

She nodded with a sexy smile. He scooped her up into his arms and rushed out of the room.

At the same moment Jillian was having an orgasm, over a thousand miles away Natalie was on her knees in Josh's office rubbing her hand over her attorney's suit pants directly over his bulging groin. That morning after filing the necessary papers with the court, he called her with the news. She rushed over as soon as she could. As she massaged his growing penis, she smiled. "So when do you think she'll get the news?"

"I have a process server scheduled for both her and her publisher for tomorrow late morning." He gave her a cocky grin. "Let's just say that a few lunches will be spoiled tomorrow."

With her eyes locked onto his, she slowly unzipped his fly. His mouth opened wide as she reached inside and extracted him from his underwear.

He watched closely as she gave him a blow job unmatched by any he had ever received before. She never pulled away, not once, and even after he finished, she kept going.

When she was finally done with him, she wiped her mouth, stood, and grinned. "When you settle this, you can touch me. In fact, you can do whatever you want to me." She leaned in an inch from his face and repeated in a whisper, "Whatever you want."

He stared at her, panting and struggling to speak. After a moment, he simply said with his voice cracking, "Okay."

At just after 6:00 p.m. in Orlando, Rob sat out by the pool and casually took in the sights of the half-dozen spectacular looking, but emotionally or otherwise unavailable, working girls as they made occasional casual conversation with him. Working on his fourth beer, he was starting to feel the effects. Carl strolled up in his swimsuit and flopped down groggily next to him. He seemed drunk or high or maybe both.

"Hey, Mr. Rodg—I mean Carl."

Carl smiled. "Blow that bonus yet?"

"Not yet."

"Hey that girl I told you about is coming out tonight." Carl eyed Rob's body a little creepily. "Yeah... I think, uh..."

"What?"

Carl closed his eyes, and Rob glanced at him, confused. Rob asked, "Carl?"

Shaking his head, Carl opened his eyes. "What?"

"Some girl, you were saying she's coming over."

"Oh, yeah." Carl ran his hand over his sleepy face. "She's coming over and depending on what kind of mood she's in, do you feel like getting together?"

"Uh, sure."

"Awesome. Keep your phone on you. I might be calling."

About two hours later, Rob was in his apartment watching television and finishing up his sixth beer when his phone rang. Checking the display, he saw it was Carl.

"Hey, Carl."

"Rob, she really wants to meet you. Can you come down?"

"Sure."

"We're in the party room—you remember where the Bachelor party was."

"Yeah."

"Hurry down here, dude. Oh and the combination to the lock is seven-one-six-seven. You got it—seven-one-six-seven?"

"Okay."

Five minutes later, Rob dialed the combination into the door lock and went inside, carrying an ice-cold beer. He found a naked young woman lounging on the chaise with Carl kneeling down and having sex with her. He was fully clothed except for his thin penis, which hung out of his fly. The woman he was having sex with was gorgeous, but she appeared a little uninterested.

"Yo, Rob," Carl said without skipping a beat. "Come in." Spotting Rob, the woman instantly perked up. She gazed at him while licking her lips and moaning. Rob walked in slowly and was mostly creeped out, but a little turned on as he watched the woman who suddenly seemed to really be enjoying the sex.

"Rob, this is Daphne. Daphne, this is the guy I was telling you about."

"Nice to meet you, Rob." She gave him a sexy smile.

"Good to meet you also."

After pulling out of Daphne, Carl walked over to the counter without bothering to cover up. "You want to do a line?"

Rob stammered, "Uh, no… thanks."

Carl bent over to the counter, snorted, then lifted back up and rubbed his nose. He looked at Rob for a moment, dizzied, before returning to Daphne. Falling onto his knees, he slipped back inside her and began moving his hips.

Daphne turned to Rob. "I feel like sucking a big cock. Do you feel like getting your big cock sucked?"

He really did, and she was hot, but this was a little weird. After pausing to mull it over, he shrugged. With the booze clouding his generally lax judgment, he unzipped his fly and pulled out his manhood. After taking a big sip, he placed his beer down on a stool next to the chaise. She stared at his penis with her eyes widened for a moment before reaching out to touch it. Opening her mouth wide, she swallowed him whole. Rob felt Carl's eyes on him as Daphne worked her magic mouth over him.

"Oh, God," Rob moaned, and he leaned his head back with his eyes closed.

Carl's phone rang. He pulled it out of his pocket and took the call while still pumping away. "Okay, I'll be right there."

She wrapped her lips around Rob's erection as Carl pulled out and walked to a door just ten feet from them. Carl fumbled with his keys as he looked back at the two of them, completely captivated by the live oral sex show. He tried to put the key in the lock then dropped the set to the floor. After retrieving the key, he unlocked the door.

He opened the door and stood with his back against it as he returned his attention to the busy pair. Groaning, Rob looked up to the ceiling as Daphne sucked him harder and harder.

Carl grabbed a box and placed it against the door to prop it open, then he glanced down to his still exposed manhood, opened his pants, and uncomfortably tucked it away. He walked to a large, secure-looking, steel door at the back of the room. He pressed a button and the door began to rise up.

Rob glanced to the left inside the propped door and spotted what looked like the door to a giant safe. It was bright steel and looked like a bank vault; he moved away from Daphne for a better look. After glaring up at him, annoyed, she adjusted her position. She returned to his balls just as the door opened fully and two uniformed security guards each wheeled out a hand truck carrying three large crates. Carl looked back to Rob, gave him a thumbs up, and Rob responded to the gesture with a weak smile.

The two guards, along with Carl, stood in the doorway watching the act, grinning and quietly commenting. Daphne glanced at them, grinned, then moved until her ass was high in air and pointed directly at the three spectators. While Carl and the guards gazed dreamily at her ass, Rob noticed that the guards were both armed, but he didn't see any markings on their uniforms to indicate what company they were with.

Rob returned his attention to Daphne as she sucked him back into her mouth and continued her work. He glanced up to the doorway every few seconds and eventually saw the guards leave and Carl push the button for the door to close. Daphne pulled away from him, took a big sip of Rob's icy cold beer, then plunged her frozen mouth over him again. Gasping, his mouth flew open. He breathed in deeply, and when he had recovered, he glanced back through the door to Carl who now stood in front of the safe, dialing in the combination on the huge mechanism. Carl pushed down the handle and pulled open the heavy door just as Daphne pulled away from Rob. "Carl, get back here. I need you."

Rob watched as Carl paused, looking into the safe, then frowned and returned his attention to Daphne. After shrugging, he reached into his pants and pulled out his penis. He stroked it as he headed back toward the room. Stopping in the doorway with one hand still working his manhood, he used his other hand to slide the box that was holding the door away. As he rushed back to her, the door closed slowly, but the box was still in its path. The door pushed the box, sliding it against the doorframe and leaving the door open about a foot.

She guided Rob back to his original position as Carl resumed his place and slipped inside of her. She groaned. With his curiosity piqued, Rob watched as Carl briefly narrowed his eyes concernedly at the open door; then he saw him seemingly put it out of his mind as he returned his attention to Daphne.

A few minutes later, when both men had finished, Rob zipped up as Carl headed back to the counter for another line. Rob took the opportunity to walk around the far side of the chaise lounge closer to the partially open door. He peered into the room through the open safe. Inside, he spotted two stacks of gold bars approximately two feet wide by two feet high by two feet deep. He did a quick count of three bars across, seven bars deep, and it looked to be about ten bars high. After glancing to Carl and finding him still occupied, he returned his attention to the safe to discover a stack of hundred dollar bills in an even larger block. Shocked, he rushed away from the door before Carl turned around.

Daphne was ready for round two, but Rob said he was too drunk and was feeling sick. Both Carl and Daphne gave him a disappointed look as he left the room. Rob slumped against the wall outside the room with his heart pounding, and it wasn't at all related to the professional quality oral sex.

16

Jillian woke up early and began writing. Brian slept in since he was currently unemployed. After two hours of writing erotica, she found herself completely wet and, for the first time on a weekday anyway, she had somewhere to turn. Grinning, she headed upstairs. When she walked into the bedroom, he was walking out of the bathroom, naked, and drying his hair with a towel.

"Oh, good you're clean."

"Why?"

"I feel like blowing you."

"Writing again?" He shot her a fake frown.

"Do you have to make that same joke every time?"

"Sorry, I'll stop."

Walking up to him, she took his penis in her hand. It was already growing before she touched it. "You don't have to stop. I still think it's cute, but it'll probably wear thin pretty soon." She kissed his chest as she massaged his manhood.

"Purely out of curiosity, what were you writing about?"

"A scene where this married couple has anal sex for the very first time."

"Sounds hot."

"It was."

She cupped his balls as she shimmied her hips. "I kinda feel like doing everything too."

"Really?"

The second she gave him a suggestive nod, the doorbell rang. She sighed. "Keep it hard, and I'll be right back." She headed for the door and turned back. Pausing, she gave him a sexy look. "Maybe we should even go around the world."

"Okay." He smiled.

She rushed to the foyer with her mind wandering, and the heat boiling up in her loins. When she opened the door, she found a young man standing there. "Are you Jillian Grayson?"

"Yes."

He handed over a large envelope. "Have a nice day."

Five minutes later, Brian was in bed tugging occasionally at his manhood, simply doing as he was told. After glancing at the clock for the fourth time with his concern growing, he was just about to go look for Jillian when she appeared in the door, wearing a frown.

"Where were you? I can't keep it hard forever."

She shook her head confused then muttered, "What?"

"What's wrong?"

"I'm being sued."

"For what?"

"Over the novel. Natalie is claiming that I created a character based on her without her permission. She's suing for defamation and invasion of privacy."

"What?" He asked as he continued to stroke his erection without thinking.

"Your ex-girlfriend is suing me and my publisher for four million dollars."

"Holy shit. How can she sue? The legal team cleared you, right?"

"Yes, but I guess anyone can sue anyone."

He nodded in agreement, while gazing at her wide-eyed, with his penis maintaining its impressive state.

She glared down to it. "What the hell are you doing?"

"I'm, uh…" He gave her a sheepish look. "Do you still want to go around… the…" After giving him a tired look, she turned, and headed toward the door.

"How about just halfway around, you know to take your mind…" His words trailed off when she was out of sight. He whispered, "Fucking Natalie."

Jillian called the publishing company and asked for the division chief of her imprint. She reached the chief's assistant instead. "Debra's in a meeting. Can I take a message?"

"It's Jillian Grayson."

"Oh, Miss Grayson. We've actually been trying to reach you. Let me transfer you to the conference room."

When she was connected, Jillian heard, "Jillian. So I've got you on speaker. We've got Howard and Melissa from legal along with

Dan Peterson, the company president. We've been discussing the lawsuit."

"Hey, Dan."

"Jillian," Dan replied. "I'm so sorry about this."

"So who is this Natalie Brookhart? Do you actually know her?" Debra asked.

Jillian paused in confusion. "Yeah."

"How?"

"Well she's the ex-girlfriend of my fiancé."

"Why is this the first we're hearing about this?" Dan asked.

"Wait. You guys know all about this. Albert told me everything was cleared through legal."

"Who's Albert?" Dan asked.

"Her agent," Debra replied and said louder, "Jillian, we don't have anything on this. We're completely blindsided here."

"There must be some mix-up. Albert had all the information. He told me he submitted it to legal and—"

"Look, Jillian, this is the first we're hearing about any of this," Dan said. "Just tell us whether the character in your novel was based on this woman or not?"

"Well, yes, but…"

"Jillian, this is Howard Adams. Are we correct when we assume that you do not have a signed authorization from her?"

"Uh, no, I—"

"So is it loosely based on this Miss Brookhart?" Debra asked.

"We changed her name and the college, but everything is based on true events," Jillian replied.

"So the question is would a reasonable person be able to determine that the character is based on her?" Melissa asked.

"I don't think so," Jillian said.

"So the cover picture of the ballerina. We assume Miss Brookhart cannot put herself into that position."

"She can. That cover was Brian's idea," Jillian replied nervously and quickly regretted mentioning him.

"Who's Brian?" Dan asked impatiently.

"Her fiancé," Debra answered. "The *technical virgin* thing, now that is all your creation, I assume." After five seconds of silence, Debra asked, "Jillian are you there?"

"I'm here."

"The virgin thing?"

Jillian sighed. "That's all her. That's her name for it. It's all true or as far as my son and Brian have told me."

In the conference room in New York, Howard, Melissa, Debra, and Dan sat around the small table with the speakerphone in the center. Everyone looked shocked.

"Your son?" Dan asked loudly.

Jillian said, "Yes, he was dating her for a while as well. Secretly and behind Brian's back. You see Brian kind of fell for Natalie when he saw her do this thing they all called *the leg thing*. She was known around campus for this particular move and—"

"Isn't that the title of the novel as well?" Dan interrupted.

"Yes, that was Bri—I mean yes it is."

"I do like the title," Debra said.

After glaring at Debra, Dan said in an accusatory tone, "So you stole the title from her as well."

"I did not, I mean…"

Dan sighed. "Let me see if I have all of this straight. You based a character completely and wholly on a young woman who was not only dating your son, but also your fiancé. The cover image is a picture of a unique ballet move that Miss Brookhart is known widely for doing. Oh, and you also used a title that anyone who knows Miss Brookhart would immediately identify with her."

The four waited with their heads cocked for her reply. After five seconds, Jillian said, "Well when you say it all like that it sounds kind of bad, but…"

With the lawyers in the room holding their heads, Dan and Debra shot each other looks while shaking their heads.

"Okay." After letting out a long slow breath, Dan shrugged. "The good news is it's selling very well. So in the event that we're required to offer a settlement in the six-figure range we still might break ev—"

Back in Miami, a switch went off on Jillian. She interrupted, "I will not give that money-grubbing whore a penny." She glanced up to find Brian standing before her with his eyes widened. After shrugging her shoulders, she returned her attention to the phone.

"Please tell me you don't use language like that in the book referring to Miss Brookhart," Howard said.

Jillian's voice took on a defensive tone. "Uh, there might be something along those lines in there."

Debra said, "I think I remember the phase, *anal whore* in reference to the Rebecca character."

"Thank you, Debra," Jillian said in a tired voice.

Dan scolded, "Look Jillian, don't speak to anyone about this. Don't give any interviews. Don't use the term *anal whore*, and don't even mention Miss Brookhart's name."

"This makes absolutely no sense. My agent assured me he had the clearance from legal."

"We never gave it. You'll need to discuss that with him," Dan said.

Howard said, "Regardless, Miss Grayson, I assure you that without a signed release from Miss Brookhart, this office would not have given clearance for this novel. And given the nature of terms like *anal whore*... I would venture a guess that Miss Brookhart would never have signed such a release."

Dan added, "We'll look at all our options and get back to you." The line went dead.

Pulling the phone from her ear, Jillian turned to Brian with her mouth wide open.

He softly asked, "Do you want some wine or something?"

"Make it a martini."

He took off toward the kitchen.

With her blood pressure rising, she dialed another number.

"Albert Blair's office."

Skipping all pleasantries, Jillian said curtly, "Get him for me... I don't care if he's in with Barack Obama discussing his next children's book. Put me through now."

Seconds later Albert picked up the call, "Jillian, what—"

"The publisher and I are being sued by Natalie Brookhart."

"Really?"

"I just got off the phone with Debra and Dan. The lawyers were there and said that you didn't inform them about any possible legal issues related to the Rebecca character."

"That makes no sense. I definitely—"

"Cut the shit Albert. Tell me what's going on here."

After pausing, he sighed. "Look, I knew they would require a release, and I knew that Natalie never would have signed one."

She shot back angrily, "So then I should have pulled all that out of the book."

"I considered suggesting that, but then, quite frankly the story would have sucked."

"What the hell do you mean?" she asked, insulted.

Brian returned with her drink.

"I mean—"

"Hold on," she growled into the phone, then placed it down.

Grabbing the drink, she took a big sip before closing her eyes a moment and taking a deep breath. She returned the phone to her ear. "So what was that Albert?"

"You take Natalie, I mean, Rebecca the superflexible, technical virgin, anal-sex loving, man manipulator out, and all you have left is a story about two tennis-obsessed, incredibly annoying complete losers."

"Losers!" She boomed, "Those two tennis-obsessed annoying losers are based on Brian and I!"

Brian's face dropped as he listened in. After shaking his head, he tiptoed out of the room.

"You know what I mean," Albert said casually.

"No, I really don't."

"Look, I figured only two things could happen… and both of them were good. Natalie never finds out, and the book sells well because it's fabulous or… Natalie does find out, sues, and you get so much publicity that the book sells like crazy."

"I don't know." She sighed and her voice softened a bit. "You should have bounced this off me."

"When Kathryn Stockett was sued by that maid over the book *The Help*, the book shot to number one on Amazon and stayed there for months. The maid sued, claiming that the character was based on her, and the judge dismissed the case."

"But did Katherine refer to the maid as an anal whore in the book?"

"She could have. I never read it," he said defensively.

"Do you *really* think she did?"

"Probably not, but—"

"This is bad. I know this is bad."

"Just trust me. Everything will be fine. Do you remember James Frey? *A Million Little Pieces.*"

"Sure."

"Oprah selected it for her book club and sure he sold some books, but when Oprah yelled at him on live television, then he really sold some books—a lot of fucking books."

"So you're saying I should piss Oprah off?"

"Could you? Do you have any idea how to pull it off? Maybe we could—"

"Albert, shut the fuck up."

After a few seconds of silence, Albert said, "Trust me on this one."

She exhaled deeply. "Okay, but what do I tell Debra and Dan?"

"I'll take care of them. And if anyone asks for an interview, you should give it. I'll e-mail you a list of talking points."

"Dan said to not talk to anyone about this."

"I'll clear it with them and get back to you."

"Wait, you have them contact me directly if they want me to give interviews. I'm not sure this trust we once had has been repaired quite yet."

"Fair enough. Hey, the book has been selling great so far."

"I know, but all that money might be going to Natalie."

"It won't."

"You know I really don't need this shit. I'm getting married in less than a week."

"Oh my God, I almost forgot about the wedding."

"Will I see you there?"

"I wouldn't miss it. Now just try to relax."

"How can I?"

"Have a drink or two."

"Okay." After putting down the phone, she chugged her martini.

Albert Blair sat in his office thinking. He picked up Jillian's wedding invitation from the desk and rubbed his chin. Glancing down at the background check report for Natalie Brookhart, he smiled. He picked up the phone and dialed a number.

After reaching his contact and getting the answer he was after, he screamed, "Gladys get in here."

Five seconds later, his assistant rushed through the door with a pen and pad ready. Albert said, "I need two round-trip plane tickets from New York to St. Barts leaving this Saturday and returning Monday. Put one in the name Tim Dale and the other is for Natalie Brookhart. Wait—put two in Natalie's name and make them first class. She might want to take a friend. And book a hotel for each of them Saturday and Sunday nights at the same hotel I'm staying in."

Gladys wrote it all down and when she raised her eyes from the pad he continued, "I need all that ASAP. Messenger Tim's over to him, but I need Natalie's hand delivered today. Call Jason."

She stood there awaiting more instructions. He glared at her. "Don't just stand there." As she rushed toward the door, he said, "Wait. Have you seen my speedboat catalog anywhere?"

She turned back to him and shrugged. Groaning, he dismissed her with the wave of his hand.

17

In all the excitement with Jillian and the lawsuit, Brian had forgotten that he had agreed to accompany Victoria to her stylist. She wanted to give him the gift of a brand new hairstyle for the wedding. He had planned on working a half-day and had it marked on his calendar at work, but now that there was no work, no calendar, and no pop up reminder, he had forgotten. When Victoria arrived, he was out by the pool relaxing. It only took a quick glare from her before he remembered. He rushed inside, quickly got dressed, and followed her out to her car. He was looking forward to a new haircut, but he had no idea of the location of all the hair she intended to be cut.

As they walked to the spa he said, "I appreciate you doing this. I could use a slightly new look for the wedding, and my hair is just too long."

"That's what I heard."

He gave her an odd look.

She smiled. "I think you'll like this place. They are very professional and have a lot of great ideas."

"Cool."

After a wash, cut, blow-dry, and style, Brian sat in the chair, admiring his new haircut, with Victoria looking on pleased. He shook his head, concerned. "I hope I can fix it this way for the wedding."

The stylist said, "Just use some of that gel and comb it out like I showed you. You should be fine."

"Thank you so much."

A thin, lithe, dark-skinned, feminine-looking man walked out from the back of the store. Smiling at Victoria, he said in a Spanish accent, "Victoria, I am ready for you."

She turned to Brian. "I have another surprise."

"What's this, I thought—"

"Just follow me," she interrupted.

They headed toward the back of the store then followed Rafael down a hall and into a small room. Rafael stood next to a padded table, pulling on a white lab coat. He smiled brightly to them both. "Victoria, I haven't seen you around in a long time."

"No reason to come in. I'm not dating all that much anymore."

"That should never stop you," he chuckled.

Stepping toward Brian, Rafael took his hand and shook it gently. "So this is your friend."

Brian cleared his throat and said in a mock deep voice, "Brian. I'm Brian." After glancing down to his hand, which Rafael still had a hold of, he pulled it slowly from his grasp.

"Nice to meet you, Brian." Rafael looked him over from head to toe. "I love your new hairstyle. Now let me work my magic on the rest of your hair. Your woman is going to love it."

Brian turned to Victoria wearing a shocked expression. "What exactly is this?"

She opened her mouth to speak, but Rafael asked first, "You want the standard male Brazilian not the Hollywood?"

Replying softly, she nodded her head. "Yes, the Brazilian."

"The what? What is that?" Brian asked horrified.

Rafael said, "A standard male Brazilian includes a full wax hair removal from the frontal pubic area, the shaft, scrotum, and anal area. It's your choice whether we leave a landing strip above the shaft, or we could take it all off."

Brian listened, dumbfounded. Victoria glanced at Brian before returning her attention to Rafael. "I'm not sure about the landing strip. What are most guys doing these days?"

"Uh, it's about half who choose the strip and half who go completely bare. I kind of like the strip. That way you don't look like a little boy." Rafael slipped on a pair of latex gloves as he turned to Brian. "So, what do you think?"

"About what?"

"The landing strip."

Leaning close to Victoria's ear, Brian whispered harshly, "Um, Victoria, can I talk to you for a second?"

Rafael exhaled deeply. "Victoria, I have another appointment in twenty minutes, so..."

She gave him an apologetic look. "We'll just be a second."

Frowning, Brian held the door open for Victoria. She shuffled into the hall, he gave Rafael a weak smile, slipped out to join her, and closed the door.

Brian narrowed his eyes. "What the hell is this?"

"He's a genius with pubic hair."

After looking at her for a few moments with his jaw slacked, he shook his head, ruefully. "I'm not letting some guy wax my ass hole."

"Oh, so you only want the Hollywood then?" She replied and waited with a wide-eyed curious smile.

He looked at her, astonished, with his mouth just about as wide open as it could get, but she plowed ahead anyway, "You see I think that's a mistake with—"

"What the fuck are you talking about?"

"We spoke about your balls a few months ago."

"Yeah, and I told you I'd shave them."

"And did you?" she asked skeptically.

"Yeah," he replied sheepishly.

"Let me see."

"Okay, I tried to once." He exhaled deeply. "But I got scared having the razor so close to my, you know, sensitive areas and—"

"I figured. So here's your solution. Waxing involves no blades of any kind."

"Yeah, but it sounds really painful. I mean ripping the hairs off your balls seems like it would kinda hurt."

"Oh, don't be a baby. It hurts for like a second."

Grimacing, he shook his head unconvinced. "I don't know."

She folded her arms. "You want more ball attention don't you?"

"Well, yes."

"And your ass…"

"What about my ass?" he asked smugly.

"You want more attention there, too?"

"It gets plenty of attention already."

She scoffed. "I heard about the sex the night of your birthday party."

"What about it? It was freaking amazing. Jillian did things to me she'd never done before."

"Are you sure?"

Moving closer to her, he whispered, "I'm sure. She actually put her tongue on my… you know and was licking it and everything."

"I hate to be the one to tell you this, but that wasn't her tongue."

"What?" He narrowed his eyes.

"That was a moistened finger."

His jaw dropped. "You're kidding, right?"

With her eyes closed, she shook her head.

"No way."

"Yes." Opening her eyes, she gave him a sympathetic smile. "She told me herself. She wanted to give you the full treatment, but when she saw the condition of the jungle, she was scared off."

"*The jungle?*"

She gave him a sincere look. "Her words."

"I don't believe it."

Rafael opened the door and gave them a tired look. Holding her finger out, Victoria turned to him. "Just one more minute."

Sighing, Rafael closed the door.

Brian slumped against the wall and gazed down to the floor.

"Jillian really wanted to please you that way, but although I haven't seen you back there personally, I've got to imagine it's a disaster."

He glared at her, insulted.

"Brian, as I've said before, no woman wants to lick hairy balls, and she certainly doesn't want to go near a hairy ass."

After shaking his head, he exhaled deeply. "I don't know."

"How amazing did it feel when she was fake licking you back there?"

"It was… just mind blowing."

Moving a step toward him, she gently touched his forearm as she spoke softly, suggestively, "Imagine what it would be like for Jillian to lick it for real and slowly move back and forth between your smooth, hair-free balls, then along your perineum…" As she described it, she traced a finger up and down his forearm. "…then back to the millions of supersensitive nerve endings of your most sensitive of areas."

Looking down, gape-mouthed, to her finger as it lingered on his skin, his pants suddenly became more crowded as he got lost in the fantasy.

"Wow." He swallowed hard and slowly lifted his chin until he was looking her in the eye.

"Just let him take a look. What could it hurt?" She gave him a hopeful look. "Let him give you his opinion. That all."

"She really told you I'm too hairy?"

She gave him a sympathetic nod.

After looking to the ceiling, he put on a weak smile. "Okay."

"Great." She opened the door for him, and he slowly walked in with her smiling widely behind him.

Rafael clapped his hands. "Okay, I've got fifteen minutes, so depending on what we're working with here, we might need to reschedule. I'm pretty booked up the rest of the week."

Victoria said, "Oh please fit him in today. He leaves for his wedding in a few days, and he needs time to heal."

"*Heal?*" Brian asked horrified.

"Let's see what we've got." Rafael turned to Brian waiting.

Brian gave him a hesitant look. "So, um, I should just drop my pants?"

"That would help," Rafael said in a weary voice.

Feeling his groin, Brian realized it was still a little excited from Victoria's erotic sales pitch. He figured that might be actually be a good thing, since he'd never been much of a shower. Now smiling semi-confidently, he slipped his pants and underwear down.

"Hello," Rafael said, impressed. Victoria smiled as she checked him out as well.

"You're a little worked up from the whole ass licking thing I told you about, aren't you?"

Brian nodded, embarrassed. Rafael slipped down to his knees lifted Brian's penis up then looked underneath. "Uh, huh." Then he lifted his balls and craned his neck down to look under them. "Oh, I see. You definitely need my help. No one is licking those and enjoying it."

After glaring at Rafael, Brian turned to Victoria to find her giving him a sympathetic shrug.

Rafael stood and looked at the clock. "Quickly remove your shoes, pants, and underwear. Then get up on the table."

Brian looked at them hesitantly. Rafael sighed, and Victoria motioned for him to hurry up. Brian pulled his shoes off and stepped out of his pants.

Rafael rubbed his chin. "He does have a good looking penis though."

Victoria smiled like a proud parent. "I know, doesn't he? I've actually held it... more than once."

Rafael simply said, "Huh."

Brian climbed up on the table on all fours, but kept his legs together and his ass cheeks closed up tight. Rafael studied his body closely. "The boys I know would love him. He has a fantastic body."

Rafael moved behind Brian and spread his ass cheeks apart. He grimaced when he got a look at the dark thick mat of hair between them. "Oh, the boys would not like this at all."

After moving in for a look, Victoria recoiled while making a sour face. "It's worse than I thought."

Brian turned back to look at them. "What's wrong?"

Rafael commanded, "Spread your legs."

Brian frowned and spread his legs, opening up everything to Victoria and Rafael as they stood behind him studying his most private of areas. He glanced back once more to them and saw their judgmental, frowning faces. Shaking his head, he whispered to himself, "I can't fucking believe I have two people staring into my slightly hairy ass."

"What was that?" Rafael asked?

"Nothing," Brian muttered.

Turing to Victoria, Rafael gave her a determined look. "I can do this, but I'm going to need to trim it first and then wax all of it. Maybe twice."

"But can you do it now?"

"I'll fit him in. It's a shame when you see a beautiful penis such as this hidden by so much hair."

"You should see his brother. Picture this body, but with a bigger penis... I mean much bigger."

"Hey, I'm right here."

She ignored him and continued, "And larger balls, like nice ones... that same firm ass, but with nothing but tiny little baby blonde hairs on all of it."

Rafael smiled brightly. "Oh, I love those baby blonde hairs."

"So do I."

"Is his brother straight?"

"He is." She gave him a confident look. "He's really, really, straight."

"That's a shame because he sounds amazing."

Brian turned to them. "Okay, can we stop fawning over my brother's perfect penis, balls, and hair-free ass? What am I—a giant hairy ape with a pencil dick?"

"No one called you an ape." She gave him a genuine smile. "You know I think you have a gorgeous penis."

With her look softening him, Brian held back a chuckle and returned to the position. Rafael clapped his hands together again. "Okay, let me get the big trimmer—the really big one."

As he walked out into the hall, Rafael screamed, "Reschedule my two thirty and my three."

Craning his neck back toward Victoria, Brian sighed. "Really?"

"You are going to love it. Trust me."

He exhaled deeply and whimpered softly.

When Rafael returned, he spent the next ten minutes trimming all the hair he could reach. When the waxing began, the bloodcurdling screams could be heard two stores away on both sides of the spa. Most people inside the spa thought it was a woman screaming, but when the screams were followed by a male voice spewing horrific expletives, they realized exactly what was happening. It wasn't the first time that a man was tricked into a full Brazilian, and it wouldn't be the last.

Forty minutes later, Brian limped to the car, exhausted and bleeding from places he'd rather not mention. He didn't say a word to Victoria during the ten-minute drive home as he sat fidgeting and grimacing in his seat. When Victoria pulled her car into the Grayson driveway, he reached for the door handle. She grabbed his arm. "Hey."

Closing his eyes, he refused to look at her.

"Look, I know this wasn't fun, but it will be worth it."

He sighed and opened his eyes. "It better be."

"When she sees your hairless parts, she's going to instantly get wet." She smiled brightly. "Wait, I know… you should not show her until the wedding night. It'll make it really special. Well…" She frowned. "You'll probably need at least three days to heal fully anyway."

"How did it look?"

"Amazing. You penis and balls looked huge not covered by all that hair. And your ass looked so good you could eat a snack off it. I saw it just before the blood began gushing out."

Grimacing, he reached again for the door.

"Wait. Don't go in there frowning. She'll know something is up. Just use the cream he gave you, and you should be fine. Take a few baths."

He painted on a fake smile. "All right."

"Do you need me to come in and take a look or change your pad or anything?"

Instead of replying, he sighed as he climbed out of the car.

"Oh, okay then."

He glanced back to her. "She better be all over me, or I'm coming over to your house so you can do it."

"Listen, Brian, if Jillian wasn't my best friend, and if I didn't just recently shove my tongue so far up your brother's ass that he couldn't breathe, you wouldn't be able to pull me off of you."

"Charming." He gave her a distasteful look. "Geez, remind me never to take a sip from your drink."

"Okay, I'm exaggerating a bit, I was mostly around the—"

"Please stop!" After taking a step away from the car, he grimaced and adjusted his shorts in the back. "Well, thanks—I guess." Frowning, he pulled down on the front of his shorts before putting on a brave smile.

"Tough it out. I promise it will be worth it."

He pushed the door closed then waddled slowly toward the house. Victoria held back a laugh as she remained in the driveway enjoying the show.

Brian struggled to walk normally as he headed into the kitchen. He found Jillian sitting at the table typing away on her laptop. "Oh, hi, you're back."

He asked hesitantly, "Is everything okay?"

"I've decided to just not think about it. Let Albert and my publisher deal with it for now. I sent the papers off to my attorney and told him I don't want to talk about it until I get back."

Finally noticing his new look, she smiled. "Oh I love your haircut! You look cute." She closed her computer and slipped off her chair and hugged him. "Let's not let it spoil our wedding." She flashed her eyes to him suggestively. "Now, weren't we going to take a trip before?"

He looked at her confused. "A trip?"

"Around the world."

"Oh yeah…"

She reached down to his groin and squeezed his package gently. He jumped back as if she had shoved a stick into an opened wound. "Ouch."

"What's wrong."

"Sorry, I just… uh, you know, balls can be so sensitive. They must have been sitting in there wrong or…"

Moving toward him, she gave him a sexy smile. "Do you want me to check them for you?" He took another step back, and she narrowed her eyes. "What the hell is wrong with you?"

"I was just thinking, maybe we shouldn't have sex until the wedding night. I think it'll really be hot to, uh, wait."

She gave him a skeptical look. "Really?"

"Yeah, we'll be so horny for each other by Sunday that we'll just go crazy. It'll be amazing."

She smiled warming to the idea a bit. "Okay. I can do it if you can do it."

He smiled halfheartedly, grabbed two beers out of the refrigerator, then headed out of the room.

"Where are you going?"

"Upstairs to take a bath."

"Really?" She put on a quizzical expression. "Okay, but remember this no sex thing means no masturbation either."

"You don't have to worry about that." He limped up the steps while clutching his balls gently.

18

On the campus of NYU, outside of Natalie's dorm building, Jason waited. When he saw her, he walked up, and although he already knew from the photo, he asked, "Are you Natalie Brookhart?"

"Yes." She looked at him confused.

He extended a large envelope toward her, and she took it. He said, "Have a good trip." She watched as he slipped away. After rushing to her room, she opened the envelope, then studied the contents. She immediately called Josh.

In Orlando, Rob was picking up carryout at a restaurant within walking distance of the apartment building. An attractive woman in her late twenties, dressed like a jogger and wearing a Georgia State University T-shirt, waited two stores away with a phone to her ear. Across the street a man in a dark suit sat in a car, and he was also on the phone.

The man watched as Rob turned toward the door. He said, "Okay now."

The woman kept the phone to her ear as she jogged toward the store. Timing it perfectly, she ran right into Rob as he opened the door and slipped outside. She tumbled to the ground as her phone skipped along the concrete. Rob's bag also flew out of his hand. After looking around in shock, he focused on the woman. "Are you okay?"

"I'm so sorry. I'm such an idiot. I was on the phone and wasn't watching. Are you all right?"

"Yeah, I'm fine."

The woman rose to her feet as he picked up her phone and his carryout bag. He handed her the phone. She smiled. "Thanks. I'll be more careful." Holding her chest out, she stood still, with the words on her T-shirt in full display. After suffering through the awkward silence, she pulled her shirt out from her waist and held it out to inspect it. "Ahh, I'm a mess."

Finally noticing the shirt, he smiled. "You went to GSU?"

"Yep. Graduated in two thousand nine."

"I just graduated this year."

She smiled brightly. "No way. I've never met any Panthers down here. Everyone seems to be from a Florida school."

He nodded. "When you live in a state with beautiful weather, why go to school somewhere else?"

She chuckled. "I'm Bridget."

"Rob."

"So did you spend a lot of time at Chubby's? Senior year we lived there."

"Sure, we were there a lot."

"I don't remember seeing you." She narrowed her eyes.

"I probably wasn't there that much in oh nine."

"So, do you live around here?"

He pointed toward the building down the street. "Yeah, right there at Blue Stone."

"That place looks nice. I'm renting a room from a friend temporarily down on Tenth Street while I look for a place."

"Oh."

"Hey, you still follow the football team?"

"Sure, but they're never on TV."

"There's this bar I know where they show all the college games. I've been looking for someone to go with to watch. You know my girlfriends would be bored, and if I go alone guys would be so... you know."

"Oh, sure," he replied while looking her over from head to toe but probably lingering a bit too long on her tits.

Ignoring his inappropriate gawking, she asked, "Would you maybe like to go sometime and watch?"

"Definitely." He smiled.

"There's a game this Saturday."

His smiled faded and he shook his head. "My mother's actually getting married this weekend, and I need to fly out for the wedding. They're getting married in St. Barts." Rob widened his eyes a little embarrassed.

"Wow, I've heard of destination weddings. That's some destination."

"I'm free the next weekend. How about we exchange numbers, and I'll call you when I get back?"

"Awesome." As Rob worked to pull his phone out of his pocket, she glanced to the man in the car and smiled.

19

October fourth was Jim's birthday, and it was a big one this year since he was turning twenty-one. After a day of classes and calls from both his mother and brother, Jim was ready for the real celebration to begin. Caroline had told him the day before that she had something special planned. She piqued his curiosity by meeting him in his dorm suite. She told him he wasn't allowed to go into his bedroom because it would spoil the surprise. Slipping back into his room, Caroline picked out an appropriate outfit for him for the night, and waited while he showered and changed.

First she took him out for dinner, then on to a bar for his first *legal* drinking experience. At just after ten, they returned to his dorm. She made him wait outside his room as she opened the door barely a foot and slid through, being careful to not let him have a glimpse. When he heard her bang some body parts into something really loudly and curse, he broke into laughter. A few seconds later, she opened the door slightly, told him to come in, then moved away from the door.

He tried to open the door, but it seemed to be blocked by some piece of furniture and would only open about eighteen inches. Peering into the dimly lit room, he saw that a single, large candle provided the room's only light; he could just make out Caroline sitting on his bed and grinning hesitantly. She said, "Sorry, I guess I should have measured before I, uh..."

"What are you up to?" Chuckling, he struggled to see what she was up to in the room. He slipped through the opening, scraping his shoulder along the way before falling onto the bed. He closed the door and steadied himself while letting his eyes fully adjust to the candlelight. Inside the room, she had created a mini feng shui massage experience with a massage table, the single large candle, and some kind of grass wall hanging. He took in the scene with his lips parted, and his heart melting. Looking back to her, his surprise was evident.

"Do you like it? I mean, it's not as nice as the one you put together for Victoria, but you know you don't have a lot of space in here, and I didn't win any money at a casino."

The room was so small that the massage table was pressed up against his dresser on one side and his bed on the other. There were only a few feet of floor space at the foot and head of the table.

"I love it."

She shook her head. "I screwed this whole thing up. It doesn't fit—it's a disaster."

"No, no. I really do love it." Leaning over, he gave her a kiss.

"Really?"

"I do."

Pointing across the room, she frowned. "There's a slight problem with the dresser. Now you can only open the top drawer. Oh, I think you can get into the bottom one if you crawl on the floor under the table."

He gave her a concerned look. "But my condoms are in that middle drawer."

"Oh, that's your other surprise."

He widened his eyes.

She returned a sexy smile. "At the beach I told you I wanted to go on the pill, remember?"

"Uh-huh."

After pausing for effect, she flashed her eyes at him. "Well, surprise."

"That might be my favorite gift."

After they shared a chuckle, he knelt up on the mattress to take in the entire room. "There's enough room—kind of. I mean, you can stand by the door for this side, then by the window for the other side, or kneel on the bed over here. It fits perfectly."

"Yeah, right, but luckily it folds up for when you actually want to live in here."

"So, what's next?" He raised his eyebrows to her.

"Not yet." Shaking her head, she held back a smile. "Why don't you get ready for your rub? You know—take it all off."

"Cool."

As she struggled to climb from the bed to the foot of the massage table, he removed his clothing. She admired his firm body in the candlelight as he moved from the bed onto the sheet-covered table and put his head comfortably in the rest.

"Is this table heated?" he asked jokingly.

"Hey." She smacked him hard on the ass.

"Just kidding."

After dribbling a line of oil over his buttocks and legs, she began to work it in. He groaned as she firmly worked his glutes. "I know you had that no sex rule at your *other* massage room, but I was thinking maybe we should waive that here."

"Oh, you do, do you?"

"Yes, in fact it's against the law to *not* have sex in the commonwealth of Pennsylvania after a massage. We're a much more liberal state than Florida."

Lifting his head up from the table, he turned to look at her, holding back a smile.

"I don't know what I'm saying. I must have had too much to drink at dinner."

He placed his head back down and exhaled deeply as she climbed onto the bed and moved to the head of the table. She dribbled oil on his neck and worked it in. "I found this special massage oil. It's oil, but it's also a personal lubricant. It can go anywhere—if you know what I mean."

He lifted his head again to look at her. "Anywhere?"

"Well, it doesn't taste so good, but it can go in all the other places."

After raising his eyebrows, he slipped back down. She dribbled oil over his back, shoulders, and arms, then worked it in for the next fifteen minutes.

"Okay, birthday boy, time to turn over."

He turned over on his back. His penis was completely flaccid. She looked at it with mock disappointment. "What? This isn't doing it for you?"

He followed her eyes to his softie. "No. I was hard before when you were doing my legs, but the upper body stuff was so relaxing that I, uh…"

She removed her clothes while he watched. As soon as her breasts were uncovered, his penis began to respond. She glanced at it. "That's better." She dribbled the oil-lubricant all over his chest and began to work it in. As she leaned over him to reach his stomach, one of her breasts grazed his mouth. He moaned; when her breast brushed his mouth again, he captured it with his lips.

She lifted up and covered his groin with a generous amount of oil. After massaging some into her breasts, she moved her hands lower between her legs and climbed on top of him. He ran his hands all over her slippery breasts, then, as she moved down on him, he cupped her ass. She slid down further, and a mini-orgasm shot through her loins. She groaned in pleasure before bending over and pressing her chest against his, rubbing her oily self all over him.

Rising upright, she slid her hands down her glistening breasts to her stomach, then to her swollen clit. She closed her eyes and groaned, simply bouncing up and down on his shaft. Moving his finger between her cheeks, he located her seam and gently pressed his lubed finger into her.

"Yes..." Opening her eyes, she nodded slowly and whispered, "Touch me there."

He slipped his finger inside while she rode him harder and faster. Her intense facial expression as he pleasured her ass was way too much for him. He pictured his penis in place of his finger there, and it pushed him over the edge. Suddenly, he groaned, and it was over. Caroline looked deep into his eyes as she held still and whispered, "I love you."

He replied, "I love you too."

She closed her eyes and began moving over him again. Jim lasted a lot longer during this session. When she finally climaxed, she slumped on to him. For three minutes they lay there recovering — panting and dripping with oil. Then she grimaced as she said, "I do love you, but if I don't get this disgusting smelly oil off of me I'm going to throw up."

He nodded in complete agreement.

20

Caroline spent the night, and Jim had an early class. After getting dressed without waking her, he looked at her bare shoulder for a long time as he stood in the doorframe. Smiling, he flashed back to their night together before he slipped away. After class, he walked past a jewelry store, and the display of engagement rings in the window caught his eye. He turned back and entered the store wearing a confident smile.

Victoria answered her front door to find a deliveryman holding a large box. She signed for it and couldn't wait to open it. It was one of the wedding gifts she had picked out for Jillian and Brian—a sexy one.

After taking his third bath in less than two days, Brian applied cream to all his effected areas. He avoided letting Jillian see him naked by locking the bathroom door.

Jillian stood outside the door frowning. "What are you doing? You never lock the door. Are you… jerking off?"

"What? No."

"We said no sex until—"

"I know. I don't trust you with this body." He cracked himself up. "You get all crazy when you see me."

Leaning against the wall, completely naked, she sighed. She traced her finger along the door molding. "Sometimes I just can't help myself."

"I think we can both make it a couple more days," he said loudly through the door. After unlocking and opening the door, he spotted her hot body. He wore only boxer briefs as he covered his eyes and shuffled past her. "This is not good for the celibacy pact."

"You're very weak you know that." She shook her head as she sauntered into the bathroom.

Turning back, he caught a glimpse of her shapely ass before she disappeared into the shower stall. He let out a sigh as he headed out of the room.

That night, he struggled to fall asleep since his new hair-free balls were literally itching and also figuratively itching for some female attention. With Jillian sound asleep next to him, he slipped quietly in to the bathroom and spent a good minute checking everything out down there in the mirror. Lifting one part up, he craned his neck to see two other parts and smiled, pleased with his new clean look. The smoothness of it all felt incredible. He couldn't wait to show Jillian and have her try out his new equipment. Rather than use a quick self-pleasuring session to try to sleep and break his word, he turned to booze. After downing a beer, he returned to the bedroom and quickly fell asleep.

The next day Brian woke up late and discovered Jillian in the great room, frowning as she watched television. She exhaled and turned it off. "The lawsuit is all over the news."

"Oh no."

"They're saying I based the character on her. Natalie's attorney, a Josh somebody, claims that Rebecca is Natalie, but the novel is filled with lies amounting to character assassination. He said they're seeking damages to ensure this never happens to another young woman. And something about repairing Natalie's reputation and helping her move on with her life. He called her a 'respectable, shy young girl who would never manipulate men or engage in the kind of sex described in the book.'"

He gave her an incredulous look. "All she did was engage in the kind of sex described in the book."

"I know." She scoffed and let out a sigh. "I think…"

"What?"

"I think we should postpone the wedding."

"But, we're flying out tomorrow." Sitting down next to her, he placed his hand on her knee. "Everything is set. Just forget about all of it."

"How can I forget? And we won't have the money to pay for any of it when she gets through with us."

She rested her head on his chest, and he stroked her hair. "Don't let her ruin this for us. It's too late to cancel it. You probably can't get any of the money back. I'll call the bank and ask for my job back."

"Don't do that." She pulled up and looked him in the eye. "I need you with me now."

They kissed, and he held her on the sofa for the next thirty minutes. Later that day the phone rang often with requests for comments and interviews. After turning them all down, she disconnected her phone. They kept the television off for the rest of the day and stayed off the Internet.

21

Jim, Caroline, and Ed and Bev Nash boarded the same flight to Miami early the next day. This was the first time Jim's parents had met Caroline, and overall they treated her well. In fact, they almost acted like normal people; it was astonishing. Neither mentioned the word *fornicate* or anything relating to religion during the flight.

Jillian and Brian met them at the gate and guided them to the correct gate for the charter flight to St. Barts. Victoria, Rob, Laura, and the rest of the wedding party, along with the local guests, were waiting there as well. All other out of town guests were flying directly from their own airport to meet them on the island of St. Maarten for the puddle-jumping flight to St. Barts.

As they waited to board the plane, a television was blaring in the waiting area. Jillian had been able to put the entire lawsuit out of her mind until the news story began on the screen:

A lawsuit against best-selling author Jillian Grayson who writes under the pen name of Jaclyn West has been filed by Natalie Brookhart, a young woman who at one time dated both Miss Grayson's son, Robert, and her fiancé, Brian Nash.

All eyes looked to the screen as the story continued.

Miss Brookhart alleges that her likeness was used in the novel without her permission. She also contends that she was painted in an unflattering, if not slanderous, light in the story. She is seeking unspecified damages that are rumored to be in the multi seven-figure range. Miss Brookhart says she can prove her claims and offers up proof with this video of her striking the exact ballet pose depicted on the cover of the novel entitled The Leg Thing.

On the screen, a split image of Natalie in the ballet position appeared next to a large image of the book cover.

Miss Grayson has yet to comment on this suit publicly, but experts we spoke to believe that there is more than enough evidence to support Miss Brookhart's claims, and there is rumored to be a large settlement currently in the works.

Jillian held her head with her eyes closed as everyone else turned to her, attempting to deliver sympathetic looks. Opening her eyes, she glanced around to her supporters. "I'd rather not talk about it. Let's just keep the TVs off the news channels this weekend."

Everyone nodded, and no one said a word as they continued to wait in the terminal. Victoria was expecting the results of the paternity test any day, and her doctor had promised to e-mail them as soon as they were available. As she was sitting in the airport, her smart phone chirped. She read the message, smiled, then looked at Jim. She decided to break the news to him the next day.

During the flight, as Victoria went over exactly how to tell Jim, Jillian spent the time with her mind reeling wearing a solemn face. After Brian tried to lift her spirits with a few witty comments that missed their mark, he gave up and decided it was best to let her work through it on her own. As the plane was descending, Jillian painted on a smile and promised that once they landed on the perfect tropical island, she would put all nonwedding-related issues out of her mind.

St. Barts, or as some call it St. Barths, is a beautiful island in the northeastern Caribbean, known for its crystal-clear blue water, fine white sand, nude sunbathing, and exclusive clientele. The Nash-Grayson group's charter flight landed in St. Maarten and from there, they met up with guests who had flown in from other airports. Then the group split up and took two smaller planes for the fifteen-minute flight to the island's Gustave Airport. The small low-flying planes gave them all a breathtaking view of the spectacular sunset, and the beauty of the tropical paradise even left Jillian with a genuine smile.

The twin aircrafts landed at the tiny airport on St. Barts just after 7:00 p.m. about ten minutes apart. Two SUVs were waiting to take Brian, Jillian, Victoria, Jim, Caroline, Rob, Laura, and the three other members of the wedding party along with two plus-ones to the house Jillian had rented. A bus transported everyone else to the Hotel Eden Rock, where the wedding was to be held in a little more than thirty-six hours. The guests of the Nash-Grayson wedding occupied nearly half of the thirty-four upscale rooms at the resort. Jillian had arranged for meals and activities for everyone attending the wedding.

The prospective bride and groom and their ten guests arrived at the huge lavish mansion that featured eight bedrooms and nine bathrooms fifteen minutes later. The house sat high on a hill overlooking the beach and town, which were a short five-minute walk away. The house included a gym room and two pools, a butler, full housekeeping staff, and a chef. Everyone dropped off their luggage in their rooms, which all featured king beds, ensuite baths, and private balconies.

After unpacking, Jillian and Brian headed to the Eden Rock to check on the guests staying at the resort. There they met with the general manager and were assured that every one of their guest's needs would be taken care of by the hotel's attentive staff.

When they returned to the house, the mansion guests met for a delicious late meal, then retired to their rooms, completely exhausted from traveling. All were looking forward to the activities planned for the next day. Although Jillian didn't mention anything related to the lawsuit, she remained mostly quiet throughout the night, and Brian was concerned about her.

Jillian stood in the bathroom of their suite just staring in the mirror while wearing a sour expression. Brian came up behind her and began to rub her shoulders. She groaned with her eyes shut. "I could really use a rub." She opened her eyes and looked at him in the mirror as she said curtly, "A good one — not one of those where you are looking for something more."

"Okay, okay. We're not supposed to do it anyway."

"Oh, that's right," she said in a tired voice.

There was a quiet knock on the door, and Jillian rolled her eyes. Rushing over, she opened it to find Jim wearing a timid expression. She attempted a smile, but failed miserably.

Jim asked, "Sorry. Is this a bad time?"

"Sure, I'm just… no, this is fine," she said, feeling a little guilty and trying a little harder to smile.

"I just wanted to speak to you both for a few minutes."

Jim moved into the room and closed the door. He began, "I know this is your weekend, and I don't want to do anything to ruin that, but…"

"What is it?" Brian asked.

"I decided to ask Caroline to marry me and…"

Jillian's painted on-smile melted away. Moving to Jim, she grabbed him for a hug and for the first time since she heard the news story in the airport, she was truly smiling. After kissing him hard on the cheek, she took a step back, and beamed without saying a word.

Brian shook his hand. "Congratulations."

A tear slid down Jillian's face. "We love her. This is wonderful. When are you going to propose?"

"That's just it. I want to do it here. It's like the perfect place to do it, so gorgeous and all, but I don't want to take any of the attention off your day. I was hoping I could do it Monday morning after the wedding."

"Don't be ridiculous. You can do it whenever you want. Announce it to everyone. We won't mind." She glanced at Brian, and they shared an approving nod.

"I wouldn't feel right about doing it before the ceremony."

She smiled. "Well, how about this. Do it Sunday night after we've left the reception. You'll both be dressed and standing out on the beautiful patio with champagne and great food. Rather than doing it some sleepy morning or while sweaty and wearing a bathing suit. You want it to be memorable."

Jim gave them a hopeful look. "You really wouldn't mind?"

"Jimmy, I can guarantee you that after we leave the reception, we won't be worried about what you guys are doing. It will be all about us." She gave him a naughty grin.

"Thank you," Jim said. Jillian hugged him again. Appearing as if his emotions were about to get the best of him, he pulled away from her while curling his lip. "I've got to get out of here before I, uh, lose it."

Brian and Jillian shared a smile, and she reached out to hold his hand as Jim left the room. Moving to him, she gave him a hug. She pulled back with her mood the complete opposite of what it had been three minutes ago. "I don't care about the lawsuit, or the book, or any of it. All I care about right now is marrying you. No matter what happens, I promise I'll be in a good mood for the rest of the trip."

He grinned. "Does that mean I don't need to give you a rub now? You know, I'm kinda tired and…"

She glared at him in mock anger. "Just get the oil."

"I was kidding."

"I know you were."

"In fact, I can't wait to sit on your perfect naked ass." He shuttered as if reliving a sexy memory. "I haven't done that in a while."

"I miss your touch." She moved close to him.

"I promise I'll be good. I won't try to slip it in or anything."

After giving him a sad look, she sighed. "If you really don't want to wait, I think I—"

"As much as it's killing me I think we should wait."

"You're right." She pressed her body to his. "What did I ever do to deserve you?"

"I'm not exactly sure."

"After the wedding…" Giving him a sexy smile, she ran a finger down his chest toward his stomach. "I'm so going to take care of you."

He gently caught her hand before it reached the problem area. "Okay, this isn't helping *things*."

"Sorry."

Turning from her, he headed toward the bathroom. "I'll get the oil, but I'm warning you, I'm keeping my underwear on."

She sighed as she pulled her shirt over her head.

The next morning, Victoria woke just after sunrise. She lay in bed thinking about when and exactly how to tell Jim about the baby. Wanting to tell him soon, she vowed that she would at the first opportunity. She moved out to the pool area with a cup of tea and curled up on a lounge chair to enjoy the spectacular weather. Jim woke up a few minutes later; he lay in bed, obsessing about the proposal. Walking out on the balcony, he spotted Victoria by the pool. He headed down, leaving Caroline sleeping soundly.

Jim sat in the chaise next to Victoria. "It's incredible here." She nodded and at the same time, they each began, "There's something I need to..." She finished that sentence with *tell you* while he finished it with *ask you*.

They shared a grin, and she said, "You first."

"Okay... I know we haven't known each other very long, but I'm going to ask Caroline to marry me."

Completely derailed by his words, she froze while he waited for her reply.

"Victoria?"

"That's uh..." she began. There was no way she could tell him now. "Wait, what did you say?" She asked simply to buy some time.

"I'm going to ask Caroline to marry me."

She wasn't sure if she was relieved to not have to tell him or simply happy to hear his wonderful news, but, after pausing another moment, a genuine smile crossed her face. "That's amazing news."

"I know. I feel weird telling you and asking you this, but I feel like I should. I mean, I already cleared it with Brian and Jillian. I didn't want to take anything away from them on this trip, you know."

She looked away, torn.

He picked up on the change in her expression. "Are you okay?"

"Oh, yeah." She shook her head. "I'm just so, you know... Wow. So what do you want to ask?"

"Jillian told me I should propose Sunday night after the wedding. Now I want to be sure it won't make you feel awkward or anything like that. We did share all that..." He batted his eyes at her. "Um, months ago, and you know I still have strong feel... uh, I'm not sure what I'm trying to say."

She looked at him with her heart melting. "You're just about the best guy on the planet. You don't worry about me. All you should worry about it making the perfect proposal. You've got to do it right. Let me see the ring."

He pulled it out of his pocket. "I was hoping you would ask. I haven't shown it to anyone yet."

After glancing around to be sure no one was watching, he handed her the box. She opened it, and her jaw dropped as she gazed at the nearly flawless and colorless, not too small, but not too large either, pear-shaped diamond. She looked at him speechless, then back to the ring. "You picked this out all by yourself?"

"I saw it in the window, and it just seemed perfect."

"I love a pear-shaped diamond."

"It's in the one carat'ish neighborhood." He gave her a hesitant look. "Do you really think she'll like it?"

"She'll love it."

She put her hand out to him, and he took it. Squeezing his hand, she gave him a sincere look that bordered on tearful. "She'd be crazy to not say yes." Their emotions began to get the best of them. She handed him back the box, and he tucked it away in his shorts as they both avoided eye contact in an attempt to collect themselves.

After a few moments, he exhaled slowly and she returned his attention to him. "Do you think you can make it through the proposal without crying like a baby?"

"I hope so." His face brightened with a realization. "Oh, so what did you want to tell me?"

Suddenly, she looked at him in shock. "Uh, I, uh… wanted to tell you that if you needed someone to bounce your wedding toast off, then just let me know. I'd like to get an opinion on my toast."

His eyes widened in alarm. "Oh shit! I completely forgot about the toast. I've been so busy worrying about…" He stood. "Thanks for reminding me."

Watching him leave, she shook her head, vowing to never tell him about the baby.

Natalie and Josh settled into their seats on the plane bound for St. Barts at the same time that Tim Dale, who was using the other plane ticket billed to Albert Blair, was heaving his heavy carry-on bag into the overhead bin just six aisles back. Albert was waiting for his plane at airport ten miles away.

Jim rushed up to his room, and while Caroline continued to sleep, he went on the balcony with a pad and paper and worked on his toast. Ten minutes later, Brian stepped out onto his balcony and saw Jim next door.

"Hey."

Jim looked up from his pad. "Good morning."

"What are you doing?"

"Working on my toast. What do you think?" Standing, Jim moved to the railing. He stretched the three feet over to Brian to hand him the pad.

Brian read out loud, "Jillian and Brian are—" After giving Jim an odd look, he shrugged. "It's short."

"I just started."

"It's a good start." After rolling his eyes, Brian handed back the pad and paused in deep thought while staring into Jim's room without really focusing. Caroline was still asleep. She was naked and one of her perfect breasts was in full view outside the sheets. Brian exhaled deeply. Noticing his brother's odd expression, he followed his gaze. When he spotted Caroline's exposure, he said, "Dude."

Brian shook his head and focused in on where his eyes were looking. "I swear I wasn't looking, well until now…wow, she's…"

"You creep."

"At least I didn't shower with her."

"Hey, I was in the shower first, Jillian's the one who—"

"Good point." Turning his head, he looked away. "I swear I didn't see her until just now. I was just staring at nothing and thinking about the wedding, and my job, and, oh… the lawsuit, and everything."

"I believe you."

Brian looked his brother in the eye. "But she's cute."

"I know, right?"

"Fuck the toast. Get in there."

They both looked into the room just as Caroline turned, exposing her adorable ass outside the sheets. They slowly turned to each other, and Jim said, "I'll just knock this out later." Brian had to take one more peek as Jim slipped back into the room and closed the blinds. Looking down to his groin, he sighed. "This no-sex rule is going to kill me."

Two hours later, brunch was served at the house, and at the resort the rest of the group was also sitting down for a meal. Soon after that, a bus transported the wedding party group to the resort where they picked up the other guests. From there, they all set out on a tour of the island.

<u>22</u>

After the breathtaking five-hour tour, everyone returned to his or her room to freshen up. Dinner and activities were planned for those who remained at the resort, but some close relatives headed to the house. After a quick wedding rehearsal on the grounds of the mansion, the group of twenty sat down at 8:30 p.m. for the rehearsal dinner.

Brian's parents and a few of Brian and Jillian's friends, who were staying at the Eden Rock, joined them for a spectacular meal featuring lobster, steak and scallops. It was all expertly prepared by the resident chef and served in the large outdoor covered dining area. The food was excellent, the mood was jovial, the alcohol was flowing, and everyone was having a blast.

All twenty guests' appetites were more than satisfied. All were a little tipsy except for Victoria, who was drinking apple juice that she claimed was white wine. Brian's parents and a few of Jillian's friends headed back to the resort before dessert was served at just after 11:00 p.m. As the crème brûlée was being tasted, Victoria felt a little nauseous. "I'll be right back. Does anyone need anything from the house?"

"Bring another bottle of that white wine," Jillian said.

Rob was seated between Victoria and Laura. Laura's hand was resting sensually on his inner thigh. At the start of the dinner it was on his knee, but as time past it traveled closer to her indented target as the alcohol had obviously accentuated her libido.

Reaching for his own drink, Rob knocked over Victoria's glass, which was half full. "Oh, sorry." With everyone chatting away, no one noticed. After dabbing up the spill with his napkin, he picked up an odd sent of apples from it and narrowed his eyes. He glanced back toward the house to catch Victoria as she stood outside the door trying to steady herself. He shook his head and surreptitiously picked up Victoria's wine glass, sniffed it, then downed what little remained, confirming that it was, in fact, apple juice.

Jillian said, "Oh, Brian, would you run in and tell her to bring the German wine, not that other one?"

"Why run in, when I can use the intercom?" He raised his eyebrows in an inebriated, yet smug grin.

"Good idea. We should totally get one of those."

"I know."

Leaning against the kitchen counter, Victoria took a several deep breaths. She smiled as her wave of nausea had all but disappeared. Turning to the sink, she grabbed a glass, and filled it with water. As she took a sip, Brian's voice came over the intercom.

"Victoria. Hey, Victoria, if you're not too drunk, please report to the intercom." The laughter of everyone outside was also flowing out of the speaker. She smiled and headed over to the box, which was on the wall. She glanced at it confused. "Yes?"

She heard Brian say, "I'm not sure how this thing works. Maybe she went to the bathroom or something."

"Can you hear me? Brian?" She studied the box, which was filled with buttons, shook her hands in confusion, then hit one button after another while saying, "Brian? Brian?"

"Oh, good. You're there. I'm in no condition to make the long trip to the house… please bring the German wine not that other crap."

"Sure thing."

"Thanks," Brian replied.

Victoria continued to hear the loud talking over the speaker until she hit a button that cut it off. Turning away, she was unaware that she'd put the system in a broadcast-only mode. She moved back to the counter and grabbed the glass of water. She opened the refrigerator, and the strong combined odor of all the food wafted out. She was quickly overcome.

She rushed to the bathroom just as Rob entered the kitchen area. He heard the sounds of her vomiting and became concerned. He knocked on the door. "Are you okay?"

"Oh yeah. I'll be right out."

When Victoria emerged from the bathroom, she spotted him standing in the kitchen. She approached him with a smile. "I think I drank too much wine."

"Uh, huh. How is that wine?" He gave her a skeptical look.

"Oh, it's really good."

He shook his head and just stared at her.

"What?"

"I know you're drinking apple juice."

She looked away. "I just switched over with that last glass."

Outside there was a lull in the conversation and laughter just as Rob asked loudly, "You're pregnant aren't you?" The sound flowed out as clearly as if he were standing right there at the table next to them. Everyone turned their attention to the box on the wall wearing stunned expressions.

In the kitchen Victoria shook her head. "I don't know what you're talking about."

"Let's see… you're not drinking and you just threw up. I haven't seen you in a bathing suit since we got here, and you're normally running around nearly naked. And your tits are huge. So unless you recently got implants…"

She glanced down to her chest with a big smile, "Really, you think they look…" Her smile melted away to a frown. "Wait. I, uh, just haven't been feeling well."

"Let me see your stomach."

She looked at him nervously. "Why?" She glanced around the corner to the door that led to the pool area and didn't see anyone. Looking back to him, she put her finger in the air, pointed out the window, then said softly, "Keep your voice down."

He glanced down to her stomach, grinned, and said in a quiet voice, "You totally have a baby in there." He paused thinking, then his eyes lit up, "That's why you had me take that blood test. There's no ancestry gift thing. That's a load of shit… I knocked you up, didn't I?"

Jillian's jaw hit the table, and Brian looked at her, concerned. Everyone else stopped eating dessert and watched the box with mouths agape as the conversation continued over the speaker. Rob added, "That night we had sex, we didn't use a condom. We, uh…" There was a long pause and he continued, "I was pretty drunk, but I remember you gave me that blow job, then I went down on you. And uh, I didn't pull out and shoot on your tits or anything…"

One of Brian's college friends, Eric, continued to listen, but also returned to eating his crème brûlée. Everyone else at the table wore disgusted looks until Laura said, "He, uh… likes to do that. It's like some kind of porn star move." The appalled looks slipped away, and they all nodded casually.

Rob continued, "You were sitting on me, and I remember exactly…"

Eric slipped a huge spoonful of the creamy custard in his mouth as Rob continued, "I shot a big load that night. It was huge… I remember it was everywhere and dripping out of you." Eric nearly gagged while everyone else exchanged sickened looks. "You're having my baby. I can't fucking believe this."

"It's not yours."

"When were you going to tell me?"

"It's not yours," Victoria repeated loudly.

"What? Then why the blood test?"

"You're not the only one who needed to take a test."

Swallowed hard, Jim looked down to the table.

Victoria said, "It's Jim's baby. All right? He's the father."

Caroline's face turned pale white. All eyes moved to Jim. He glanced around the table in shock. Rising up, he headed toward the intercom box. "Brian, show me how to turn this off. This isn't—"

Caroline, Laura, and Jillian all said in unison, "Don't touch it."

Just as Jim reached the box, Victoria said, "I love him."

Rob asked, "What's he doing here with Caroline if you guys are together?"

Back in the kitchen, Victoria exhaled deeply. "He doesn't know about the baby… or how I feel. He's in love with her, and I don't want to do anything to spoil that. You cannot tell him. He's going to ask her to marry him after the wedding."

"How do you know?"

"He cleared it with Brian and Jillian. He didn't want to steal their day. He even asked if it would be weird for me. He's so thoughtful and caring and sensit—"

"This *is* a guy were talking about right?" Rob shot her a look of disgust.

"Yeah..." She glared at him. "The most amazing one on the planet."

Outside, a tear fell from Caroline's eye as she just stared at Jim. He returned and knelt down beside her. He breathed out hard and opened his mouth to speak the instant the intercom blasted out Rob latest gem. "I can't believe he knocked you up. There is no way he shot more than I did that night. It had been like a week since I jerked off if I remember correctly. How much did he shoot?"

Standing, Jim glared at Brian with the veins popping out of his head. "Turn that fucking thing off now." Brian rushed over and turned it off as Jim returned his attention to Caroline. "I'm so sorry. I didn't know."

"Obviously..." She folded her arms. "Were you really planning to ask me to marry you?"

"Yes."

"Look me in the eye and tell me you don't love her."

"I love you."

"That's not... what does it matter. You two are having a baby. She's in love with you. I know you still have feelings for her." Caroline stood just as Rob and Victoria walked out the back door. Looking at Victoria, Caroline growled, "I've got to get out of here."

Laura rose to her feet. "I'll go with you."

Rob and Victoria reached the dinning area just as the two women stepped on the path toward the house. Laura and Caroline stood glaring at Victoria. Victoria and Rob scanned the faces of the silent crowd and were completely at a loss.

After she caught Jillian's glare, Victoria asked, "What the hell is going on out here?" No one said a word until Caroline looked at Victoria and said in a voice dripping with sarcasm, "Congrats."

Laura added, "Are there any guys here you haven't banged?"

Victoria scanned the room a moment, instinctively, and did a quick count while thinking, "I haven't even slept with half the men here — well unless you count holding Brian's penis, but, shit, who would count that?"

Laura slapped Rob hard across the face as everyone looked on in shock. Pushing past him, she rushed toward the house. Victoria looked completely mystified as her eyes went from Jim to Caroline, then to the group staring at her from the table.

Brian said, "Uh, the intercom was on when you two were talking... we kinda heard everything."

Victoria's mouth fell open. "Look, I, uh—"

Caroline interrupted, "He's in love with you. I hope you'll be very happy together." She turned to Jim. "You should know that I slept with Jeff a couple weeks ago. It just happened. Evidently I still have feelings for him. So now you don't need to feel guilty at all."

Jim looked at her, crushed.

"Come on, let's go," Laura called out to Caroline, while giving Rob another icy stare.

Rob turned to Laura. "We weren't even going out when this happened. How can—"

Laura sneered at him and yelled, "You'll never touch me again. I don't want to see you or speak to you ever again."

Caroline disappeared into the house as Rob rushed to Laura. "I made a mistake. I love you." As they stood alone near the house, she leaned in and whispered while glaring at him like she wanted to kill him, "I'm not really mad. This is pretty hot, right?" He looked at her confused as she continued softly, "Let's have amazing make-up sex."

"What?" he asked softly.

"Just go with it."

He took hold of her arm gently. She pulled it away and yelled, "Don't put your hands on me." Laura whispered, "I'm going to find a hotel, and I want you in my ass."

Rob whispered, "Really?"

Everyone at the table was straining to hear what they were saying, but not getting a word of the good stuff.

He grinned for a moment, and she said softly, "Don't break character."

Rob said loudly with a slightly lame performance, "Yes, well... I'll die if I can never see you again."

"Well, I guess you'll die then."

Rob whispered, "Nice touch."

She moved close to his ear. "When we fuck, be angry. I don't want to be able to walk when you're done."

She pulled away, and he nodded. He leaned in and whispered, "I'm so hard right now."

Laura sighed, as she glanced down to his bulge. After looking him in the eye, she growled something unintelligible at him and headed toward the house. She turned back, rushed to him, and said softly, "I'll text you the hotel and room number... Uh, I'm sure the hotels here are really expensive, do you have any cash?"

He leaned in and whispered, "My wallet's in the room."

She scoffed in mock disgust and slapped him even harder across the face. Everyone at the table gasped. Rob rubbed his jaw as he stared at her, desperate to be inside her instead of watching her walk into the house.

All eyes returned to Victoria. Her gaze traveled from face to face until landing on Jillian. "It was that night Rob found out about you two, and I was thinking about David. I was drunk, and it just..."

Jillian just shook her head as Brian put his hand on her shoulder.

Eric said, "Well this is a rehearsal dinner that you'll never ever forget." All eyes went to him. He shrugged. "What?"

Victoria glanced back to Jillian who refused to look at her. She sighed. "Sorry everyone for spoiling an otherwise beautiful evening." Then she walked toward the house with everyone watching.

23

As Victoria sat on the sofa in her room crying there was a knock at the door. Wiping her eyes, she tried to pull herself together. "Come in."

Jim opened the door, spotted her and gave her a weak smile. "Are you okay?"

"Yeah."

"You want to go for a walk?"

They walked down the long driveway toward the beach, and he asked, "When were you going to tell me?"

"I tried a few days ago, but then you told me about proposing to Caroline, I thought that maybe I should wait—perhaps forever."

"So, you're going to keep it?"

She looked at him a little shocked. "Yes, definitely."

"No, I meant were you considering adoption?"

"Oh, no... I guess I still was going to tell you at some point before..."

They shared a look as they continued toward the beach in silence. When they made it to the sand, they slipped off their shoes. She said, "I'm sorry about Caroline. I..."

He exhaled. "She probably wasn't going to say yes. You heard her. She had sex with Jeff again. He's her first love. I guess she wasn't really—"

"She'd be an idiot to say no."

He paused while staring out at the moonlit ocean and said in an uninspired tone, "Thanks."

Back at the mansion, Rob rushed through a quick shower and while still dripping wet, checked his cell phone for a message from Laura. There was nothing. He grabbed a towel and raced to get dressed.

Just a short walk from the house, the girls found adjoining rooms available at the Hotel Le Villiage St Jean. After they checked in, Caroline and Laura stood on the respective balconies of their rooms talking—both working off a mild buzz. They gazed out to the ocean, then Laura looked through Caroline's sliding door. "Wow, I can see right into your room. This isn't very private."

"Don't worry, I don't plan on having any sex while I'm here."

"I do." Laura flashed her a naughty smile.

"Are you really going to find some random guy?"

"No. Rob's coming over."

Caroline gave her a look. "I thought you guys were—"

"It was just an act. I want to have some make-up sex. I'm not really mad. We were broken up when he, uh, you know."

Caroline looked out over the waves. "You know. I'm not really mad either. I mean, I wasn't dating Jim at the time. It's just weird. I don't dislike Victoria. I'm just having a hard time accepting that the guy I love is going to be the father of someone else's baby."

"I know." Laura shook her head. "It's hard to hate her. She's so nice."

"I heard she lost her husband a few years ago."

"Yeah."

Caroline sighed. "And I didn't really sleep with my old boyfriend."

"Then why'd you say it?"

"I mean, I kissed Jeff, and I thought about having sex with him, but I stopped him. I've been feeling really guilty, and I guess I just wanted to hurt Jim a little." Laura gave her an understanding nod and Caroline said, "I just don't want to see Jim right now. I'm just... I'm jealous of her, but it's weird, I don't really dislike her."

"I know. I feel the same—you just can't hate her."

"Well, I do hate her tits. I mean who has tits like that at her age? And her body—she looks like she's twenty-eight."

Laura made a face. "And she probably won't get all fat after the pregnancy. She'll end up with even bigger, more perfect tits and the same exact body."

"That bitch," Caroline said, as they both shared a chuckle. "So, when is Rob coming over?"

Laura's eyes widened. "Oh, I need to send him a text."

"You don't need to stay with me. I'm fine."

Laura said quietly, "It's not that. I kind of promised him something in the heat of the moment."

"What?"

"Have you ever done… anal?"

"Almost once. I, We… Let's just say that it's on our list of things to try again."

"I'm trying to psych myself up, but I need something first." Laura gave her a hesitant smile. "Do you smoke pot? I think I need a lot of pot."

"Now that's something that I did exactly once."

Laura widened her eyes. "Do you want to?"

"You have some?"

Nodding, Laura smiled.

"I won't even ask. " Caroline grinned. "You're a bad girl."

Back at the mansion, Rob sat on his bed fully dressed, simply staring at his phone. He exhaled deeply, then stood and started pacing. He pulled down his shorts and inspected his junk. Finding it a tad hairy, he grimaced and headed back into the bathroom.

Back at the hotel, the girls were halfway through their joint. Still on their respective balconies, passing it back and forth. They were getting there…

Caroline asked, "Has Rob ever licked you back there?"

"What? No… that's. No."

Caroline took a big hit and simply nodded to her wearing a naughty smile.

"Really?"

"Make him do that first. Your head will explode."

"So, Jim does that?"

"All the time. When he first got together in Atlantic City, he couldn't do any of that very well. But when… after he was with Miss Perfect Tits, he was like… It's like he has a master degree now in licking everything. I've never cum so hard." Caroline took another hit and passed the joint. "Wait, do you have any lube?"

Laura took a big hit and shook her head no. "Where can I get some?"

"I saw condoms at store in the lobby. I'm sure they have something."

Laura gave her a naughty look. "There was one other thing that Rob and I always wanted to do…"

Caroline put her hand out for the joint as Laura continued, "We want to have someone watch us have sex."

"Really?" Laura nodded as Caroline took a hit. "That sounds kinda hot."

"You, uh, want to watch us? You can stand there and see right to the bed from where you are."

"I couldn't." Caroline said halfheartedly.

"All right, but…" Laura took a deep breath. "I think I'm ready now, but I need to run down to get the lube. Oh, I probably should take a shower. Shit, he's waiting."

"I'll go to the store. You text him, jump in the shower, then I'll toss the lube on your balcony."

"Awesome. And I'll leave the curtain open just in case you want to watch…" Laura gave her a smile. "In the back of my mind, I'll think you're out there, and it'll make it so much hotter. Maybe I'll tell him that there's this hot couple next door watching."

Caroline pondered this with a sexy smile.

"Oh, and if it gets a little loud over here, don't be concerned. We're just role paying."

After nodding, Caroline asked hesitantly, "Do you have more of that pot?"

Laura smiled. "Be right back."

On the beach, Jim and Victoria walked along the edge of the water.

He sighed. "I love you both. I'm so confused."

She gave him a tender smile. "Caroline is an amazing girl."

"Have you ever been in love with two people at the same time?"

"No, but I think I understand what you're feeling." Crossing her arms, she rubbed her hands over them. "I'm a little cold. You mind if we go back?"

Five minutes later, Jim and Victoria were sitting together on the sofa in Jim's room. He looked into her eyes. "Did you mean it when you said you loved me?"

She breathed out deeply. "I did. I do. It's just, I don't want to stand between you and Caroline."

"There's obviously nothing to stand between."

She shook her head. "You don't know that."

"Don't I?"

"Maybe she's just in love with the both of you too."

He acknowledged that she had a point with a sigh. Then, he looked her body over closely. "Can I feel your stomach?"

She nodded.

"Can you feel it kick?" He placed his hand on her stomach through her shirt.

Glancing down to his hand, she felt her pulse quicken simply from his gentle touch. "Not yet. I read that during your first pregnancy you usually can't feel it until the twenty-fifth week."

"How far along are you?"

"About fourteen weeks." Lifting up her shirt, she rubbed her hand gently over her small bump with a smile bordering on tears. "I never thought I could get pregnant. I didn't do this on purpose."

"I know."

Her smile brightened a bit. "I thought I'd be depressed, but I've never been happier."

He looked at her small rounded belly, and he began to get emotional. "Jesus, I, uh…" He squeezed the bridge of his nose and shook his head. "Sorry, I'm such a chick."

Gazing at him, she was also on the verge of tears. "I've been a bit emotional lately myself. It's all the hormones."

"At least you have an excuse." After they shared a laugh, he smiled. "You look stunning pregnant."

"I feel like a fat cow."

He scoffed. "You can barely tell that you are. I just think you look sexy."

"Oh, stop." Grinning, she waved him away with her hand.

Laura showered while Caroline picked up two small bottles of KY from the store. She received an odd look from the clerk, but she couldn't have cared less as her high was in full swing. When she went out on the balcony to toss it over, she discovered Laura standing in the room with a white robe around her shoulders glancing into the mirror. She watched as Laura pulled the robe off her shoulders and looked at her reflection with a slightly perplexed expression. Caroline studied her nude body breathlessly. She had never really thought about being with a woman, but Laura was hot. Maybe it was the pot, but she felt really horny. Laura spotted her, smiled, then walked to the door.

"What do you think robe or no robe?"

After slipping it back over her shoulders, Laura paused, then pulled it off, and waited for a reply. Caroline's gaze traveled down her breasts to Laura's perfectly coiffed pubic hair.

"So what do you think, off or on?"

Caroline snapped out of her trance. "Uh, I'd leave it on. Give him something to take off of you."

"Good idea." She slipped the robe back over her shoulders and moved out to the balcony. Caroline handed over the lube. There was a knock at the door and Laura smiled. "Wish me luck."

Back on the sofa in Jim's room, he said, "Can I, uh, put my ear to your belly? I wonder if you can hear the heartbeat or movement or something."

"Knock yourself out."

Kneeling on the floor, he leaned over and placed his ear carefully on her stomach. He paused, listening. "I can't hear anything."

Victoria moved her hand to his head and gently ran her fingers through his hair. He gasped as he stared down to her still taut, perfect legs and that familiar feeling of heat bubbled up in his loins. He placed a hand on her knee.

Her body trembled as she softly said, "I, uh, haven't been with anyone since we…"

"Really?" They remained in that position with his ear pressed to her stomach, and her gently stroking his hair.

"I haven't really met anyone plus it just doesn't feel right with me being pregnant."

"Oh."

"It's killing me. The hormones are making me so horny. My breasts are huge, my pussy is always wet, and I, uh..."

Sliding her hand down his back, she slipped it under his shirt, and touched him tenderly. His hand wandered from her knee, up her thigh, until it came to rest less than an inch from her panties. She gasped as he slid his other hand under her shirt to one of her full breasts.

"You weren't kidding about your..."

Leaning her head back, she moaned. He pushed her shirt higher and lifted his head up from her stomach. He gazed breathlessly at her bra, which was stretched across her swollen chest. He sighed and simply said, "Wow."

Back at the hotel, Caroline turned the lights off in her room and arranged a chair on her darkened balcony so it faced directly into Laura's room. She was working through the second joint as she watched the action unfold next door.

Wearing only the robe, Laura stood before Rob as she said convincingly, "You bastard. You fucked her didn't you?"

He looked at her confused. "Didn't we already go through this?"

Exhaling, she gave him a tired look.

"Oh, sorry..." Then he attempted some acting—some bad acting. "Yes, uh... I did fuck her."

Caroline giggled softly as she stared wide-eyed into the room, enjoying the show.

Laura glared at him. "You're going to do everything I say. Got it?"

He nodded breathlessly.

"Don't you dare ever fuck anyone else again."

"I won't. I swear."

Slipping down to her knees, Laura rubbed her hand over the lengthening bulge in his shorts as it ran down his leg. He looked to the ceiling and moaned.

"Did she suck your big cock?"

Looking back to her, he said convincingly, "I forced it down her slutty throat."

"Nice touch."

"Thanks."

Caroline chuckled before slipping her hand under her skirt.

Laura unbuttoned his shorts and pulled them down. He wore no underwear, and his nearly hard penis sprang up close to her face. Caroline's eyes locked on it, and taking in his impressive size she gasped. Licking her lips, Laura gazed at it as she held it with both hands. She glanced out to the balcony, and spotted the faint glimmer of Caroline's burning joint. Grinning, she turned her attention back to Rob.

Caroline looked away for a moment self consciously, and when she looked back, Laura had slipped her lips over him. Putting his hands on Laura's neck, he sensually rubbed her as she sucked him with conviction. He pushed the collar of her robe open, and it slid off her shoulders and down her body, exposing her luscious curves.

Caroline put the joint out and focused more closely as Rob reached down and squeezed Laura's nipples firmly. After a few moments, Laura stood, then moved to the bed. Getting on her hands and knees, she thrust her ass in the air and commanded, "Now lick my ass."

"What?"

"Lick it. Now. If you want to put your cock in there, you've got to taste it first."

Gasping excitedly, he quickly removed the rest of his clothes as she waved her ass slowly in front of him.

"I'm waiting," she yelled back.

He slipped down to his knees, placed one hand on each of her cheeks, and spread them apart gently. Moving his tongue tentatively to her, he did as she asked.

"That's it," Laura said as her eyes rolled back in her head. He kept at it, and she groaned. Pulling his head back, he took a quick look at her beautiful parts as she let out a sigh.

Caroline moved closer to her balcony's railing and focused on Rob's body. She watched as he continued licking Laura. Caroline slipped her fingers under her panties and between her legs. Discovering she was completely wet, she gasped. She rubbed her clit for a moment, then slipped her finger down past her pussy and placed it directly on her tiny pink hole. She made small circles around it, as her mouth opened wide, and her eyes were still locked on the horny couple.

"Now fuck my pussy," Laura ordered.

He stood and in one quick motion slipped inside her. Caroline watched for a moment, then shut her eyes, fantasizing that she was under Laura licking her as a penis moved in and out of her. It was Jim's penis and not Rob's that was sliding into Laura though.

Moving her fingers back to her own vagina, Caroline slipped them inside as her brain remained locked in her fantasy with her eyes slammed shut. Hearing Laura say, "*Put it in my ass,*" brought her back to reality. She gazed closely as Rob applied the lube to himself then moved to Laura. He pushed forward gently, with his eyes locked on the sight of his erection pressing against her tight hole. Caroline moved her finger back to her own puckered seam and pressed it inside just as Rob pushed into Laura.

Caroline watched the horny couple, mesmerized. Laura looked back with a wide, satisfied smile. Tearing her eyes from them, Caroline looked into her darkened room. Suddenly wondering what Jim was doing and missing him terribly, she stood and slipped quietly inside.

<u>24</u>

Victoria lay on her back with her hands clutching Jim's hips as he hovered above her face with her as his guide. A few minutes earlier, they both had climaxed after ten minutes of intensely passionate missionary position sex. Afterward, she pulled him up and refused to let him go as she pleasured him with her mouth while he struggled simply to hold on for the ride.

As he experienced a second thunderous climax, she pulled him closer and he could no longer take it. He pulled away quickly and lay next to her with tingles flowing through his body.

"Oh my God," he said.

Her heart pounded. Turning to him tenderly while clutching her chest, she replied, "Yeah." They stared into each other's eyes; their noses only an inch apart with their heads rocking slightly as they struggled to recover.

Closing his eyes, his mind immediately went to Caroline. What had he just done? He loved them both, but what now? He rolled onto his back and stared up to the ceiling. His heart beat faster and sweat dripped down the side of his face as the panic overtook him. He had to get out of there if for no other reason than to think. "Uh, I'm all sweaty. You mind if I take a shower and then we can talk?"

She shook her head no.

He headed off toward the bathroom with conflicting emotions clouding his thinking. Standing in the shower, he leaned against the wall thinking about Caroline and Victoria and the baby. What the fuck was he going to do?

After slipping her clothes back on, Victoria walked through the open sliding door out to the balcony. She gazed at the lights of a nearby hotel and struggled to listen to the sounds of the waves crashing on the shore. Hearing a door open behind her, she turned to look into the room. Caroline entered but didn't see her. Victoria hid behind the blinds and peered back inside. She watched as Caroline removed all her clothes. Victoria focused in on her perfect heart-shaped, firm, young ass. "Lucky bitch!" she whispered to herself.

Caroline slipped into bed and lay facing the bathroom door waiting for him to appear. Jim walked out, while working the towel through his hair. He glanced quickly at the nude woman in his bed and began. "Vi—" but stopped when he saw who it was.

She glanced at him confused, and he recovered, "Vir you are. I mean, there you are."

Victoria moved closer to the wide open door to listen. After moving his eyes around the room nervously, he returned his attention to Caroline. "Uh, you're back."

"I missed you. Come lay next to me."

Making his way to her, he took one last look around the room.

"I didn't have sex with Jeff."

"You didn't?" he asked while attempting to hide his disappointment.

"We just kissed." That's all. I mean, I thought about it, but we didn't... I was just mad, and I didn't really think. I, I, just said it."

Victoria closed her eyes, devastated.

He gave her a hopeful look. "You can tell me. I won't be upset. Did you give him a blow job or—"

"No."

"A hand job?"

"What? No!" She gave him a sexy smile. "You're not one of those guys who likes to see his girl having sex with someone else are you?"

"No, of course not."

"Good."

He grinned. "Unless we're talking about another girl. Are we talking about..." She glared at him with mock anger, and he added, "Just kidding. Look I'm sorry. I..." He looked closely into her eyes. "Are you stoned?"

She giggled. "A little."

Victoria chuckled softly and shook her head.

"Where did you get it?"

"Laura."

After closing his eyes, he sighed. "Okay, um, I didn't know that she was pregnant. I haven't even seen her since we all had dinner together at school. I—"

"I know. Look, I love you. I know you love me, but you also have this connection with her, and now you two are having a baby,

I… I'm not sure what all this means. Maybe I'm too high to know what I'm saying, but—"

"You seem really clearheaded."

"Thanks. I don't hate her. I want to hate her—I mean she has those perfect tits and body, and she's like the nicest, most down-to-earth woman in the world. I get why you're in love with her."

Outside on the balcony, Victoria slumped against the wall with her heart melting. She sighed, rubbing her hands over her face.

Caroline put her hand on his chest as she continued, "I… look, I'm going to leave tomorrow. I don't want to, but I just can't stay for the wedding. You stay. I can't face Victoria yet. When you come back home, we'll talk. I know you haven't had sex with her since we became serious. I believe you. I do." She looked deeply into his eyes.

His lips parted, desperate to stop her, to tell her everything, but she kept going with her pot-induced, heartfelt and poignant speech. "If you still want to marry me, I will marry you, but you must be true to me. You can love her or admire her from afar. Whatever you want, I can deal with it—I think. But you can't have her ever again if you still want us to be together. We'll deal with the baby thing. I might not want to baby-sit at first or throw her a baby shower or anything, but I'll figure out how to deal with it. It'll probably be the cutest damn baby in the world. I mean look at you two."

Outside, still listening, Victoria smiled widely gazing through the blinds at the adorable couple. She watched as Caroline moved her lips to Jim's. After kissing her briefly, he pulled back. "Wait. There's something I need to tell you."

"Let's not talk now. Whatever you have to say can wait. I want to…" She sighed. "Let's do everything tonight. I want you to… you know."

He looked confused. "What?"

"Don't make me say it. Over there in my purse… I bought some lube. Go get it."

Swallowing hard, he got it all right. As he got out of bed, Victoria drank in his tight body and perfect penis as he headed toward the purse. He glanced toward the open balcony door, unsure whether he saw something out there or not. Victoria moved away and he shook his head as he retrieved the purse.

Caroline said, "Hey, lock the door and turn the TV on loud. I plan on making a lot of noise."

Just as the television began to blare, Victoria looked over the balcony and considered her options. Looking down to the pool, she thought that she could probably jump from there and actually make it into the water. If it weren't for the baby, she might have actually considered it. She glanced to the left at the balcony to the adjoining room. They were only about three feet apart. That she could pull off in her condition. Climbing over the railing, she kept one hand and foot on that side as she extended the other foot and reached with the other hand to the opposite balcony.

She grabbed the railing tightly and smiled as she straddled the two balconies. After making the mistake of looking down to the twelve-foot drop, she became instantly frightened, then looked into the adjoining room. Inside the room, of course, was Brian walking nude from the bathroom toward the bed. He spotted her, and his face dropped as he instinctively covered up his junk with his hands. She moved her hand and other foot over to his balcony. After smiling proudly at her small victory, her feet slipped, leaving her dangling off the railing.

Brian rushed to the door, ripped it open, then went to her still not wearing a thing. Reaching over the balcony, he grabbed both her wrists. "What the fuck are you doing?"

"Oh, I just wanted to get some fresh air."

Her face was between two spindles and eye level with what was left of his pubic hair. She looked right at his penis, which was no more than a half-inch from her nose.

"Hey, I haven't seen it since the spa. It looks great."

"Gee, thanks."

She breathed in. "God, you Nash boys smell good."

"Just showered." He grinned and gripped her wrists tighter. The television blared from the next room and Brian glanced over curiously. "What the hell are they doing in there?"

"Something really fun."

Jillian walked into the room and quickly spotted Brian's naked ass as he stood toward the side of the balcony. She rushed out.

"What are you doing?" Jillian stood shaking her head confused as she discovered him leaning over the balcony holding something.

Straining, he looked back and grumbled, "Trying to save her life... Help me!"

She moved to him and looked over to see Victoria hanging there with her face pressed up against his penis. Jillian rolled her eyes. "I should have known."

Victoria glanced up to her meekly. "Oh, hi."

Adjusting his stance, he braced his hips against the railing, smashing his parts all over her face. This startled Victoria and tickled her skin; she shook her head and blew out of her mouth while blinking her eyes.

Jillian scoffed. "Would you please get your lips off my fiancé's penis."

Victoria glared up at Jillian. Shaking her head, Jillian reached over and took hold of Victoria's elbow. Together they pulled her up until her feet were securely on the balcony's edge.

Breathing out deeply, she smiled. "Thanks."

They each held one of Victoria's hands and an elbow securely as she lifted a leg over the railing. When she was safely on the balcony, Victoria and Brian stood grinning while Jillian put her hands on her hips and frowned. Brian glanced down to his coiffed pubic area. "Oh shit." He quickly covered it with his hands.

Jillian glared at him. "Oh, now you're shy. Go put something on." She watched him, shaking her head as he walked inside still covering his groin.

Victoria gave her a remorseful look. "Sorry."

"What the hell are you doing hanging from the balcony?" When Victoria opened her mouth to reply, Jillian cut her off, "Forget it. I don't want to know." Scoffing, Jillian walked away from her and into the room.

Victoria rushed after her. "Jillian wait." Jillian turned to look at her, not giving anything away.

25

What separated Jillian, Brian, and Victoria from one of the most passionate simultaneous oral sex experiences ever was simply your standard two-by-four studded sheetrock wall. In Jim's room, the young, loving couple was rounding the corner of eight-minutes of slow oral pleasure, having moved into position number five. During the first solid minute, Jim felt like a worthless lying sack of shit, but it's really hard to maintain self-loathing when *one* of the women you love has her gorgeous pussy parked right in front of your face and is also licking your penis so sensuously that your head is about to explode.

The television was blaring some horrible action movie, but the two blocked it out until Caroline lifted her head away from him and said, "I've got to shut that thing off."

Coming up for air, he wiped his face. She grabbed the remote and turned off the television, then returned her attention to his huge erection. Holding the bottle of lube, she kneeled up on the bed between his legs. She slathered an incredible amount of the slick substance on his erection, as he weaved his head around dizzily enjoying her touch.

"I want to try this position I read about."

He nodded breathlessly. He was up for anything.

"It's just like the one we always use, but… uh… I'll show you."

She lay next to him on her back and lifted up in a reverse crablike fashion, sliding over until she was hovering above him. He gently held her sides as she slipped down until her back was resting on his chest and his manhood was sticking straight up between her thighs. She lifted her lower half up, supporting her weight with her legs. Reaching between them, she took hold of his erection and guided it until it was pressed up against her virgin hole.

Feeling it throbbing against her, she gasped. "Oh, Jim…"

She slipped down over him and held perfectly still, struggling to adjust to his intimate presence within her. With eyes rolling back in her head, she turned to kiss him. They connected, their lips fighting for the right angle, and their tongues stretching to find their way.

"I love you," she whispered.

"I love you, too."

Moving her hips up, she held her position as she groaned, "I've never felt anything…"

Next door, Victoria glared back at Jillian. "You know this your fault."

"What's my fault?"

"Me and Rob having sex."

Jillian looked at her like she wanted to kill her. "How the hell—"

"Maybe if you had actually told Rob when you had the chance instead of having him find out by introducing him to your rape-fantasy experience, none of this would have happened."

Jillian snarled, "You mean the, uh, rape-fantasy experience that you arranged?"

"Well, yes, but… that's really a kind of chicken or the egg thing."

Emerging from the bathroom wearing a T-shirt and shorts, Brian had a huge smile on his face. Jillian noticed. "What the hell are you smiling about?"

"Uh, I… It's really kind of funny, but maybe you're not in the mood for…"

With her blood boiling, Jillian said in an angry sarcastic tone, "I could really use a good joke right now. My best friend in the world had sex with my young, innocent son and, I…"

She stopped mid-sentence when she saw the looks of complete incredulity on their faces.

"Innocent?" asked Victoria, her voice heavy with skepticism.

"Well…" Jillian shook her head quickly and corrected her statement. "He's my young son anyway." She returned her attention back to Brian. "Oh and after you tell me your joke, why don't you tell me again why the hell you were just outside naked."

He shot back, "I don't appreciate your tone, I, uh…" He stopped talking when she gave him a look that said you'll tell me or this will be your last day on earth.

She folded her arms. "The joke first."

He took a deep breath, paused, then began with a smile, "Well, I was just in the bathroom thinking that Victoria had already held my, you know, so you could call that technically a hand job. Just now, she had her lips on it... so you could call..." He looked at Jillian's deathlike stare. "Maybe I should, uh, finish it later."

Victoria's face lit up with a grin as Jillian shook her head and said without a hint of anything resembling a smile, and with so much sarcasm that you could cut it with a knife, "It's funny so far. I want to hear the rest. Really."

He continued, treading lightly. "So her lips, um, I guess you could technically call that a blow job. Maybe when we go to that nude beach on Monday, she'll fall on me, it will accidentally slip in and then we'll finally go all the way."

Covering her mouth, Victoria started to lose it.

Jillian's expression didn't change at all. "Funny. You should go on tour." She gave him a curious look. "And, uh, why were you outside with no clothes on?"

"Well, I, uh was just out of the shower, and I saw a woman hanging off a balcony and I..." His confidence built with every additional word, "...was naked AND rather than take the few minutes required to get dressed, I chose to SAVE her instead. I ran out in what I happened to be wearing at the time... which was nothing."

After clearing her throat, Victoria said softly, "Thank you for that."

"You're welcome!" He stood wearing a proud smile, but as Jillian stared him down, his smile melted away.

She slowly moved her evil gaze back to Victoria.

"Oh me now." Victoria began. "Look, I told you that was the day I was depressed about David, and Rob and I were both drinking... a lot. It was stupid. We haven't done it since, and I don't know what to say. I made a mistake. No one is dead and—"

Jillian held her hand up to stop her. "Tell me that you never slept with George."

"George?" Victoria looked like she could crack up at any second. "You're ex-husband George?"

Narrowing her eyes in offense, Jillian nodded.

"Oh, gross I would never—"

"He's not gross," she said defensively.

Victoria's smile faded as she said unconvincingly, "I mean he's not my type." Then she added with a dash of sarcasm, "I assure you I never had sex with your precious George."

"Okay, good," Jillian said with her arms crossed and her nose held high.

In the next room, Jim began slowly moving his hips up and down as Caroline moaned, "Don't stop."

Her hands had a death grip on his shoulders as she hovered over him. She gazed dreamily at the ceiling as he picked up the pace.

"Fuck," she purred.

"Oh, you're so…" He began as she started moving her hips with him in perfect rhythm.

She either experienced two big orgasms back to back or one of the longest single climaxes ever. As it grew stronger, her cries grew louder and louder. She cried out, "Oh… Oh… God… Oh…" Her eyes rolled back behind her lids. She held still while he continued on faster and faster into her. He reached around and touched her clit, and that was it. The orgasm overtook her body fast and strong. Her nails dug into the flesh on his shoulders.

She bit her lip, panted, and kept moving over him. She wasn't done. She lifted her hips up and down as he continued working her with his finger. She screamed, "OH, GOD. YES. JIM."

Next door, Jillian and Victoria were now in the midst of a big hug as the scream reverberated through the wall. The girls pulled back from each other, and Brian cracked up.

Victoria said casually, "Well, they seem to be having a lot more fun over there."

Jillian broke into a laugh and sat down on the bed. When they heard another loud cry, which began but cut off mid-thought, "JIM, YOU REALLY—" Jillian slumped to her side and cackled like a teenager. Brian and Victoria joined her on the bed, crying from laughing so hard.

Pulling herself together first, Victoria said, "Finish that thought. Jim you really... know how to please a woman."

Cracking up, he took his turn. "Jim you really have an amazing supercock."

After another laugh from the three, Jillian held her hand up. "Jim you really..." Pausing she bit her lip before letting it fly, "you really need to get the hell off of me because enough is enough already."

Next door, Jim and Caroline sat up in bed completely spent and sharing an odd look in response to the loud laughter spilling through the wall.

He said, "They're really having some fun over there."

In the next room, the three were lying face up on the bed and wiping their tears while wearing huge grins.

Jillian asked, "What the hell were you really doing hanging from the balcony."

"Oh, I was just talking with Jim, and I walked outside his room when he went into the bathroom. Then I saw Caroline come in, and I didn't want her to get the wrong idea so I..."

"So you risked your life to save having to explain yourself?" Jillian's smile faded. "You just had sex with him. Didn't you?"

Victoria sat up and folded her arms. "I did not, and I'm offended that you would even suggest that."

Jillian looked up to her, unconvinced. "No more lies."

"I'm not lying." Scoffing, Victoria stood up. "Do you think he could have performed like that if I had just worked my magic on him no more than ten minutes ago?" Motioning with her head toward the adjoining wall, she made a face.

Jillian and Brian shared a knowing nod, and Jillian said, "She does have a good point."

Brian added, "There's no way."

Victoria maintained her stone face while inside she was a basket case. She paused thinking, *How the hell did Jim just pull that off? He came twice with me. I even did the ball thing to him and everything. He must be superhuman.* Turning away, perplexed, she shook her head. "I'm tired. I'm going to bed."

26

Jillian gave Brian a quick kiss goodnight and retired to another bedroom. They had agreed that they would spend their last unmarried night apart so that the wedding night would be even more special—well at least she had suggested it, and he went along with the idea. They had also not done anything sexual in just about a week. He had promised not to masturbate during that entire time, and he was pretty proud of himself since he only fell of the wagon three times.

He found it a tad difficult to keep his word while being so close to so many attractive women in St. Barts. Not to mention he had to deal with getting dressed in the same room with Jillian and her spectacular body, seeing her come out of the shower, and generally walk around naked and in various superhot underwear ensembles. She was lucky he didn't jerk off three times a day given his surroundings.

He planned to be a good boy on this last night especially. After turning the light off, he settled in. He didn't reach down and begin adjusting or scratching anything, which he usually found led to trouble. Plus he hated it when Jillian was in a bad mood. It turned him off. She seemed to be so on edge and was treating him like he was an idiot. She really was acting like a complete bitch.

He knew she was just nervous about the wedding and a little upset that her best friend, her friend with the body of a playmate, had lied to her and had sex with her son. He pondered exactly what Rob and Victoria had done together. He wondered if she did that thing where she licks—He pulled the plug on that line of thought when things started happening under the sheets. Without bothering to check his condition, which he was almost sure was nearing the problematic stage; he drifted off to sleep.

Two minutes later Jillian slipped back into the room. Turning on the light, she made her way to the bed, and knelt on the floor. He was already asleep and breathing deeply when she kissed him and jarred him awake. "What's wrong?"

"Oh nothing, I just… I'm sorry I've been such a bitch today."

He turned on his back. "Oh, you haven't been at all."

She gave him a look, and he agreed with his eyes. She sighed. "I'm sorry. I was already losing it today… then I find out Rob and Victoria did God knows what."

"I know. I know." In support, he ran his hand gently on her arm.

"I've been treating you like garbage. I didn't laugh at your Victoria joke and it was really funny."

"It was, wasn't it?"

She gave him a big nod. "And I yelled at you for being naked outside. You were just saving her. Thank you for saving my best friend, even though she probably had my son's pen—"

He widened his eyes, and she stopped.

After taking a deep breath, she rubbed his chest gently. "And you've been such a good boy. We haven't done anything for days. I know it's been hard."

"It has been really *hard*."

"I'll bet…" She gave him a sexy look. "I'm so proud of you saving it for our wedding night. I'm going to take such good care of you. I have something so special planned, that I—" She shimmied her hips as a little mini-O traveled through her loins. Flustered, she shook her head. "I'd better stop."

"Yeah, this isn't helping me."

She smiled at him. "You're the best thing that's ever happened to me, and even if I'm losing it or acting like a lunatic sometimes, just know that I love you more than anything."

"I love you, too."

"Goodnight." She kissed him gently on the lips. He smiled. Sighing, she moaned, "Maybe we should just…" Taking hold of the covers, she pulled them down below his boxer shorts. She reached for his waistband. His eyes widened and he covered up quickly with his hands desperately protecting his new look down there.

She chuckled. "Are you shy?"

"What are you doing?"

"I just want to see it before I go to bed. So I can dream about you and *him* all night."

"That's probably not a—"

"I just want to see him."

"Okay, but, um, use the flap. That's probably safer."

"Really, I can't see if all?" She gave him a disappointed look.

"No, I know how you are."

"All right." Frowning, she reached through the flap, and carefully extracted his semi-hard penis. She smiled at his face, moved her lips to it, and placed two tiny wet kisses right on the tip. He craned his neck to watch her, captivated.

"You do have one gorgeous cock." She slipped him back inside the boxers and pulled the covers over him.

"I wasn't going to let Victoria be the only one to kiss you there tonight." She broke into a big smile. "She would probably love to wrap her lips around your penis. She's probably pretty good at it."

"I would think so," he said. Jillian glared at him, and he tried to repair the damage, "Oh, but I'm sure you're much better."

Smiling, she looked away. "Remember when she wanted to do that threesome with us?"

"I do."

"I wonder who would have made you cum—me or her."

His eyes widened. "I, uh, really couldn't say."

"We probably would both have been fighting over who put her lips on you to finish you off," she drawled sexily.

"Uh-huh." Gasping, his jaw dropped.

"I can't wait for tomorrow night." Gazing into his eyes, she said slowly, "I'm so horny and freaking wet right now." After rubbing her hands together, her lustful, hazy look evaporated. "Anyway," she said, completely switching gears—every drop of sensuality present in the last forty seconds of her X-rated exposition snuffed out like a candle stepped on by an elephant.

He glanced at her, dizzied and wondering where all that sensuality had gone. Just because she'd turned the corner didn't stop his breathing from becoming labored, his heart from pumping like mad, and his brain from directing every ounce of blood it could spare to his now fully-rigid penis.

She put her hand to his cheek. "Now I can dream about you all night. Will you dream about me?"

"Well, probably now I will." He gave her a weak smile and rolled over to hide his disappointment.

She kissed him on the cheek. "Goodnight."

"Night."

She slipped out of the room. He lay there for almost sixty seconds before he reached down and felt how still unbelievably hard he was. He muttered to himself, "How the hell can women just turn it off like that? You can't wait until tomorrow night... a man would say why wait!" He sighed, tossed off the covers, then headed toward the bathroom.

Once inside he pulled down his boxers and looked at his impressive penis for a moment before looking in the mirror. "You know I was fine before—she had to see it... she had to kiss it and start with the threesome stuff. Geez." After squirting hand lotion into his hand, he began to work off the pressure...

Victoria was walking toward her room carrying a drink. She met Jillian in the hall, and they shared another quick hug before saying their goodnights. Standing in front of her door, she waited until Jillian disappeared into her room. She headed to Brian's room, knocked once softly and slipped inside. Seeing the light on in the bathroom, she headed over quietly.

She stood outside and listened to Brian moaning and obviously running some X-rated scenario through his mind as he said, "Oh, Jillian, I love when you suck my cock. Now girls don't fight... There's plenty of me for both of you... Oh... Victoria, that's it—lick my balls."

Grinning, she pushed open the door a little and caught the reflection of Brian in the mirror with his death grip on his erection while his other hand massaged his balls. His face was all contorted and serious. She broke into a giggle. He spun to look at her, in heart-stopping surprise, as he covered his groin. "What the hell are you doing in here?"

She gave him a mock angry look. "I can't believe you're using me to fuel your spank bank!"

He grabbed a towel and wrapped it around his waist. "What the fuck?"

She glanced down to the towel and his still protruding penis. "I just wanted to talk to you. I can wait until you're done if you want. It looks like you really need to finish."

Looking to the problem area, he frowned. "I don't need to. This is all Jillian's fault anyway." He sat on the toilet and sighed.

She gave him a sexy smile. "So you had me licking your balls while she was blowing you?"

"No, I didn't."

"I heard you say it." Her smile morphed into a frown. "Why the hell am I relegated to ball-licking duty?"

He sighed and admitted sheepishly, "I was just about to switch you two up."

"Good." She shook her head with a grin.

"Look, Jillian was just in here teasing me. We haven't done it in like a week and—"

"Saving it for the wedding night?"

"Well that and I've been recovering…" He made eyes directing her to his groin.

"Oh, I completely forgot about." She cringed. "So did everything stop bleeding?"

"Yeah." He looked at her desperate for understanding. "She actually kissed it and said something about you having your lips on it when I… *saved your life…* then she mentioned that threesome you suggested a few months ago."

A wide smile spread on her face. "She mentioned it, huh?"

"Yeah. She even wondered which one of you would make me cum. And which one of you would be better doing that… Jesus, she says all this sexy dirty crap and leaves me in bed, obviously unable to sleep on my stomach." He shook his head. "…and then she expects me *not* to whack off. Is she nuts?"

"I can't believe she really wants to have a threesome with me."

"What? I didn't say that. Don't you dare tell her I told you any of this."

"So, who did you think would be better at it?"

"Of course I said she would."

She gave him a skeptical look.

"I'm serious." Glaring at her, he scoffed. "Don't say anything."

"Relax." She glanced at his lap, which had returned almost to normal. "Look, everything is back down. Can we talk now?"

"Can I at least get dressed first?"

"Sure."

"Could you turn around?"

She gave him a look that screamed, *seriously*.

"Oh fuck it." He tossed the towel down exposing his not completely flaccid manhood while he gave her a tired look and pulled on his boxers. She grinned the whole time. Walking past her, he sighed and got into bed.

He was up against the headboard as she sat on the mattress. "I need some advice."

"On what?"

She gave him an apologetic look. "I did just have sex with Jim."

He looked at her shocked. "Just now?"

"No, before. Right before he was with Caroline."

"So you lied to Jillian. I can't believe —"

She raised her eyebrows. "Yes, I lied. You should try it sometime. The right lie can save a lot of hurt feelings."

"So you guys did it, then ten minutes later he was having sex with her. How the hell does he do it?"

She added proudly, "He even came twice with me."

"Twice?" His jaw dropped wide open.

"Yes, he's a machine. Can I get you to focus on the problem?"

He stared right through her. "God, I wish I was twenty-one again."

She slapped him lightly across the face.

"Really?" He glared at her. "What the hell?"

"Listen!"

"What?" he grumbled.

"Are you listening?"

"Yes."

"When he asks you for advice on this —"

"What makes you think he'll..." He stopped when he saw her tired expression.

She began again with a scolding voice, "WHEN HE asks you for advice on this, you tell him to never tell Caroline that we slept together again."

"You really think he didn't tell her?"

She raised her eyebrows as if to say he was a complete moron.

"Right." He nodded. "She had sex with him and all, so of course he didn't tell her."

Closing her eyes, she shook her head. When she opened her eyes again, she wore a bored expression.

"Sorry. Most of my blood still hasn't returned to my brain. I'm still recovering and not thinking all that clearly."

After nodding in agreement, she took a deep breath. "You tell him to take this to his grave, and you do the same. If you do tell someone, especially the judgmental and perfect angel Jillian, the next time my mouth is near your penis, I'm going to bite down—hard. You got me?"

He nodded a little frightened.

"And when Jim tells you he loves me, and he also loves her, and he's confused about what he should do, you tell him that he needs to stay with Caroline and marry her. As much as I love him—or think I do. I don't know exactly." She sighed. "All I know is that when I was on the balcony listening to them… she said things that, that… let's just say if he doesn't marry her, then I might have to ask her out."

"Now there's a honeymoon I'd like to see." With his eyes glazing over, he appeared to be somewhere far away. "Wow, with your amazing tits and her spectacular ass, you put those together in bed and that's…"

She was momentarily sidetracked as well. "I wish I had her ass. Could you imagine me still with these?" She pointed to her chest. "And her ass… I wouldn't be able to leave the house." After pondering that for a moment, she snapped back to reality but he remained trapped in his trance-like stare. "Hey, are you with me?"

"Sorry." He shook the cobwebs out of his head and opened his eyes wide. "I haven't had sex in a week."

"Anyway where was I… Oh, you tell him that she's the one for him. Tell him that I'll be fine, and everything will work out. Tell him not to worry about the baby. That we'll figure out some arrangement. You get all that?"

He nodded.

She gave him an angry look, "Don't fuck this up. Have some balls. Your brother's happiness depends on it." She emphasized this with a medium-strength backhand tap to his groin.

Slumping over in pain, he let out a groan.

She cringed. "Sorry about that, just trying to…you know, make a point."

"I got it," he whimpered.

Her expression morphed into one of genuine concern. "Oh God, sorry I've been so flaky lately. I'm acting like a total bitch. It's the hormones I think, I don't know…"

"Are you okay?"

"Uh-huh."

Some mild anger returned to her voice. "I just want what's best for Jim. So if I, well— Did I say thank you for saving my life earlier?"

"I'm not sure, but you're welcome," he said hesitantly as he covered his groin with both hands.

She took a deep breath. "Ok, I'm better now. I'm so proud of you for marrying our Jillian. I know you'll make a great husband."

"I love her."

"I know you do… I wish I could have what you two have, but I don't think I can… I know I would screw things up for Jimmy and me… Help me out here. Talk to him."

"I will."

She gave him a hesitant look. "Are your balls okay? You're really going to need them tomorrow."

"I think so." After feeling around down there, he nodded.

"Good." She smiled and said in the sweetest motherly tone. "Now go to sleep. You have a big day tomorrow." She lifted up the sheets, and he slipped under the covers. He looked ten years old as he curled up with his pillow. Sighing, she kissed him tenderly on the cheek.

When she reached the door, she turned back and whispered sarcastically, "Hey, fantasy boy, do you need me to finish you off?"

He chuckled. "Get the hell out of here."

She grinned and slipped out of the room.

About three minutes later, he got up, locked the door, and went into the bathroom. Ninety seconds later he was done, smiling and back in bed. About twelve seconds after that he was sound asleep. The last thought that crossed his mind was, who needs Ambien when you've got the most natural sleep aid available in the palm of your hand—well, if you're a guy anyway.

27

Early the next morning, Caroline woke Jim with a kiss. Fighting his way back to consciousness, he noticed she was fully dressed. "What are you doing?"

"Going home."

"Why?"

"I have to go." Kneeling down, she took his hand in hers.

"Are we okay?"

"Yes, we're good. I was able to get a flight, but I need to leave now. Please apologize to everyone for me."

He sat up in bed and wiped his eyes. "You sure?"

"I just can't be here right now."

"Okay, but let me go with you to the airport."

"The cab is already outside and you have a lot of things to do today."

"All right. I love you."

"I know you do." She smiled.

I'm so sorry, about—"

"Don't." Placing her hand to his lips, she touched him gently. "Remember what I said last night, and I'll see you when you get back."

She kissed him again and slipped out the door.

A few hours later, Jim sat by the pool thinking. He spotted Brian walking and called to him. Jim took off away from the house and motioned for Brian to follow. When they were safely away, Jim said, "I had sex with Victoria last night after Caroline took off with Laura. We were just talking, and I touched her belly and one thing led to another and, uh…"

"And?" Brian asked impatiently.

"And then Caroline showed up, Victoria disappeared, and I had sex with her." He whispered, "We even did…" he checked around, found it clear, then continued, "anal."

Brian made a face. "You did anal with Victoria. Oh… wait you didn't go ass to mouth did you?"

Jim paused to think. "No, not Victoria. I went mouth to ass." He nodded confidently. Plus, I took a shower between the two."

"Mouth to ass... that's okay, and the shower... well that makes it slightly better."

"How am I supposed to live with myself? I mean one minute I'm having an orgasm inside Victoria's you know, oh and then a second one in her mouth, then ten minutes later Caroline was going down on me and then..." He punctuated the unfinished thought with raised eyebrows and a knowing look.

Brian shook his head, still unable to grasp how he could perform like this. "Who are you — some kind of sex god?"

Giving him a tired look, Jim shrugged.

"No, really, I want to know how you could perform three times in like ten minutes. Is it some supplement or exercise reg —"

"I really need you to focus here," Jim interrupted in an angry tone.

Brian sighed. "Okay. Yeah, sorry. So I assume that you didn't tell Caroline about Victoria?"

"No, but I really think I need to."

"You can never tell her. No matter what you do, don't tell her."

"I feel so guilty."

"Did Victoria tell you if she had sex with anyone else since you guys last did it?"

Jim looked confused. "What does that matter?"

"Did it come up?"

"She said she's been with no one else."

"Okay good, then you don't need to feel guilty."

"What?" Jim scoffed. "Why?"

"You know they say that once you have sex with someone, you've also had sex with all the people that person has had sex with?" Brian crossed his eyes confused for a moment and continued, "Also all the people that the people they've had sex with have had sex with. It's like, once you've slept with someone, you've all of a sudden had sex with ten thousand people... unless of course you do it with a virgin." He shook his head pleased with getting that all out semi-coherently.

"What the hell does that have to do with anything?"

"Here, follow me. So if Victoria hadn't had sex with anyone new, then you haven't added to your count, and now that you've had sex with Caroline, you haven't added to her count either. So technically there's nothing for you to feel guilty about."

Jim glared at him. "Wait, you're an idiot. Using your logic I could go around screwing nothing but virgins, and I wouldn't need to feel guilty about it."

"Yeah, that doesn't sound right." Scratching his head, Brian gave him an apologetic look. "Sorry, I'm losing it. I haven't had sex in like a week — well, not with someone else."

"Oh, come on, dude." Jim grimaced.

Brian kept plodding along, "Jillian's running around practically naked and teasing me with talk of threesomes." Brian moved in close to Jim and grabbed him by his shirt. "I know she's not serious, but you don't joke around with a guy with blue balls about a threesome… you just don't do it." Looking at Brian like he might need some professional help, Jim shook his head. Brian sighed and released his shirt. "I'm also nervous about the wedding, and the lawsuit, and I quit my job and —"

"You quit your job? Why?"

"Because my boss was an asshole, and I hated sitting in that office. And I think I'm going crazy. I got a fucking full Brazilian wax like five days ago, and my ass itches so bad that I feel like scratching it with a cheese grater."

"You got waxed?"

Brian simply said, "Victoria."

Jim nodded as if to say, 'Nuff said!'

Cringing, Jim asked, "Anything else you want to share?"

"No."

Jim rolled his eyes. "I thought we were supposed to be working on my problems, but since you mentioned yours let me knock them out for you. You are marrying the most beautiful, amazing woman on the planet, so everything will be fine. I'm pretty sure you'll be getting laid tonight so tough it out and jerk off again if you really need to. Um, the job? Jillian has lots of money so no worries there. Oh and for your ass, try some baby powder." After nodding in agreement after each suggestion, Brian finally looked relieved.

Jim asked, "Can we get back to my issue?"

"I think I'm still waiting for you to tell me exactly what the issue is."

Jim glared at him. "Uh, I'm in love with two women. One of whom is carrying my child. Oh and I had sex with both of them in the space of a long commercial break."

"Do you really love Victoria? I mean lust is one thing, but love is another. Every guy would probably want to have sex with her. I imagine that she's just some kind of acrobatic, thinking-outside-the-box, sexual genius. It would be pretty easy to mistake lust for love when someone's doing things to you that, while they feel amazing, are illegal in most countries."

"Sure she's amazing in bed." Jim paused, pondering it all. "But there's something else about her. I love her. I'm sure of that."

"And Caroline?"

"I love her, too." After exhaling deeply, he looked to Brian desperate for understanding.

"Look, Caroline loves you. She's amazing. She's *your age*... Victoria is a financially secure, independent woman who doesn't really need or want one man in her life. She can survive and overcome anything."

"I know. I know."

"Does Caroline have a problem with Victoria having your baby?"

Jim sighed. "I mean, she's not crazy about the idea, but she said we'll find a way to make it work. She said she'd marry me if I can commit to her. She told me to figure it out and decide."

"And I assume the sex with Caroline is..."

"Oh my God, it's amazing, too. I, uh—"

"Then it's simple. Victoria will never settle down with one man again. That part of her life was over when her husband died. You figure out exactly how to deal with the baby thing, and go get Caroline. If you lose her, you'll want to hang yourself."

"Okay. You're right." Jim gave him an appreciative smile.

Brian looked away, thinking, then glanced back to Jim. "Seriously what kind of vitamins do you take?"

Grinning, Jim grabbed Brian around the shoulder putting him in a headlock.

Jim knocked gently on Victoria's door. She opened it wearing only a short robe. She smiled sweetly. "Hi."

"Can we talk for a minute?"

"Sure."

Sitting together on the bed, he asked, "What happened to you last night after, uh, we... When I came out of the shower, you were gone."

"I panicked. It was too much too soon, and I freaked out and went back to my room."

"Oh." Pausing a moment, Jim looked at the floor. "Caroline came back last night. She told me she didn't sleep with Jeff. She was just making it up to—"

"Well that's great news. She loves you."

"She flew back this morning. Says she can't see you right now, and she didn't want to spoil the wedding." He looked her in the eye. "I didn't tell her about us."

"And you never should. That would devastate her."

"I don't know what to do. I know I love you. It's not just lust. I mean, sure I can't look at you without getting hard, but it's more than that. You're intelligent, kind, giving, sexy, and the nicest, most—"

"Look, I love you too." She felt her cheeks getting flushed, and her pussy getting wet. These damn hormones, she thought. She really wanted him inside her again, but she fought that feeling back. After taking a deep breath, she gave him a sweet smile. "I do, but I don't think I can ever settle down again."

"I think you're just afraid to let yourself be happy."

She nodded. "Maybe. I think you only meet your soul mate once in this life, and I met mine and he died. Your soul mate is on a plane right now, thinking about nothing but you. She loves you. She wants to marry you, but she wants to know you don't have this other thing always hanging around in your mind. If you screw this up with Caroline, you'll regret it for the rest of your life. You'll wake up one day and realize that someone else is married to your soul mate—the one person who gets you. The one person who completes you for lack of a noncliché thing..."

"But the baby, I need to—"

"You can be a part of this baby's life, but what are you going to do—drop out of school and transfer to Miami? Give up all your dreams?" She looked at him, wearing a sad expression.

"We could make it work." Taking her hand, he gave her a hopeful look. "We could be together, but only if you really want to be with me. I could get a job and support you and the baby."

She sighed. "I have over four million dollars in the bank."

"What? Really?"

"Yes, so I don't need any financial support."

"I'll say, but I still could—"

"Are you hearing me? I know I'd screw us up. I get bored easily. I'm not built to be someone's girlfriend or wife. You have one chance with Caroline—don't be an idiot and blow it."

Turning away, a tear fell from his eye. He stood, wiped his face, then looked down to her while desperately holding back his emotions. "I can't believe that this is what you want."

With no response from her, he moved to the window and looking out let out a sigh.

Hanging her head down, she was the one now looking to the floor for answers. She realized that all she'd need to do would be to reach out and touch him and they'd be in bed together making love again. He'd move to Miami, they'd have the baby, and everything would be perfect for her... but what about for him? What about twenty years from now? She shook her head. No, she couldn't do it to him.

He turned to her. "You... you look me in the eye and tell me you don't want me, and that you want me to be with her."

After closing her eyes and letting out a breath, she met his gaze.

He waited for her reply with his breathing labored. "Tell me you want me to be with her and not you."

She shook her head no, but her heart screamed for her to not say it. It came out anyway. "She's the one for you. I want you to be with her. I would mess us up. I know that."

He breathed out deeply; his emotions plainly tearing him inside out. He curled his lip while rubbing his hand over his chin and sighed. After shaking his head no, he painted a slight smile on his face.

He walked to her and gently kissed her cheek. "Okay."

She watched as he slowly walked to the door. Turning back, he opened his mouth to speak, but no words came out. She closed her eyes. When she opened them again, he was gone. Slumping on the bed, she silently and completely lost it.

28

A few hours later, Jim was in the lobby of the hotel wearing his tuxedo and waiting at the front desk. Next to him were two men talking. The older man, who wore a suit, said, "Tim, just make sure you're in position when she walks down the aisle."

Jim nodded his head thinking that this must be the wedding videographer.

The younger skinny man held an expensive-looking video camera and said, "Got it."

"If you miss her reaction, it will cost me two hundred thousand dollars at least." Jim looked at both men closely and became a little confused. The older man handed over an envelope. The skinny guy opened it, and Jim spotted a wad of cash.

"I won't miss it."

The older man said, "Pull it off, and there's an extra grand in it for you." Jim watched as the men walked away.

Ten minutes before the ceremony was scheduled to start, Jim and Brian stood together talking. The older man Jim had seen an hour earlier approached and shook Brian's hand. Brian said, "Albert this is my brother Jim. Jim this is Jillian's agent, Albert Blair."

Albert shook Jim's hand. "Nice to meet you, Jim. You're getting quite a sister-in-law."

"Yes I am." Jim smiled.

"Well, I'd better get to my seat."

As Albert walked away, Jim said, "I saw him speaking with your videographer earlier today, and it was stran—"

"What videographer?" Brian looked at him confused.

"The skinny guy with the video camera."

"We didn't hire one."

"Maybe I misheard them or something."

The hotel's wedding coordinator approached them with her face beaming. "They're ready for you."

Five minutes later the three-piece orchestra began playing a slow and romantic song as Brian stood in his black tux before the outdoor altar, looking down the aisle toward the crowd of nearly forty guests. Behind Brian was the gorgeous white sand beach and perfect blue ocean, and in front of him the striking profile of the hotel Eden Rock's breathtaking structure, which appeared to be carved out of the hill.

Eric, the first groomsman, walked down the aisle with his bridesmaid. Then Lisa followed with her groomsman, followed by Rob and Laura, then finally Jim and Victoria. They all took their places on either side of Brian as the processional music grew louder. Then Jillian appeared on the arm of her long-time editor, Roland Pike.

She looked gorgeous in her tea-length, strapless, taffeta sheath dress, which was accented by a facial blusher veil. Jim fought to hold back his emotions as tears streamed down Victoria's face. Jim noticed Albert as he signaled to someone behind him. When Jim looked back, he saw the skinny cameraman moving closer to the altar with his camera pointed at Jillian.

Gazing at his wife to be, Brian smiled sweetly while also struggling to hold back his emotions. As Jillian reached the middle of the crowd, Natalie removed her sunglasses. Brian instantly recognized her and without thinking, called out, "Natalie!" Jillian's eyes immediately moved to the smiling witch. Rob looked over as well. The cameraman moved in position and Albert watched the scene unfold, wearing a grin.

Jillian glared at Natalie. "What the hell are you doing here?" The music screeched to a halt as everyone looked to the bride.

"I have an invitation," Natalie replied smugly as she stood.

Brian rushed toward Jillian.

"There's no way." Jillian shook her head. "First you sue me, and now you try to ruin my wedding!"

The cameraman moved in and got a great shot of Jillian smashing the bouquet of flowers into Natalie's chest. Losing her balance, Natalie tumbled backwards, taking her chair down with her as she fell to the ground. Natalie glared up to Jillian as she struggled back to her feet. "What the hell is wrong with you, you old bitch?"

Brian was two feet away as Natalie dove into Jillian, nailing her with a perfect shoulder tackle down to the turf. All eyes watched the girl fight, mesmerized as they pawed at each other while rolling around on the white runner.

The cameraman got every second of the stunning scene. Brian moved to Jillian and pulled her away. Natalie's date, attorney Josh Roth, helped her to her feet. The two men stood holding back their women as Brian glared at Natalie. "What the hell are you doing here?"

"I told you already. I received an invitation." Natalie gave Jillian a snide look. "I thought you brought me here to apologize, you know for all the lies in your—"

"Apologize?" Jillian interrupted as she stared at her, dumbfounded. Suddenly noticing the cameraman, she pointed at him. "Get that camera away from me."

Jim headed angrily over to Tim. The skinny guy put his hand up defensively and pointed the video camera to the ground. Jim noticed the wide smile on Albert's face and the realization hit him. He rushed to Brian. "That's the guy I saw earlier. He was talking to her agent. Albert handed him an envelope full of money."

All eyes went to Albert. He stood and put on a hesitant smile. "I, uh…"

Jillian stormed up to her agent. "You hired this cameraman?"

He stammered, "Remember there is no such thing as bad publicity."

Tim looked around to be sure he wasn't being watched, then began recording again as Jillian gazed at Albert dumbfounded. "But, how'd you know there'd be something to… Wait. Wait… You *knew* she'd be here."

Natalie yelled out, "Someone sent me the invitation and plane tickets. Oh and also the book." Brian glanced at Natalie. Putting his hand out to Brian, Josh said, "Hello, I'm her attorney, Josh Roth."

After dismissing Josh with a look, his gaze moved to Jillian. Her face was blood red as she snarled, "You set this whole thing up. You ruined my wedding and for what? To sell a few more books. You goddamn bastard."

Brian stared at Albert with his anger building. Rushing over, Brian punched him right in the jaw. Albert went down hard, taking chairs with him. After covering her mouth in dismay, Jillian smiled proudly at Brian. Never pulling her eyes from Brian, Natalie shook her head wearing a smile and seemingly turned on as she once again witnessed his dark side.

Albert looked up groggily to the cameraman. "Tell me you got that?"

"You bastard." Jim headed toward Tim.

Grabbing his case in a panic, Tim took off toward the resort. Jillian glared down at Albert. "You even think about pressing charges against Brian, I'll make sure you don't see a dime more from this book. I'll even pull it just to be sure you don't." She turned toward Brian and sighed.

"Are you okay?"

"Are you?"

After nodding, the angry expression returned to her face. She turned her attention to her agent. "Oh, and you're fired."

Albert stood and brushed himself off. "I'm waiting on a call back from *The View* I think I can—" He shut up when Brian took half a step toward him. Albert put his hands up to protect himself. "Okay. Okay."

"Maybe you should skip the wedding," Brian snarled. Albert straightened his tie and slinked away with all eyes on him.

Victoria stood directly in front of Natalie and stared down to her angrily. Natalie grinned uneasily, grabbed Josh's hand and rushed away. Victoria grinned then walked over to Jillian. Looking at her from back to front, she took in the condition of her dress, which was a mess and covered with grass stains. "It's ruined."

Jillian wore an odd smile as she looked down at her dress. Shaking her head, she spotted a chair and took a seat, looking like she could either burst into laughter or have a giant meltdown any second. Brian's gaze slowly traveled from Jillian's face up to the ominous dark clouds quickly approaching from behind the crowd. Victoria and Jim spotted the approaching storm just as Jillian chuckled. "I'm pretty sure the worst is behind us. I mean, what else could, uh..." She stopped talking when she saw the concerned looks in front of her. After looking behind her skyward, she turned slowly back to Brian.

Brian shrugged. "Don't they say rain is good luck for a wedding?"

Jillian nodded casually as huge drops began to fall. Everyone except Brian and Jillian took off running toward the resort. Instead they simply looked at each other with silly grins as the rain pelted them. She screamed over the rain drops, "Rain might be good luck, but bar fights generally aren't."

"You're taking this all in stride. I'm proud of you," he yelled back while nodding casually. He held his hand out to her. "Shall we?"

She stood and moved to him. The crowd watched from inside the resort all wearing smiles and shaking their heads in disbelief. He swept her up in his arms, and they shared a long kiss that went on for a good thirty seconds. When they finally pulled their lips apart, their clothes were completely soaked. After sharing a laugh, they turned toward the resort and smiled at their audience. Oblivious to the driving rain, he picked her up and carried her at a leisurely pace toward the building. Jim held the door as they slipped inside. He placed her carefully down, and they stood dripping wet just shaking their heads.

Brian announced, "I think we'll, uh, need to move the wedding inside." He walked to Victoria and motioned for Jim to join them. "Are you guys okay?"

"Yeah."

"We're obviously going to go change... Can you guys get everything set up and make sure everyone is comfortable? We'll be down in twenty minutes."

Victoria pointed to Jillian's completely wet, drowned-rat hairstyle. "Better make it at least thirty."

Holding back a laugh, Brian nodded. He walked to Jillian, took her hand, and they headed toward the elevator.

29

Jillian and Brian booked the honeymoon suite for the night. They had dropped their bags off before the wedding with the intention of changing midway during the reception, but now things, of course, had changed. Once in their suite, they both stripped out of their soaked clothes while laughing hysterically.

She glanced down to his groin and noticed something a little unusual. "You look different."

Brian covered up with his hands. "I, uh…"

"You shaved down there didn't you?"

"Not shaved exactly." He cringed. "It was supposed to be a surprise for later."

"You look so cute. Let me see it."

"Waxed."

"You waxed… show me."

Sighing, he moved his hands away. She slipped down to her knees for a closer look. "Oh wow. It looks great." She glanced up to his face. "When did you get this done?"

"On Tuesday. Remember that string of a couple days when I couldn't sit down?"

"Oh, yeah."

"Victoria took me to her spa. They gave me the whole treatment. It was a complete nightmare."

"I wondered what was going on with you. Usually you're running around the house with your penis hanging out."

He nodded. Returning her gaze to it, she lifted his penis up and cupped his balls with her other hand. "It looks huge, and your balls are so clean—just like a baby's bottom."

"Speaking of a baby's bottom." He gave her a smug look. "They did the back as well."

"No way. Let me see."

He turned and bent over. She moved close to him and checked out everything from the back. She parted his cheeks slightly, felt his balls from the back, then wore a big smile. "I just got wet… I mean my, you know."

He was getting a little excited himself as she continued running her hands over his parts.

"I'm so going to be all over you later. And I'm not going to drink much. I want to remember it all. This is going to be fun."

She stood, and he turned toward her with his erection huge and sticking straight out. They both looked down at it, equally impressed. He said, "It does look bigger doesn't it?"

She said breathlessly, "It really does."

"I don't think I'm going to be able to fit that in my pants without, uh…"

She looked up to his face and shrugged. "They kind of have to wait for us anyway. What's a few more minutes?"

He smiled.

"Just a quick one. Even though I can't wait to get my mouth down there… Let's just—"

Before she could finish, he scooped her up into his arms. Carrying her to the bed, he placed her down carefully. She spread her legs, and he was inside of her in less than two seconds. Gazing into each other's eyes, they slowly made love. Closing her eyes she moaned, and he quickened his pace.

"I've missed you," she said.

He nodded with a determined look as he flexed every muscle in his body. She wrapped her arms around his neck as he reached his hands down to scoop her up by her ass cheeks. He lifted her like she weighed next to nothing, and she remained impaled on his erection. Standing up straight, he bounced her up and down on his length. She sucked gently on his neck, and he groaned loudly.

Moments later she came hard with a huge climax. She screamed. While she moved her taut body faster and faster over him, he held his breath. His mouth opened wide with a silent scream as he exploded deep inside of her while still lifting her up and down over him. Exhausted and spent, he stopped moving and just held her tight as they stared into each other's eyes, struggling to catch their breath.

She grimaced. "Ouch… Okay, put me down."

Releasing his grasp, he allowed her to slip to the floor.

"That was amazing, but now we have to move." She took off into the bathroom, looked in the mirror, and screamed, "Oh my gosh. Have you seen my hair?"

"It doesn't look that bad."

She stepped out of the bathroom wearing a wide-eyed expression with her hair a complete mess. "Put your suit on and get down there. Send Victoria up. Tell her it's an emergency."

She put on a bra and panties, then went back into the bathroom to battle her hair, as he quickly got dressed. Poking his head into the bathroom, he saw that her hair somehow now looked even worse. He tried to hide his expression, but she saw his look and asked, "What?"

He glanced at himself in the mirror and recovered by saying, "I just got a look at my own hair. Shit."

After working gel into his hair, he quickly pulled a comb through it, then took off. Turning back, he slipped into the bathroom and kissed her. "I love you. You look amazing."

Brian located the guests in the banquet space, which had now been rearranged to accommodate the wedding. The minister and wedding party stood in the front, and all the guests who remained after the fracas were in their seats. He rushed to Victoria. "She needs you up there now. It's her hair. It's bad, really bad."

Victoria took off. Brian made the rounds to check on all the guests. He thanked the minister for his patience, and fifteen minutes later Victoria appeared wearing a smile. Brian looked sharp in his dark blue suit with a yellow tie, which matched Jillian's stylish yellow one-shoulder stretch satin sheath dress, which she had planned to wear for the reception. Brian beamed for the second time in less than an hour as the three-piece orchestra repeated their processional song. Feeling his emotions getting the best of him once again, Jim looked away from Victoria to focus on Jillian. That made matters worse, so he moved his eyes to the crowd instead and took a deep breath in an effort to pull himself together.

The service was moving, yet concise. When it came time to say their vows, they had prepared their own. Brian spoke first, "Jillian, before I met you I was lost inside the confusion of my own thoughts. As soon as I saw you, everything became clear, and I fell in love. As I grew to know you better, I fell deeper." Jillian gazed into his face, with her emotions bubbling up just below the surface. Both Victoria and Jim were close to losing it as well. Brian continued, "I'll spend the rest of my days trying to be the man you deserve. I love you completely."

Fighting back tears, Jillian took a deep breath. "Brian, when you met me I was a basket case. I couldn't write a word. I couldn't think. I needed something, someone to show me the way. You showed me that life could be amazing and that love could be special again. I thank God every day for delivering you to me. I'll love you always."

Victoria and Jim didn't stand a chance and curling their lips didn't stop the tears from rolling down their faces. And as the crowd looked on, immersed in the ceremony, you could count the dry eyes in the place on one hand.

30

Since the wedding was delayed by more than an hour, Jillian decided to have everyone eat before there were any toasts or dancing. After a glorious meal, Jillian and Brian made the rounds and personally thanked everyone for their infinite patience and for sharing this day with them. After the newly married couple returned to the table, Jim stood and sheepishly tried to get everyone's attention by tapping a knife against his glass. It didn't work. Victoria noticed, put her fingers to her mouth, and blew out a piercing whistle, much like a sailor. The room quieted instantly, and all eyes went to Jim.

Turing to Victoria, he gave her half a smile. "Thanks." Jim held his glass as he began, "When I met Jillian, I thought she was beautiful, kind, and amazing. As I saw the way she looked at my brother, Brian, I wondered what the heck was wrong with her. I mean, did she take a blow to the head or..." Everyone burst into laughter as Brian grinned looking up to his brother. "I'm just kidding. These two crazy kids are in love." Turning to face them, he added, "When you look at them you can tell they love each other and that it will last forever. Most people dream about meeting the one person..." He stopped when he felt his emotions taking over. Glancing at Victoria, he cleared his throat then returned to look over the room of guests. "...the one person in this world that is made for them. For these two, the dream has come true." Jillian looked up at him while her lip fluttered, then she and Brian shared a smile.

Jim raised his glass along with everyone else. "The rest of us should be so lucky. Cheers."

Moving to Brian, Jim shook his hand. Jillian stood and gave him a big hug. Jim turned away and faced the window for a moment as he collected his emotions before returning to his seat.

Victoria stood and all eyes went to her. Grinning, she took a moment to look down to Jillian and Brian. She held her glass in the air as she began, "When I met Brian for the first time, I was wearing this little see-through, sheer white bikini. I happened to be stretching, and my bikini bottoms fell right off..." Bev and Ed Nash shared a horrified look as grins spread across the face of most in attendance.

Victoria nodded casually. "It happens… anyway, this amazing young man was such a gentleman that he hardly looked at all." She nodded to the crowd with a proud smile. "And that was before these two wonderful people fell in love. Now I'm sure I could take my top off, and he wouldn't even notice because there is no other woman in the world for him. Here I'll prove it…" She placed both hands on the top of her dress, and Beverly Nash gasped. "Just kidding… although I've known Jillian for only two years, she's like a sister to me. From the moment Jillian met Brian, she hasn't been the same. She's truly happy, and they make a perfect couple." Holding her glass higher, she turned to see Brian and Jillian huddled close together. "If you want to know what true love looks like, well, take a good look. You won't see it often… I love you both and wish you the very best." She took a sip and everyone did the same.

Smiling, Jillian and Brian stood. After hugging Victoria, Jillian moved to Jim as Brian grabbed the sexy maid of honor. Jim got out of his seat and embraced the bride once again. The orchestra began playing a song, and the happy couple headed out to the dance floor as the guests looked on wearing slightly envious smiles.

Half way through the song, Jim stood and put his hand out to Victoria. She smiled, and they walked out to the dance floor. He held her close as their bodies pressed together moving to the rhythm of the music. Her stomach, with his child growing inside, was against him. Closing her eyes, she held him tightly and sighed. Opening her eyes, her lips parted as if she had something to tell him. Without uttering a word, she closed her eyes and simply held on.

As he danced with her, Jim's thoughts clouded his mind. He wondered how a nerdy guy who just three months ago couldn't get a girlfriend to save his life, now found himself in love with two incredible women, both of whom he was sure loved him back. He wanted them both, and the baby. He wanted to carry Victoria up to one of the rooms and make love to her all night. He wanted to fall asleep with his hand resting on her growing belly.

The rest of the wedding party joined them on the dance floor. A member of the hotel staff held a phone and waited out of sight while wearing a bright smile. When the song ended, Jillian and Brian returned to their seats, and the hotel employee approached them. Jillian shook her head no as the employee conveyed what apparently was good news. She sighed and looked to Brian. He shrugged, and she reluctantly grabbed the phone. Heading to a quieter spot, she spoke to the caller. Her expression went from a frown to a look of surprise to a huge smile. A few moments later, she rushed back to Brian and whispered in his ear. Beaming, he walked with her to the stage and motioned to the orchestra to hold the music. When the music stopped all eyes were on her.

Jillian spoke into the microphone, "It's been an interesting day. You've probably seen some things you've never before seen at a wedding." She received a chuckle from the crowd and smiled. "As you are painfully aware, I recently published a novel, and it's been, uh, selling fairly well. As you also know, a young woman *you met* a little earlier today has sued me over the book. If you're confused, she's the one I was rolling around with on the grass." She shook her head with a grin as the crowd giggled. "That was my publisher on the phone. Since the story broke a few days ago, sales of my book have been incredible, and it moved into the top ten on Amazon. Well, since the video of the altercation at the wedding hit the Internet and the cable TV newscasts, sales have spiked just a bit. *The Leg Thing* hit number one on Amazon about two hours ago and—" The crowd cheered as Jillian shook her head, bewildered. "I hate to share sales figures, but what the hell... sales through yesterday were just over seven hundred thousand copies. Today we've sold almost one hundred and fifty thousand copies, and my publisher estimates we'll blow through the one million mark before midnight."

Nearly everyone in the crowd gasped as she continued, "To give you an idea of what this means, I've sold more copies in the last three days then I've sold of any book ever... oh, and I was told we should put on the Darcy Gray show right now, she's..." Turning to the hotel employee, she pointed to the large television screen as she asked, "Do you get CNTN in here?" The employee nodded and rushed to a turn on the TV as Jillian continued, "Darcy evidently is a big fan and seems to be on my side. And God knows I need as many people on my side now as I can get."

In Natalie's hotel room, the flexible ballerina soaked in the large tub behind the closed bathroom door as Josh sat pouting on the bed. She'd been in a really bad mood since they were asked to leave the wedding. Natalie informed him that he'd be sleeping on the floor that night. He had the television on, and a story caught his attention. He rushed into the bathroom. She screeched, "Get out of here." He froze looking down to her amazing body as she covered her chest with her hands.

"I said get out of here." She waved him away with her hand.

"What? No, you've got to see this."

He grabbed the remote and tuned the television to the proper channel.

On screen they both watched the section from the wedding video where Natalie was knocked to the ground after Jillian smashed her with the flowers. The reporter said, "*That is a clear assault and should bolster the case of Miss Brookhart against Miss Grayson.*"

After smiling at him, she moved her hands from her breasts and returned her attention to the screen. The reporter continued, "*The book at the center of this lawsuit has vaulted to number one on Amazon, and it's reported to be closing in on the one-million-sales mark.*" An image of another man appeared on the screen who commented, "*I believe that Miss Brookhart has a compelling case and she should soon be fielding an offer for a settlement in the seven-figure range.*"

Sliding up higher in the tub, she stretched her arms around the edge exposing her breasts to him fully. "Do you want to get in?"

Back in the banquet room, the television brightened to the image of Darcy sitting in front of the camera with her big hair, way too much jewelry and her signature bright pastel colored pleather jacket. On this night, it was a vibrant blue. Half the screen was Darcy, while in one quarter appeared an image of a man wearing a suit, and the final quarter showed a loop of two sections of the wedding video. The first section was of Jillian nailing Natalie with the bouquet, then Natalie taking a tumble over the chair. That was followed by Natalie charging and tackling Jillian to the ground. Then it showed the twenty seconds of them rolling around on the runner and spilling over on the grass.

Darcy commented, "*That looks to me like assault. How can you be suing someone and expect to win if you are in the process of beating them up? It just makes no sense.*"

The man commented, "*That is a gutsy strategy, but some might argue that when Miss Grayson threw the flowers causing Miss Brookhart to fall over, she was the one committing the assault.*"

Darcy gave the camera a tired look. "*Mitchell, who in their right mind would argue that? Someone would need to be an absolute moron to believe that. Just plain stupid.*"

The video loop went to the scene where Brian punched Albert and knocked him to the ground. Darcy commented, "*Now here is a knight in shining armor if I ever saw one. Coming to the aid of his beautiful fiancée and socking the man who reportedly hired the cameraman. We believe that the man taking the blow was Miss Grayson's agent who purposefully destroyed her wedding day to create some sort of shameless publicity stunt. What a lowlife scum. This man should be shot, but a good punch to the jaw will help me sleep just a little better tonight. Thank you Mr. Brian Nash. Now let's see that again.*"

After the punch was replayed, Darcy continued, "*He is quite a hunk.*" Darcy stared into the camera. "*Oh and Miss Grayson, I love your work, but if you don't treat that man right, I'll be giving him a call. So you take good care of him, you hear.*"

There was a loud chuckle from the crowd then Jillian motioned for the employee to turn off the television. After the screen went black, Jillian grabbed Brian. "You can tell Darcy that I will be taking care of my hero." She kissed him, and the crowd moaned, "Awww." Jillian looked back to the group. "Oh and my publisher said there will be no settlement. We're taking Miss Brookhart all the way to trial if she so chooses. So Natalie, wherever you are, suck on that, you little tramp." The crowd broke into laughter and applause.

In Natalie's tub, the little tramp just happened to be sucking on it right at that moment. She worked her mouth excitedly over Josh's stiff manhood as he kneeled in the tub. Pulling her mouth off of him, she trailed kisses up his stomach and chest. She kissed him full on the lips and leaned back in the tub as he slipped into the water. Moving both her feet to his erection, she gently massaged him between her toes. She smiled. "Josh, have you ever had anal sex?"

"Uh, no."

"I'm really good at it."

"Really." He swallowed hard.

"I didn't bring my special lube so we'll just have to do it naturally." She ran her tongue seductively over her lips. "I think I can get you slick enough so that we can pull it off. How does that sound?" He didn't respond. Instead he got to his feet and quickly reached for a towel.

Two minutes later, Josh lay flat on the bed as Natalie kneeled between his spread legs with her mouth hovering just above his erection. She tore her eyes away from it to look him in the eye. "Do you think they'll really offer us a settlement?"

"I would be surprised if I didn't have an offer on my desk within a week."

Grinning, she returned her attention to his penis, running a finger around the ridge. "Josh, you really have an amazing cock. The head is slim like a cute little triangle. Just perfect to slide right into a *tight* space." She placed her mouth over the head and sucked it gently. He groaned desperately until she pulled up and added, "Yet, it's so long…"

She traced the length with her finger as she gazed into his eyes.

"Uh-huh," he replied, mesmerized.

Sliding her hand to the base, she held it firmly. "…and so thick at the bottom for when you really want to be filled up."

He nodded breathlessly.

"I really want to be filled up Josh. Will you... fill me?"

"Yes."

Natalie was able, somehow, to get him slick enough for the sex she craved. Josh's head was spinning as she took control. In the middle of it all, she held still over him and asked, "Is it too late to sue for more money?"

"God, no," he cried.

She grinned and moved her hips up, then back down once more. She held still again, pressing hard into him and asked, "Ten million?"

He narrowed his eyes and said confidently, "Twenty." She gasped and went back to it. He slammed his eyes shut as she slowly rode him. When he finally exploded, he experienced the most intense orgasm of his life. When they finally went to sleep that night, he wasn't on the floor.

31

In the banquet room the wedding was in full swing. Brian and Jillian were making the rounds again as Jim, Victoria, Lisa, Eric, and his girlfriend, and the rest of the wedding party remained together at the main table. Lisa was in a particularly bad mood, even for her. She was clearly tipsy. She and Eric had been trading jabs at each other all night. Lisa was an opinionated conservative Republican while Eric's political leanings were much further to the left. He was a big Obama fan.

Jim was attempting to hold it together for the night and not have some giant meltdown related to his current love-life debacle. He decided the way to accomplish this was to drink a lot. It certainly put him in a good mood, but also brought his mind's filtering capabilities way down.

Victoria was, of course, completely sober and picking up on some tension between Eric and his girlfriend, Annette. She had noticed it at the rehearsal dinner as well and figured their relationship was dead or at the very least on life support. As she watched Eric and Lisa's heated political discussions, she could picture them together. There was a fiery passion there. She knew Lisa didn't have a lot of experience with men, but she didn't know quite how critical the situation was. Victoria figured if Annette hadn't been on this trip, she could see these two hooking up for the night.

Thirty minutes later, everyone except Jim, Victoria, and Lisa had left the reception and retired to their rooms. Victoria was sure that many of those who left were already enjoying some hot passionate sex after the romantic wedding. She was jealous. She loved weddings; they always made her horny, but who was she kidding—everything made her horny. She figured even Eric and Annette were probably going at it. As she glanced at Lisa and Jim, she figured that the three of them would be the only people associated with the wedding who would not be getting laid that night.

The bartender came over with three drinks: a glass of wine and a half bottle for Lisa, another gin and tonic for Jim (his sixth), and a mineral water for Victoria. He smiled, told them he was closing up, then headed off. Jim really didn't need another drink but began working on it anyway.

Lisa's mood could probably use another couple drinks, and she took a large sip as she eyed the bottle. Victoria didn't touch her mineral water. After finishing off her glass of wine, Lisa poured another. "You know, I'm going to be thirty-six in a month, and I'm still a virgin."

Victoria perked up as she lied, "I would never have guessed."

Jim mumbled, "I was a virgin up until about six months ago."

Lisa nodded to him dismissively and took another sip. "In fact I've never made it to the third date with any man."

Now this surprised Victoria, and she asked, "You've never been in love?"

"I didn't say that."

"Tell us."

"When I was a senior in high school, I met this guy who was in college. We had dated a few times, then he took me to prom. We had a great time that night. We kissed for hours, and I, uh, fell in love with him."

"What happened?" Victoria asked.

"We never saw each other again. I waited and waited for him to call me, and he never did. I left him a couple messages, but…"

"Oh, that's awful."

"I really wanted to sleep with him that night, but I was scared. I'm glad I didn't because I would have felt much, much worse."

Lisa took another sip of wine as Victoria gave her a sympathetic look. "Why do you think you've never dated anyone?"

"I find most men to be annoying and not very attractive. I guess none will ever measure up to my Doug."

Victoria frowned. "I think you're too picky. Most men have something to offer. You just need to open yourself up. If you don't, you'll never be happy."

"Maybe, but I usually say the wrong thing to men. I can be sorta opinionated."

"Really?" Victoria asked with mock skepticism.

"Yes, when I start talking about politics or religion, I kind of lose it a bit."

"You should really steer clear of those subjects when you're around a guy you like. And I watched you eat... that's not how you eat when you're on a date is it?"

Lisa looked at her offended.

"Sorry, I'm just trying to help. You, uh, really like shrimp don't you?"

Lisa gazed at her dumbfounded. "Well yeah."

Victoria shook her head. "Let's forget about the eating for now."

"Okay."

"I think you must miss the signals men send out. That's part of your problem."

"What are you talking about?"

"For example, I think Eric likes you."

Lisa looked at her shocked. "Eric? No way. He's got a girlfriend, and he's not very good looking."

"I think he's cute, and those two are about to break up. You guys would make a good couple."

Lisa sneered at her. "One... he's a Democrat and two he's not tall enough."

Victoria scoffed. "You are way too picky. You just need to get laid. I think that would change your whole outlook on men."

After taking a sip, Lisa gave her a hesitant look. "You know I've never even touched one."

Jim perked up. "A guy?"

Lisa sighed and whispered, "No, a penis."

"Is that why you left the bachelorette party?"

Lisa nodded. "I knew you had a stripper and I couldn't stay."

"You missed out because you could have touched one there—a *big* one."

Jim chuckled. "You had a stripper at your party?"

Victoria shook her head with a grin. "No not a stripper—a famous porn star. He was hung like a horse."

After taking a sip of his drink, he gave them a disapproving look. "You girls are disgusting."

Victoria raised her eyebrows. "And what did you guys do at the bachelor party?"

"Uh... I don't want to talk about it."

Victoria gave him a smug look and turned her attention to Lisa. "So not even Doug's?"

"No, we made out that night, and we dry humped I guess they call it, but no."

"Wow, I've seen probably more than thirty." Lisa widened her eyes as Victoria continued, "I couldn't imagine my life without a penis every now and then. I always hope for more now than then." Victoria winked and they shared a grin.

"Well, obviously you're pregnant and all," Lisa said. "Oh sorry." Covering her mouth, she looked to Jim.

He scoffed. "Don't worry about it. I'd help you out with the penis thing except I've already got way too many women in my life." He motioned with his eyes to Victoria. "This one I'm still in love with, and, as you just painfully reminded me, is carrying my child. Oh, and there's Caroline who left this morning."

Lisa nodded.

He took a sip of his drink and shook his head. "But did you know last night that I had sex with both—"

"So Lisa…" Victoria interrupted narrowing her eyes at him.

He rolled his eyes and returned to his drink.

"Lisa, you really should consider Eric. I think I can get you guys together."

"I have to think about it. I don't want to marry a man who is short. Our kids could be short."

"He's like five-eleven," Victoria said incredulously. "Plus first you need to actually make it to the third date with a man before you can ever even think he might ask you to marry him. Not to mention you need to have sex before you can have a baby. You've got to take some baby steps, no pun intended… and obsessing about a guy's height is not getting you any closer to getting laid."

Lisa sighed. "I know I'm a messed up bitch. I was the youngest child, and my parents filled my head with how perfect and beautiful I was. It really screwed me up. I don't think anyone is good enough for me."

Victoria shook her head. "You need to give a blow job. That's what you need. Nothing centers you more than sucking on a big dick."

Both Jim and Lisa looked at her in shock.

"I'm serious." She gave them a defensive look. "You think no one is good enough for you, and you're nervous. You need a big hard cock coming at your face. That'll give you some perspective. You should have casual sex with a few guys, then maybe you can focus on having a serious relationship."

Lisa paused; her appalled look morphed into a one of uncertainty. "I guess, but I'm scared."

"Of what?"

"I really don't know." Sighing, Lisa picked up her glass and emptied it.

The sexless trio took a cab to the house. Jim was out of it completely, while Lisa was pretty tipsy but able to function for the most part. The two women helped him up to his room with Victoria doing most of the heavy lifting.

Once they were inside, Jim gazed dreamily at Victoria. "You know I do love you. We should move here and have the baby. We could live in a shack on the beach. You could make puca shell necklaces, and I'd sell them to the tourists."

The two women shared a wide-eyed look. Victoria said, "He's adorable. Drunk, but adorable."

Shaking her head, Lisa smiled.

They watched as Jim swayed a bit while he removed his jacket and shirt. He lowered his pants, and as he went to step out of them, he fell back against the bed. The women chuckled. Victoria said, "He could use some help."

They helped him sit up on the bed. Victoria got on her knees and pulled his shoes, socks, and pants off as Lisa pulled off his T-shirt. Jim grabbed Lisa around the neck. "You are pretty. I think you can get a guy, just don't be so mean to them. They, uh, don't like... *meanness.*"

"Okay," she replied with a laugh.

With his eyes barely open, he pulled his boxer briefs down. "Here you can look at my penis if you want. Don't be scared."

Lisa waited a moment before quickly glancing at his groin and shyly looking away.

He rubbed his hands on his face and gave them a silly smile. "It's too hot in here anyway."

Lisa returned her gaze to him and studied his lean body. He climbed higher in the bed to rest his head on the pillow. Victoria looked him over too, and they both watched as he closed his eyes and took a deep breath.

Tearing her eyes from him, Victoria said, "So now you've seen one."

"It's kinda nice."

Victoria gave her a naughty smile. "You want to see it get hard? Then you'll really see what you've been missing all these years."

Lisa gave her a vaguely revolted look. "Are you going to touch it or…"

"No, no. That would be wrong… on so many levels—really, really, really fun, but wrong. He's the one who took his underwear off, and he said you could look at it, so what I'm about to do isn't wrong at all. Just watch this."

Grinning, Victoria leaned over and whispered dirty stuff in his ear. She knew exactly what would get him going.

He moaned while moving his head around and wearing a sexy grin. His penis began to move as it expanded in size. Lisa stared at it, mesmerized. Then, she glanced up at Victoria and grinned for only a moment before her eyes returned to the main attraction.

Lifting her head up, Victoria checked the progress. She smiled proudly before leaning back in and whispering something even filthier.

Rising to her feet, she looked to Lisa. "That should do it."

Jim's penis was now at about half-mast and with each beat of his heart it throbbed and expanded even more. Victoria kneeled down near his midsection for a front row seat to the show.

Lisa gazed down at her, astonished. "You're just incredible."

"I know." Victoria looked down proudly at her accomplishment.

"What did you say?"

"Trust me." Victoria shook her head. "You're not ready."

Lisa nodded and went to her knees on the opposite side of the bed. They both stared at Jim's manhood as it grew right before their eyes. Victoria said confidently, "He should be reaching down to play with it any moment now. Men just can't leave it alone. I guess I can't blame them." As if on queue, Jim's hand wandered down, and he began pulling hard on his penis. The women shared a silent chuckle as the demonstration went on.

Lisa was captivated and said breathlessly, "He's, uh, got a nice one. Not that I would really know, but…"

"No, you're right. He does."

He moaned and whispered, "Oh, Caroline lick my balls again."

Lisa looked at her shocked. "Wow does that bother you?"

"No, if I had balls, I'd want her licking them also. She's hot."

They watched as he took a deep breath and his hand fell away from his erection. As it began to slowly deflate, Victoria frowned. "It's sad when they go back down."

"I'll bet."

"I can't believe you've never had one of those in your mouth or your pussy… or your ass."

"Ass?"

"Oh, God yeah. You haven't lived until you've had a hard cock gently penetrating you there." Lisa returned a sour face as Victoria looked past her and said slowly, "It's, uh, really… yeah…" Shaking her head, she tore herself from the image. "But you should take baby steps. I wouldn't start with anal."

"No." Lisa nodded matter-of-factly.

Victoria rose to her feet and took one more admiring look at Jim's body. After exhaling, she covered him up.

Victoria stood with Lisa outside of her room. Victoria whispered, "We'll both certainly be thinking of Jim when we masturbate tonight." Lisa returned an almost infantile look.

Victoria made a face. "Tell me you plan on giving yourself at least two orgasms after what we just witnessed."

"I, uh…"

"You do touch yourself down there, don't you?"

Lisa paused with her mouth open and said halfheartedly, "I have."

Sighing, Victoria shook her head. "How do you get out of bed every day?" She didn't wait for an answer. "You probably have never had a big orgasm. If you can't give yourself one, you can't expect a man to give you one."

"Really?"

"Look, I'm just about to get my master's degree in psychology. In a few months I'm opening my own office. I'm going to be a sex therapist. I could help you if you want."

"How can you help?"

"I want to show you how to touch yourself. Give me twenty minutes, and you'll be humping the leg of the next man you see."

Lisa looked at her a little put off.

Victoria smiled. "Just kidding about the humping thing."

"Okay…" Lisa nodded, relieved. "I think I'd like to learn."

32

In the luxurious honeymoon suite, Jillian climbed out of the tub and left Brian behind to wash everything really, really well just one more time while she prepared. She slipped on a sexy baby-doll top with the matching V-string panty she purchased especially for the night. Two thin straps held up the satin cups, which perfectly accentuated her breasts. From there, a luxurious see-through tulle sheath hung down to just below the tiny satin panty. After placing his perfectly wrapped present on the bed, she stretched out next to it, fluffing her hair up and trying out various sexy poses. She settled on a pose seconds before he entered the room wearing only dark blue silk boxer shorts. She eyed his lean, muscular body up and down. He spotted the present on the bed. "Wait—we're doing presents now?"

"If you want."

"I've been dying to give you yours." Grinning, he headed to the closet and pulled out the large wrapped picture frame-shaped gift along with a separate smaller box. He placed them on the bed next to the other present and climbed up.

"You look amazing. Is that new?"

"It is." She knelt up in bed. "Do you want to go first?"

He answered her by ripping off the wrapping paper and pulling the lid off the box. Inside were three superexpensive tennis racquets that he'd had his eye on for months. He smiled. "I love them. I can't wait to use 'em."

"Open the envelope." Holding her balled up hands under her face she smiled excitedly.

He opened the envelope and pulled out airline tickets. "Phoenix?"

"Yes, I'm taking you back to the Phoenician, but this time I blocked off a lot of time on the grass court. We're going at the end of November."

He leaned over and kissed her. "These are the best gifts ever."

"Okay, now mine."

He handed her the small box and she shook her head. "So, I want to open the big one first."

"I'm not sure you'll like the other one. Open this one first so it will..." He frowned. "...cushion the blow if necessary."

After giving him a curious look, she opened the box. When she pulled out the three-quarter carat diamond earrings, she beamed. "Oh they're perfect. I love them, but okay now the big one. I kinda saw it in the closet earlier and I just can't wait anymore."

"I can't believe you." He scoffed.

"I didn't shake it or anything."

He handed her the wrapped frame. After feeling the weight of it, she tore the paper off. In awe, she studied the expertly rendered charcoal sketch of her naked on a bed with her arm draped lazily over her breasts; the delicious curve of her hips had been captured brilliantly. Moving her gaze to the image of her face, she shook her head in appreciation of the amazing likeness he had been able to capture. "Wow..." She looked at him blown completely away and returned to the drawing. "This is incredible."

He admitted, "I, uh, kind of took a class."

"I can't believe you drew this."

"I was inspired."

"How did you do this? From memory?"

"Victoria helped."

She looked at him, confused.

He gave her a hesitant smile. "Well, do you remember that girls' weekend and the photo shoot? She uh—"

"She told me the pictures didn't come out." She scoffed. "That witch."

"Well they did, and they were incredible. This was my favorite of all the, uh, *safer* ones. Some were pretty X rated."

"Really?"

"How did she convince you to get in those poses?"

"I was a little drunk."

After nodding casually, he returned to look at his drawing. "I could stare at you forever. Especially when you're naked."

"The drawing is amazing. I didn't know you were so incredibly talented. But..." She frowned. "Do you really like your gift? Victoria said it sucked. Wait... but that's when she was trying to trick me into doing the photo shoot. She's a really good liar."

"The best. She should run for president."

They shared a chuckle and her frown returned. "But your gift is so much more personal than mine, I, uh…"

Scoffing, he looked at her like she was crazy. "You wrote a whole freaking novel about me. How much more personal does it get?"

Jillian shrugged, unconvinced.

"Come on there's like a whole chapter about how crazy in love with me you are, then there's that entire paragraph about now much you love my penis."

"Two," she said smugly.

"What?"

"I wrote two whole paragraphs about your penis."

"You see… I love the racquets and can't wait to take the trip."

"Okay." She gave him a bright smile.

Slipping off the bed, he moved the gifts to the dresser. "Now I think we should forget about gifts and novels and drawings and lawsuits—" He cringed. "Sorry, I didn't…"

She smiled. "Nothing could spoil this night. But since you brought it up…" She put on a serious expression. "I'm convinced Natalie is in love with you."

"What?" He climbed back in bed.

"Why else would she have come to the wedding? She can't get over you."

"I don't think so, she's—"

"Oh, I do." An evil look crossed Jillian's face. "I love that you're mine, and she wants you and can't have you. I'm going to totally…" She shook her head, too embarrassed to say it out loud.

"I love when you're angry—like at my parents house. You were on fire."

"I remember," she said with a faraway, sexy look.

"Hey, I think my mom was looking at you funny during the reception." Folding his arms across his chest he nodded. "I bet she doesn't want you to lay a finger on me."

"You know, I think you're…" Looking at his face, she saw he was holding back a laugh. "Wait, I see what you're doing, and I like it." After kissing him hard, she pushed him down on the mattress.

He said, half kidding, "Just don't hurt me."

"Too much?" she asked calmly.

"Maybe a little. I mean go with it, but just dial it back a notch."

"Okay," She moved on top of him, pressing her lips to his and giving him a tender kiss. Pulling up from him, she looked into his eyes.

"I love you."

"Oh…" She curled her lip, and her voice cracked as she said, "I love you too."

Down the hall, Victoria sat in a chair near the bed in the brightly lit room. Lisa wore only a bra and panties as she drained the final sip from a glass of wine that Victoria had retrieved for her. After taking a deep breath, she slipped off her panties. Victoria eyes opened wide as she took in Lisa's overgrown pubic region. Lisa noticed her expression. "What's wrong?"

"When we get back to Miami, I've got to take you to my bikini wax guy."

"Uh, okay."

"Pick up the mirror and take a look." Victoria shook her head. "No offense, but can you even find your clitoris in all that hair?"

Lisa picked up the hand mirror and cringed as she took a cautious look between her legs.

Victoria sighed. "I think if we're going to do this tonight, we need an emergency shaving."

"I don't know about that."

"Honey, if you're not giving yourself a satisfying orgasm, that jungle has to be part of the reason."

"I'm not sure I'd like it with no hair."

"Are you planning on going to the nude beach tomorrow?"

"I was."

"You can't go like that. Trust me." Victoria stood. "Would you like to see mine?"

"Okay," Lisa replied hesitantly.

"Now bear with me because I'm in desperate need of a waxing. With the pregnancy, I'm really overdue." She pulled up her dress, pushed down her panties, and spread her legs a bit. Gazing at her nearly hairless parts, Lisa asked skeptically, "*You* need a waxing?"

"I know. I just feel… yuck."

"No, I mean that looks clean and sexy."

"I'll definitely be touching it up before tomorrow." Victoria ran her fingers across some small random hairs and shook her head with a frown. "I think you'll like this look." Victoria gave Lisa an uncertain glance. "Since you've seen the front, would you mind taking a look at the back? I'm trying to decide if I should get my anus bleached, and I'd love another opinion."

Lisa gave her a look that screamed that she had no idea what Victoria was talking about.

Back in the honeymoon suite, Brian kissed his way down to Jillian's neck while peeling one of the tiny babydoll straps from her shoulder to uncover her full breast. Moving his lips to her nipple, he sucked it gently. She closed her eyes as she ran her fingers through his hair pulling him closer to her with her legs that were wrapped around his abdomen. Lifting the fabric from her other shoulder, he slid his lips over to explore her other magnificent breast. He sucked her nipple and ran his tongue around it roughly, feeling it harden. He moved back and forth between each breast as she spread her legs, and he pressed his body into her satin-covered pussy. Pulling up from her, his gaze traveled down her body, stopping first at the sheer tulle top, which lay bunched up at her waist, then moved to her satin-covered panty.

He sighed as he pulled the baby-doll top down her body. She lifted her hips off the bed, and he slipped it down her legs.

She wore only the V-string now and looked nothing short of breathtaking. He knelt up for a better look and paused, just drinking in her entire body. She watched him while fluttering her eyelids bashfully and after ten seconds she whispered, "What is it?"

He shook his head slowly, with his lips parted and his breathing labored, as his eyes traveled back to her beautiful face. "I can't believe you're mine."

She smiled. "Believe it."

"I'm never going to stop trying to make you happy."

"That's what I want to hear, but could you please start right about now?"

Grinning, he took hold of both sides of the V-string and slowly pushed it down her legs; as it reached her ankles, she kicked it off seductively. She placed her hands on the waistband of his silk boxers, and he kneeled up so she could push them down. His erection sprang out, and her eyes locked on his silky smooth shaft and balls. She sighed as she cupped the twins with one hand, then circled his shaft with the other. "I really love you like this."

He leaned back as she continued to stroke him. Sliding her hand back farther under his balls to his ass, she gently stroked him with her finger.

"Oh, man," he moaned.

She climbed off the bed and guided him to the position she wanted: on his hands and knees near the bed's edge. She kneeled down and studied his parts for a moment while licking her lips. After thinking, *Victoria was right; this could be fun,* she went to it.

More than an hour later, Brian was panting as he collapsed on his wife, abandoning his attempt for a third orgasm. He lay on her for a moment, then slipped off to the side to recover from their passionate coupling. After a moment, he said with a straight face, "I heard married sex was supposed to stink, but this... wow."

They shared a grin, which grew into a chuckle. He moved his hand to caress her stomach. She glanced down to his penis, and his eyes followed along. Reaching out to touch it, she smiled. "I really like everything this way. Do you think you'll keep it?"

"If you had asked me an hour ago, I would have said there's no way, but now..."

"Was it very painful?"

His eyes widened. "Imagine what it feels like to have the hair ripped from your balls." After they shared a grimace, he added, "Maybe they can drug me next time."

In Lisa's bathroom, Victoria walked her through the emergency clean up. They did what they could with the tools they had available. Victoria said that when they returned home, she'd snap up Rafael's next two appointments for the both of them. Returning to the bedroom, Lisa studied her new look in the mirror and was delighted. Victoria sat near the bed and instructed her in finding her G-spot, exploring the wonders of the clitoris, and appreciating her now smooth and hair-free female parts.

As Victoria held the hand mirror, Lisa brought herself to a mind-blowing climax. When her work was done, Victoria slipped out of the room and left Lisa panting on the bed, wishing she'd kept the two dildos and the rest of the items in the pink and white striped bachelorette party gift box.

33

The next day the flight back to St. Maarten didn't leave until late afternoon so everyone was invited to the beach at Grand Saline. It was widely believed to be one of the five most beautiful beaches in the world and was the only one in that class where clothing was optional. Victoria joked that she would only allow people from their group to go if they agreed to exercise the option. Using her unique powers of persuasion, she managed to convince them all.

As Victoria was heading down the hall with Lisa, she spotted Jim walking into his room. "Come on, let's go. The bus is waiting."

Turning to her, he frowned. "I think I'm going to stay here."

She looked at him, shocked. "What?"

"Yeah, I'm tired and I just—"

"You get your ass down in that driveway right now. We're about to leave for the most beautiful beach in the world, and you don't want to go?" He opened his mouth to speak, but she blurted out, "Jillian will be there, naked, and uh, Jeff's girlfriend, she's got a nice ass, I think. Well, we will soon find out."

Shaking his head, he held back a smile. "What the hell is wrong with you?"

"Come on! It will be fun. I'll splash cold water on Brian's penis, and it'll shrink up like a frightened turtle, and then you can strut around. You know how much he hates that you're bigger than he is."

Lisa raised her eyebrows. "Yeah, you've got nothing to be ashamed of."

Turning to Lisa, he made a face as a flashback shot through his brain. He gave Victoria a curious look. "How drunk was I last night?"

"You were pretty out of it, but we made sure you got back to your bed safely. We even helped you out of your clothes."

The women shared a knowing giggle.

He gave them a hesitant look. "Did I do anything stupid?"

"No." Victoria smiled. "Are you coming or not?"

"You promise you'll embarrass Brian?"

"I'll figure something out."

He chucked. "Okay then."

Victoria glanced at Lisa. "Can we meet you down at the bus? I'd like a minute."

"Sure." Lisa headed down the stairs.

Victoria gave him a serious look. "We're good, aren't we? I mean, we talked and, uh…"

He nodded. "We're good."

"Great. I'd hate for us to be angry with each other."

"Who could ever be angry with you?"

"You know, you're right about that. I'm just amazing." After putting on a big grin, she put her arm around him. "Now let's go see some dicks and tits. I'm hoping for more dicks."

"I'd prefer tits."

After stopping off at the hotel, the bus picked up Brian and Jillian and a few other guests from the house. Rob convinced Laura to go to another beach because he thought it would be just a little creepy to be naked with his mother and new stepfather.

The bus dropped them off, and the group set out on an exhausting five-minute walk down a tree-lined path. The path was long and deceptively grueling, especially considering the incredible beauty that lay at the end of it. Midway through the walk most of the group wondered why the hell they had agreed to go.

But when they reached the gap between two dunes and spotted the crystal clear water and fine white sand, everyone's eyes widened. As they moved past the dunes to take in the entire spectacle of the most pristine, untouched, perfect beach in the world, they gasped.

Jim looked at Victoria. "This is… nice." As everyone else watched, Jim quickly pulled off all his clothes and ran to the water and dove in.

Victoria said, "Wow, he's not shy."

After Brian, Jillian, and Victoria shared a grin, they dropped their stuff in the sand and began pulling off clothing. Brian was in the water next, closely followed by Jillian. Then, Victoria showed off her new larger breasts as she slowly made her way to the water. Some others from their group joined them in the ocean while others stayed on the beach simply watching the nude frolickers. Lisa hesitantly removed her clothes and sat on a towel checking out her hair free vagina.

An hour later, everyone was thoroughly lathered with sunscreen and basking in the brilliant sun. Lisa wore sunglasses and spent most of her time studying male parts. It was hard to spot, but Lisa did log some time gyrating her hips as she sat on her towel proving Victoria was right—she did feel like humping something.

Brian brought his pad and was sketching Victoria as she posed for him, lying on her side in a sexy position. Jillian watched him draw, impressed. When he was done, he showed it to Victoria. She beamed. "That is amazing. Can I have it?"

"Sure."

Lisa looked at the sketch. "Wow, Brian, you are really good." Jim glanced at it and thought that he'd really like to have a copy, but he was sure Caroline would not be on board.

Jillian said, "Bri, you want to go for a walk?"

He agreed. Victoria and Jim watched as he got up and followed her toward the ocean. Halfway there, he stopped and said something to Jillian. She nodded and went on without him as he rushed back to Victoria.

Getting up, Lisa told Victoria that she was taking a walk herself to show off and also to checkout the packages of a group of attractive guys who were down near the water.

Brian dropped down to the sand next to Victoria and glanced back to be sure Jillian was still by the water. "Her birthday is coming up... and I want to get her back for, you know, that trick she played on me at my birthday... I think I have a plan, but I need your help. Will you help me?"

Jim looked on with a grin, and Victoria's face brightened into a huge smile. "You know I was hoping you would get her back. I'd love to help."

Brian gave her a suspicious look. "Wait, how do I know you aren't messing with me? I mean, you're her best friend, and you'll probably double-cross me or something."

She glared at him. "I can't believe you would think that. When she pulled that on you, I... I was shocked. It was mostly her idea. When she came up with the police women thing, I thought she was going a little to far."

"She told me the police thing was your idea."

Victoria shook her head. "Look, do you want my help or not? I think it would really be good, and God knows she deserves it. How many times did she send you running naked to my house?"

"Uh, three."

"So are we doing this?"

After gazing into her eyes looking for any hint that she was screwing with him, he couldn't find anything. "Okay. Yeah."

"Great, we'll discuss the details when we get home."

Brian smiled brightly as he headed off to meet Jillian.

Jim spotted the evil look on Victoria's face. "Hey what are you up to?"

Leaning back with her hands in the sand and her breasts pushed out proudly, she smiled. "The fly just landed in my web."

"What?"

"I feel so bad. He's such a good guy, but Jillian and I have been waiting for him to pull this revenge thing."

"What are you going to do?"

"Uh, he's going to end up naked once again in front of a group of people."

"Yeah so. Who cares? Everyone's already seen him naked once—some more than once."

She shook her head. "Not this way they haven't."

"What the hell do you mean?"

She grinned and glanced behind her to find an older couple sitting within listening distance. She motioned for Jim to come closer, then leaned and whispered in his ear. After about twenty seconds of explanation littered with obscene hand gestures, his eyes widened in shock. She shook her head confidently and returned to whispering. When she was done, she pulled away from him and gave him a proud look. "So?"

He shook his head. "You guys are bad."

"It's mostly my idea. Jillian's not that creative."

"How do you come up with this stuff?"

She shrugged. "The plan is almost perfect. I just need to figure out some plausible way to make him think he can get Jillian naked in my house."

They both mulled this over a moment. His eyes widened and he smiled. "Hey, tell him to tell her that they can use the massage room. She'll need to be naked for that."

"That could work."

"Have him suggest they go outside to your hot tub after the massage, then he'll think you'll have everyone waiting out in the living room."

She looked at him, impressed. "You're good."

Victoria glanced down to his penis. "And did you see how small Brian was when he was over here talking to us about all this? He must have been really nervous or cold... or both."

"Yeah, I noticed that, but I wasn't going to say anything."

They shared a chuckle, and Victoria said, "Let's get you pumped up a bit, then we'll walk past them as they head back. He'll be dying."

"Awesome. But how are we going to do it?"

"I'll just turn over, and you can look at my ass. In no time you'll be hanging halfway to your knees."

"Yep." He shrugged. "That will do it."

She turned onto her side for thirty seconds. When she glanced back, she saw that had in fact done the trick. "Looks like you're ready."

They headed off toward the water just as Jillian and Brian turned to head back. Victoria glanced down to his sizeable showing and grinned. "You're a lucky guy."

"Thanks." He checked out her shapely ass and smiled. He thought, since they reached the beach he'd spent about ninety-five percent of his time staring at Victoria's body, about four percent glancing at Jillian, and maybe the remaining one percent checking out the other nude women, many of whom were really attractive. He wondered what that meant.

When they were about thirty feet from the approaching newlyweds, Brian spotted Jim's impressive hanging appendage first, and his expression morphed into an envious stare. Jillian was in the middle of telling Brian something when she noticed it too and immediately lost her train of thought. She simply gawked at it opened-mouthed. As they got closer, Victoria and Jim both unabashedly looked directly at Brian's groin, wearing grins. Brian flashed them an evil look. Jillian didn't take her eyes off of Jim until they were right on top of each other. As the couples were five feet apart, Brian sneered. "Show off!"

Victoria replied, "You're just jealous."

The couples walked past each other and didn't look back.

Brian murmured under his breath, "Lucky bastard."

Glancing down to Brian's equipment, Jillian put a hand on his shoulder. "Yours grows just fine."

"Thanks."

After smiling, wearing a faraway look, as she evidently was picturing it in its fully-grown state, she said. "Do you think we have time to get back to the house and squeeze in a quickie before the flight?"

"Probably not." He frowned.

Further down the beach, Victoria glanced down to Jim's equipment and sighed.

Out of the corner of his eye, Jim looked Victoria over from head to toe and thought, *It doesn't get any better than walking on the most beautiful beach in the world with a near boner next to one of the hottest women on the planet who just happens to be carrying my baby.*

He exhaled and looked straight ahead, thinking that he could grab Victoria and tell her he loved her and couldn't live without her. Maybe if he begged and pleaded long enough, she'd agree. Turning his head to the ocean, he thought about Caroline, the incredible sex they had experienced only two nights ago, and the amazing three months they had spent together. He wondered what she was doing. He missed her terribly. Maybe Victoria was right, and Caroline was the one.

34

An hour later they were all dressed and on the bus heading back. There was no time for a quickie, and the group made it to the airport just twenty minutes before take-off. They boarded the two small planes for the short flight to the airport in St. Maarten and switched to their chartered flight back to Miami.

Victoria and Jim sat in the row behind the newlyweds, who snuggled and touched each other semi-inappropriately. Peering between the seats, Victoria grinned as she attempted to spy on them, but Jim was oblivious as he stared out the window, his mind racing. Victoria watched as Jillian whispered something to Brian. Suddenly, Brian stood and walked past her to the back of the plane. Holding back a laugh, she shook her head. Victoria pretended to be asleep twenty seconds later when Jillian walked past her obviously on her way to join an exclusive club.

Lisa sat across the aisle from Victoria. In front of Lisa sat Eric and Annette. Lisa nudged Victoria during one of Eric and Annette's arguments. Victoria returned a knowing nod.

Two minutes later, Jillian had her legs wrapped around Brian as they fucked in the tiny bathroom. They were smashing up against the door pretty hard, and Beverly was nearby, giving the bathroom door a strange look. He was close to finishing when she placed one hand on the counter for support, then unfortunately her head crashed into the door latch. One last thrust knocked the newly married couple out of the bathroom, but he was somehow able to keep his balance. They remained upright and still *connected* as they stood just looking at their guests sheepishly. Luckily Jillian's skirt hung down over her ass and no naughty parts were on display.

All eyes, including the flight crew were glued to the demonstration. There were grins and shakes of heads all around, and even Beverly and Edward actually cracked a smile.

Jillian said, "Sorry."

Brian said, "We'll, uh, be right out."

He shuffled carefully back into the bathroom. After closing the door, they burst into laughter. Brian gave her a hopeful look. "Can I finish?"

She looked at him unsure.

"We can't really claim we did it unless I…"

"Okay, just hurry up."

It took three more minutes, but they both came pretty hard. After cleaning up, they walked out together, holding their heads high. When they reached the center of the plane, there was a loud ovation. Suddenly embarrassed, they slipped back to their seats and huddled together laughing like middle schoolers who just heard a good fart joke.

An hour later the plane landed in Miami. Victoria, Jillian, and Brian headed home. Jim and his parents waited at the gate for their flight to Philadelphia, and Rob drove Laura to her apartment.

Caroline was soaking in a bathtub at her parent's house in New Jersey. She grimaced in pain as she slipped into the steaming hot water. A few minutes later, her cell rang. Checking the display, she smiled when she saw it was Jim. "Jim, are you on the plane?"

"No, but we should be in a few minutes."

"How was the wedding?"

"Well did you see the news?"

"No, I haven't watched any TV at all."

"It was really nice once it got started. I missed you at the wedding. I wish you had stayed. You didn't get to hear my toast."

"Did you cry?"

"No, not at all."

"Right." She grinned into the phone.

"I can't wait to see you. What are you doing?"

"I'm at my parent's house taking a bath… I'm in pain."

"What's wrong?"

"I think for our first *experience*, um… I should have taken it a little slower. I think we maybe over did it a little."

"Experience? What are you talking about?" He asked clueless.

"Um, do I need to say it?"

"Oh, oh, my God. Are you okay?"

Caroline slipped lower in the tub and put her legs up on the edge. "I will be. I just need a little time."

"I guess maybe we shouldn't do that again," he said unenthusiastically.

"But it was amazing."

He perked up. "I thought so too."

"I think we just need to wait a little while and then take it slow."

"Sounds good."

She asked hesitantly, "So…how's Victoria? Did you guys talk?"

"We did, and she's so smart and together and—"

"I know. I know."

"Sorry, I love you, and I thought about everything that you said, and I'm coming home to be with you. I can't imagine my life without you in it."

"Me either."

"I want to ask you a question when I get back—"

"A question?"

"Yeah, it's a question you may have already heard secondhand over an intercom possibly… but I want you to forget that you heard it."

"Uh, okay. Yeah—that question."

"I want to do it right—a nice dinner, flowers, and a whole down-on-one-knee kind of thing. I'll plan the perfect night, and we'll try to put the rest of this behind us for now anyway."

"I can't wait to see you."

"Me either so just get your ass ready."

"Jim!"

"I'm kidding."

"Will you hold me all night?"

"I'll give it a shot, but you know how overheated and sweaty we both get when we try that."

She chuckled. "I know. Meet me at my dorm."

"Cool. Love you."

"Bye."

After parking the car in front of Laura's apartment building, Rob carried her luggage to the door.

"Do you want me to stay over?" he asked. "I have to work tomorrow, but I could drive back early in the morning."

"No, I really want to get some sleep."

"Do you want to come to Orlando next weekend?"

After pondering it for a moment while wearing a frown, she said, "Maybe. I'll call you."

He shrugged. The couple stood together, him not knowing what else to say and her looking around as if she had something better to do. After an awkward silent moment he said, "I guess I'd better go then."

"Okay." She kissed him on the cheek then slipped into her apartment.

He got in his car and drove away. After two blocks, he realized he'd bought her a bracelet on the island and had forgotten to give it to her. Returning to her apartment, he knocked on the door. There was no answer. He walked around a large bush so he could peer in the window and saw her luggage on the floor, but no sign of her. As he moved back around the bush, he noticed movement in the apartment directly opposite hers. He spotted Laura sitting on the sofa. He looked curiously at her and noticed a tall good-looking guy sitting on the sofa next to her. Laura turned to look out the window.

Quickly Rob ducked down behind the bush, waited a few seconds, then rose up to look again. They were only talking. Sighing, he slipped down again and thought that maybe they were just friends. Deciding to knock on the door, he stood. His eyes shot open with the discovery of Laura on her knees in front of the young man. He watched with his mouth opened wide as she rubbed the guy's penis through his shorts. When she began to unzip his pants, he turned to go.

He sat in his car gazing at the bracelet and feeling his emotions get the best of him. After slapping his face, he ran his fingers over his nose and sighed. He looked up to Laura's new boyfriend's window and saw that the blinds were now closed.

"Fuck," he said then let out a long slow breath.

He slumped against the steering wheel, dreading the four-hour drive to Orlando because this new development would obviously be all he thought about. Then it hit him. He smiled as he pulled out his cell phone, located Bridget's number and hit send.

"Hey, Rob."

"Bridget, I, uh. I just flew back from the wedding."

"How was it?"

"It was nice."

"I'm driving back to Orlando now. Do you feel like getting together? We could go for a swim, or we have a steam room in the building. Whatever you want to do. I should be home about eleven."

"Definitely. Call me when you get home."

"Bridget?"

"Yeah."

"I…" After glancing at the beautiful multicolored jeweled bracelet, he shrugged. "I bought you something."

"Really?"

"Just a little thing I saw when I was on the island. It's really not a big deal. I just thought of you when I saw it. That sounds creepy doesn't it?"

"No."

"I mean we just met, and here I am buying you a present, and I uh—"

"Well the more you keep talking, the creepier it's starting to sound."

"Oh sorry."

She chuckled. "I'm kidding. Call me, and I'm looking forward to the present. I'm a big fan of presents. As long as it didn't cost more than like fifty dollars, I think it won't be too inappropriate at this stage of our relationship."

"Oh no, it's nothing extravagant." He pulled the receipt out of the bag and looked at the $689.13 total. "See you around eleven."

"Can't wait."

Victoria relaxed in a large bubble bath. She ran her soapy hands down her huge swollen breasts to her protruding belly. Cradling it gently, she began to cry.

Brian and Jillian went up to their bedroom and turned on the light. He headed to the bathroom as she stood in front of the sitting area with her mouth wide open. There was a black sex swing hanging from a heavy-duty hook in the center of the small room. A large red bow was tied around it. Walking up to it, she felt the thick leather straps. She shook her head confused. "Is this from you?"

He called back, "What?"

"Is this from you?"

He poked his head into the bedroom, saw her standing in front of the contraption, and broke into laughter. He joined her next to it as she repeated, "Is this from you?"

"No, I, uh, didn't buy this."

They turned their heads slowly to one another as they said in unison, "Victoria."

Noticing a card on the seat, she picked it up. She opened the envelope and read the enclosed note out loud, "Hope you enjoy this. Just be careful. I pulled a muscle last time I used one. Congratulations! Love, Victoria."

They shared a chuckle. He grasped one of the ceiling straps, mesmerized. Pulling hard, he checked if it was sturdy. "Wow, this thing is heavy duty."

She grinned. "I am *not* getting in that thing. It looks dangerous."

"Maybe I'm supposed to be the one who gets in it."

She gave him a skeptical look as she pointed to the leather stirrups. He glanced down to the stirrups and gave her half a shrug. "I mean I think both partners can use it. It looks like fun."

She shook her head no as Brian looked around the room. He spotted some papers and said cheerily, "Oh, here's the manual."

He studied the pages as she walked away toward the bathroom shaking her head and holding back a laugh.

THE END...

Follow the continuing story of Victoria, Jillian, Brian, Jim, Caroline and Rob in FRIENDS WITH EXTRA BENEFITS (An excerpt is included).

To contact Luke or to be placed on a mailing list to receive updates about new releases, send an email to lukebyoung@gmail.com

To find out more about the author and his work, see http://www.lukeyoungbooks.com/

ALSO BY LUKE YOUNG

SHRINKAGE
CHOCOLATE COVERED BILLIONAIRE NAVY SEAL
CHANCES AREN'T

The Friends With... Benefits Series:
FRIENDS WITH PARTIAL BENEFITS
FRIENDS WITH FULL BENEFITS
FRIENDS WITH MORE BENEFITS
FRIENDS WITH EXTRA BENEFITS
FRIENDS WITH WAY TOO MANY BENEFITS (releasing
12/17/2013)

FRIENDS WITH EXTRA BENEFITS

1

Brian Nash walked out of the bathroom wearing only boxer shorts. Glancing to the bed, he found it empty. He shook his head confused then turned to discover his new wife, Jillian, sitting naked in their sex swing—a wedding gift courtesy of Victoria. His favorite gift by far.

He headed toward her and scoffed. "Hey, I thought you weren't getting in that. And didn't you say you were tired?"

She smiled. "I got a second wind... and I've been kinda mean to you lately, and this is just my way of starting to make it up to you."

He painted on a frown. "You have been really short with me and so preoccupied with all this lawsuit crap."

"I know. I'm really sorry."

"I think it's going to take a little more than one go around in the swing to make up for—"

"Shut-up, get over here and lick me." Jillian shot out as she glared at him.

Brian raised his eyebrows in mock offense.

She smiled, spread her legs wide and ran a finger slowly between her legs. "I mean... Brian, please use your amazing tongue on my pussy."

He rushed over to her while licking his lips. "God, I love you... I kind of like when you order me around during sex, but you should really try to be in a better mood when we're not having sex, too."

Smiling sweetly up to him, she said, "I promise I'll work on it."

"Whenever you start to think about the lawsuit, think about my penis instead."

"I'll try." Jillian licked her lips as she dipped a finger inside her juicy folds. He stared down at her, admiring the sight in a near trance-like state.

She glared impatiently up at him. "What the hell are you waiting for? Lick me now!"

He snapped out of it, grinned, and then moved closer to her. Jillian's legs rested comfortably on the harness supports and her pussy was incredibly accessible in the leather contraption. He ripped down his boxer shorts, and his nearly-hard cock sprang before her.

She whispered, "Uhhh... maybe I want you inside me first."

He shook his head no. "I'm tasting that sweet pussy; then maybe if you're lucky, I'll give you the full treatment."

Her mouth dropped open. She enjoyed when he took charge, as well. Brian reached up, quickly unhooked one of the ropes and yanked hard. Jillian's body rose quickly. He stopped pulling when her gorgeous parts were right in line with his face.

She sighed, a little dizzied. "Wow. How the hell did you —"

He raised his eyebrows. "I've been reading the manual."

She grinned as Brian secured the rope. He pushed her legs further apart then shoved his tongue between them.

"Oh my," Jillian groaned. Her eyes rolled back in her head as his tongue slowly explored her delicious folds.

After nearly a minute, he pulled his head back. "This is awesome. No neck pain. I could lick you for hours like this."

She gave him a sad look. "Don't stop now."

He obeyed her request then after almost ten minutes, she came hard, and wave after wave of orgasmic pulses flowed through her. He moved to her thighs and placed tiny kisses over them while she slowly recovered.

She gasped. "Please... lower me. Put it in... I need it."

Grinning, he slowly lowered her until she was in line with his throbbing erection. He secured the ropes, and then carefully slipped inside her. Nodding breathlessly, she stared up at his face. "I love your cock."

He said, "I want to put it in your mouth after. I want you to taste how delicious you are."

She licked her lips. "I want you to cum in my mouth. Will you save it for me?"

Brian nodded as he began slowly pumping in and nearly all the way out of her. He gently held her legs, as she remained suspended in the swing while they continued to make love. Reaching out, Jillian put her hands on his chest. She felt the muscles in his chest straining and wandered to one of his nipples, squeezing it hard.

Faster and faster, he moved inside of her. She closed her eyes, savoring the sensation of him filling every inch of her, while she sat in the swing, feeling almost weightless.

It went on and on until he hit just the right spot. Then her eyes opened wide for only a moment before slamming shut as the huge orgasm swept through her loins. Jillian squeezed the ropes even harder as he kept going. Her eyes rolled back in her head as either an aftershock of the first orgasm or a second mini-climax rippled through her. She wasn't sure which, nor did she care.

He held still, pressed as far inside of her as he could go. She opened her eyes and stared at him for a moment before glancing down to their connection, nodding breathlessly and licking her lips.

Pulling away from her, he stepped between the ropes to move closer to her face. Jillian leaned back and held the ropes while he brought his erection to her mouth. She opened wide, and he slipped inside. She groaned. He began pumping slowly between her lips. Moving one hand to his balls, she squeezed them gently. His head tilted toward the ceiling as he moaned loudly. She kept on pleasing him as he tensed every muscle in his legs, desperately fighting to push it out.

She felt him throb between her lips, then the first gush exploded into her mouth. Cringing, she pulled her mouth from him and finished him with her hands.

He stared down at her face, half in shock and half in ecstasy, as she spit out and then wiped his semen from her lips.

"Hey, what was that?" he asked.

"What?"

"Um... the 'cum in my mouth' stuff. You—"

She grinned up at him while still gently massaging his erection with both hands. "Sometimes you say things in the heat of passion that you don't really mean." She ran her tongue around her mouth with a grimace. "Have you ever tasted that stuff? It's not that great... especially today."

"I did eat a lot of spicy food at the wedding."

"Maybe if you went on an all-pineapple diet, I would really do it."

He smiled. "But you know..." He shut his mouth as she began running her hands over him more forcefully. He sighed. Then after composing himself, he grinned. "This is no way to begin a marriage."

"Really?"

Fighting to keep a straight face, he added, "You, uh, you sit on a swing of lies."

She struggled to hold back a chuckle, and they shared a smile.

She widened her eyes. "How's *this* for a way to begin a marriage?" She quickly pulled him back into her mouth.

He groaned loudly. "Yeah, this is... a great way..."

Reaching up, Brian took hold of the ropes with both hands. He closed his eyes and drifted away in complete ecstasy as the pleasure continued.

Jim arrived at Caroline's dorm at just about the time Jillian was begging Brian to help get her the hell out of that 'thing'. Jim used his key and found the lights out. He saw her in bed, smiled and then stripped down to his boxers and slipped under the covers next to her. Exhausted, he took a deep breath as he struggled to get comfortable.

Pretending to be asleep, Caroline, not wearing a thing, lay on her stomach. She groaned with mock sleepiness when Jim placed his hand on her back. She grinned when he moved his hand lower. When he found his fingers resting on the delicious curve of her naked ass, his heart rate increased. He felt the heat rising inside him as blood rushed to his groin. She moaned as he cupped her ass cheeks gently. Slipping on top of her, he kissed her shoulder. She feigned waking up and whispered groggily, "Jim."

"Yes."

"I missed you."

He kissed her neck. "I missed you, too."

"You body feels so good."

"How's your..."

"Oh, it's ok I think, but you can check if you want."

He grinned as he slipped down toward her ass. She spread her legs. Her pussy was very wet. She wanted him badly. He began lightly kissing her cheeks, and she responded by shimmying her hips and moaning softly.

He put his chin between the cheeks of her ass and whispered, "You smell great."

"Yeah, I took a bath. I wish you—" She lost her train of thought when he placed a gentle kiss between her cleft.

He pulled up and asked, "Are you sure you're ok?"

"You can kiss it to make it better... if you want."

Spreading her cheeks with his hands, Jim moved his lips lower to her. After exploring her parts with his tongue, she begged him to put it in. He didn't need to be asked twice and slowly kissed his way up her back then slipped inside her. He put his head beside hers and she turned to kiss him. Their mouths connected with their tongues stretching to play together as he began slowly pumping into her.

She whispered breathlessly, "I love you."

"I love you, too."

He lifted his upper body away from her and went up on his toes. She adjusted her hips lower to get even more stimulation where she needed it. She groaned loudly as he slid deeply into her with one long, slow stroke.

"Oh, Jim... harder."

Following her command, Jim began pumping harder and harder. It went on and on, with him driving into her and Caroline rocking her hips up and down as her climax drew closer. Suddenly her orgasm was upon her, big and thunderous. Moments later he exploded, collapsing on her in a heap and kissing her shoulder gently as they both lay there recovering.

She said, "I was waiting for you."

He nuzzled her neck and then whispered, "I could tell."

End of excerpt

Made in the USA
Middletown, DE
10 March 2020